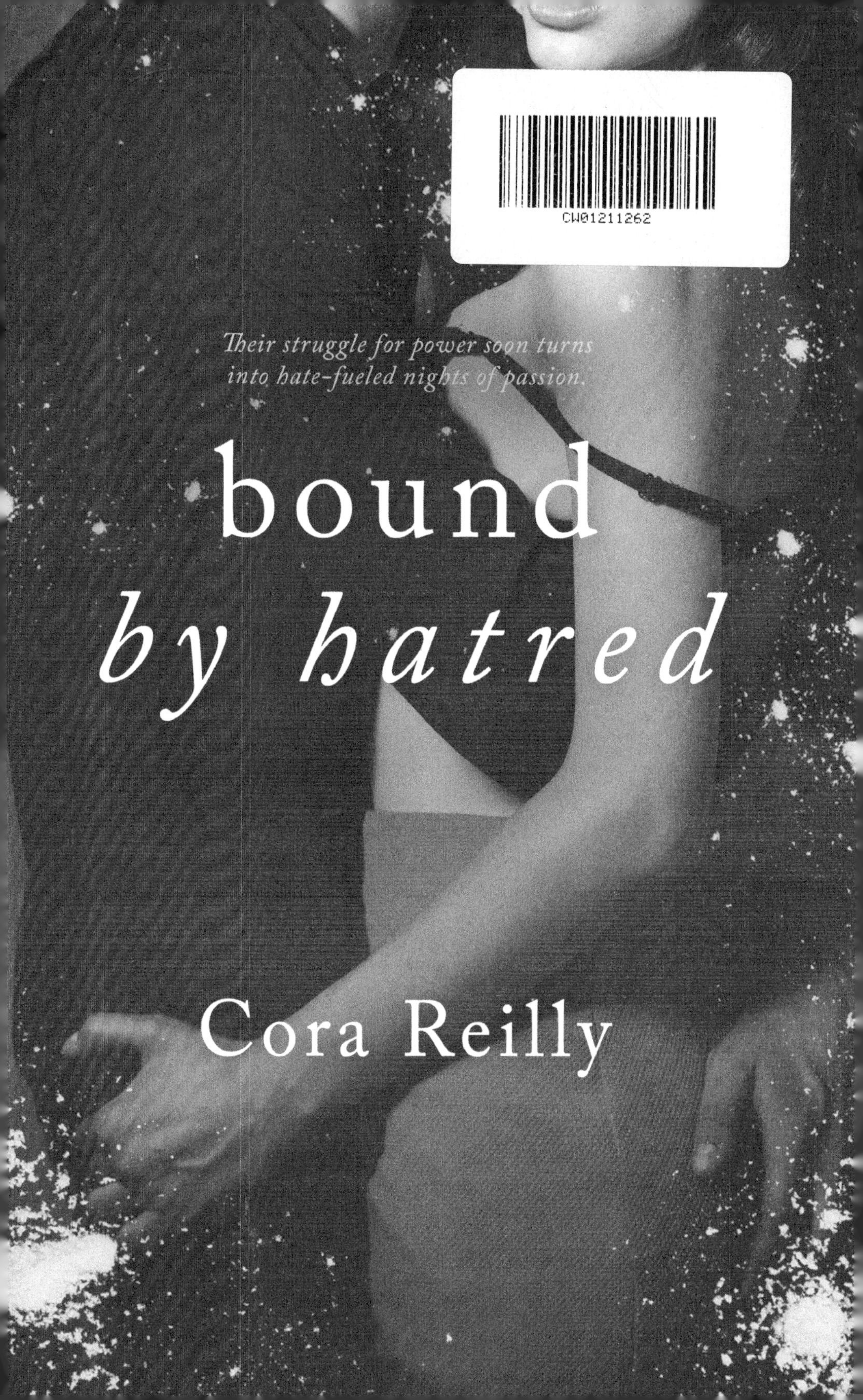
Their struggle for power soon turns into hate-fueled nights of passion.
bound
by hatred
Cora Reilly

Subscribe to Cora's newsletter to find out about her next books, bonus content and giveaways: www.corareillyauthor.blogspot.de/p/newsletter.html

Cover design by Hang Le
Book design by Inkstain Design Studio

bound
by hatred

prologue

—GIANNA—

My reflection could have been the opening scene of a horror movie. Blood covered my chin and more blood dripped from the cut in my lower lip and onto my white shirt. My lip was already swelling, but I was happy to find my eyes dry, no sign of a single tear.

Matteo appeared behind me, tall frame towering over me, his dark eyes scanning my messed-up face. Without his trademark shark-grin and the arrogant amusement, he looked almost tolerable. "You don't know when to shut up, do you?" His lips turned into a smirk, but it looked somehow wrong. There was something unsettling in his eyes. The look in them reminded me of the one I'd seen when he'd dealt with the Russian captives in the basement. Something dark and twisted lurked in their depth.

"Neither do you," I said, then winced at the pain shooting through my lip.

"True," he said in a strange voice. Before I had time to react, he gripped my hips, turned me around and hoisted me onto the washstand. "That's why we are perfect for each other."

Back was the arrogant smile. The bastard stepped between my legs.

"What are you doing?" I hissed, sliding back from the edge of the washstand to bring more distance between us while pushing against his chest.

He didn't budge, too strong for me. The smile got bigger. He grabbed my chin and tilted my head up. "I want to take a look at your lip."

"I don't need your help now. Maybe you should have stopped my father from busting my lip in the first place."

"Yes. I should have," he said darkly, his thumb lightly touching my wound as he parted my lips. "If Luca hadn't held me back, I would have plunged my knife into your father's fucking back, consequences be damned. Maybe I will still do it. I'd fucking love it."

He released my lip and pulled a long curved knife from the holster below his jacket before twisting it in his hand with a calculating look on his face. Then his eyes flickered up to me. "Do you want me to kill him?"

God, yes. I shivered at the sound of Matteo's voice. I knew it was wrong, but after what Father had said today, I wanted to see him begging for mercy and I knew Matteo was capable of bringing anyone to their knees, which excited me in a horrifying way. That was exactly why I'd wanted out of this life, why I *still* wanted out. I had the potential for cruelty regardless of how I tried to convince myself of the opposite, and this life was the reason for it.

"That would mean war between Chicago and New York," I said simply. Not that I gave a damn about peace. The men would find a reason to tear into each other soon enough. Someone always managed to insult someone else's honor and then all bets were off.

"Seeing your father bleed to death at my feet would be worth the risk. You *are* worth it."

chapter I

—MATTEO—

The first time I saw Gianna, she was a scrawny fourteen-year-old with a too big mouth, a splattering of freckles on her face and untamed red locks. She was everything a proper Italian girl wasn't supposed to be, which was probably why I found her entertaining. But she was a kid, and though I was barely four years older, I had already been a Made Man for five years, killed several people and fucked my fair share of women. The moment Luca and I were back in New York, busy with mob business and easy society girls, I didn't give the rude redhead a second thought. We had enough trouble with the Bratva trying to sabotage our drug labs, and our father had grown too old to handle things as they needed to be handled: with unrelenting brutality. It was time for the old man to die and hand the job over to my brother. Luca was the perfect man for brutality.

I'd pretty much forgotten all about Gianna when Luca and I returned to New York three years later for his wedding to Aria.

Luca had gotten it into his head that he wanted to see Aria before the wedding. The official explanation being that he wanted to make sure she was on the pill—which was bullshit. I knew it was because he was eager to see how she'd grown up. And damn, the girl had filled up nicely. When she appeared behind her younger sister Liliana in the doorframe to their suite in the Mandarin Oriental, my eyes didn't know what part of her to check out first. Long blonde hair, stunning blue eyes, narrow waist, lean legs, nice butt and tits. She was smoking hot. She was also Luca's fiancée and so firmly off-limits. Not to mention that she was a bit too demure for my taste. The way she cast down her eyes whenever Luca looked at her would have driven me insane. Luca was an intimidating fucker, and the girl had been dealt a heavy blow for having to marry him, but she needed to grow a spine if she wanted to stand a chance against Luca. He was used to bossing people around.

Of course, the moment I entered the suite, Aria was the last thing on my mind. My gaze settled on the girl with the flaming red hair who lounged on the sofa, long legs casually crossed and propped up on the coffee table. At once the long-forgotten memory of her rudeness resurfaced and with it my interest in her. She wasn't the awkward, scrawny girl she used to be.

Definitely not scrawny.

She had developed all the right curves in all the right places, and her face had gotten rid of her freckles. Unlike most girls I knew she didn't seem impressed by me. To be honest, she looked like I was a cockroach she wanted to squash under her boots. With a grin, I headed straight for her, never one to shy away from a challenge. Especially a hot challenge. What was life without the thrill of getting burned?

Gianna straightened in a jerk, her black boots landing on the ground with a thud, and then she narrowed her eyes at me. If she thought that would stop me, she was thoroughly mistaken. Unfortunately, the youngest Scuderi girl stepped in my way and gave me her version of a flirty smile. "Can I see your gun?" she asked in that voice caught somewhere between girl and woman.

Had Gianna asked that question, a myriad of inappropriate replies would have been on the tip of my tongue, but Liliana was a bit too young for them. What a waste of opportunity.

"No, you can't," Aria said before I got the chance to come up with a reply fit for younger ears. Always so proper, that girl. Thank God, Father had chosen her for Luca and not for me.

"You shouldn't be here alone with us," Gianna muttered, her eyes moving from Luca to me. Damn it. She was something else, really. "It's not appropriate."

Luca didn't seem too impressed with her. It was obvious that she grated on his nerves, already something she and I had in common. "Where is Umberto? Shouldn't he be guarding this door?" he asked.

"He's probably on a toilet or cigarette break," Aria said.

I almost laughed. What kind of idiots worked for Scuderi? Things in Chicago seemed to follow very different rules. I could tell that Luca was on the verge of an outburst. He'd been on edge for days, probably because his balls were bursting. He'd fucked Grace far more often than usual to bridge the time before he could fuck Aria.

"Does it happen often that he leaves you without protection?" he asked.

"Oh, all the time," Gianna snapped, then rolled her eyes at her sister. "You see, Lily, Aria, and I sneak out every weekend because we have a bet going who can pick up more guys."

Big words for a girl who'd never seen a cock in real life. From the look Luca gave me, he thought the exact same thing. Gianna really didn't know anything about my brother if she thought it was a good thing to taunt him like that.

Luca stalked toward his little fiancée who flinched as she always did when he acted like a berserk. "I want to have a word with you, Aria."

Gianna jumped to her feet like a tigress determined to protect her young. "I was joking, for God's sake!" She actually tried to get in between Luca and Aria, which was a fucking bad idea. Before Luca could lose his shit, I grabbed her wrist and dragged her away.

Gianna's blue eyes flashed with fury. I'd been wrong. Her face hadn't gotten rid of all of her freckles. This close up I could see the soft dusting of freckles on her nose, but somehow they made her look even more beautiful.

"Let go of me, or I'll break your fingers," she hissed.

I'd love to see you try. I released her with a grin that seemed to enrage her only further if the narrowing of her eyes was any indication.

Luca started leading Aria away. "Come on. Where's your bedroom?"

Gianna's gaze flitted between Luca and me. "I'll call our father! You can't do that."

Of course, Luca didn't give a fuck. Scuderi would have given Aria to him years ago; he definitely wouldn't care if Luca sampled her goods a few days before the wedding. The door fell shut and Gianna stalked toward it. I gripped her hand again before she could piss off Luca even more. This girl really didn't know what was good for her. "Give them some privacy. Luca won't rip Aria's clothes off before the wedding night."

Gianna shook me off. "Do you think that's funny?"

"What are they talking about?" Liliana asked.

The door to the suite swung open and Umberto stepped in, sending a glare my way. The old man still hadn't forgiven me for insulting his wife three years ago.

"Gianna, Liliana, come here," he said sharply. I cocked one eyebrow at him. Was he worried I'd hurt them? If that were my intention, they definitely wouldn't be standing next to me unscathed. Romero rolled his eyes behind Umberto's back as he stepped in behind the man, and I smirked. Of course, the old man caught it and his fingers moved a bit closer to his knife holder.

Do it, old man. It's been too long since I had a good fight.

Liliana obeyed at once and walked toward her bodyguard. As expected, Gianna stayed beside the door to her sister's bedroom. "Luca dragged Aria into her bedroom. They are alone in there."

Umberto started to head toward the door but I blocked his way. Romero was close behind him. Not that I would need him to stop the old guy. Umberto tried to stare me down. He was at least four inches shorter than me, and no matter how good of a knife fighter he was, I'd cut him open with my blade before he could even blink. My fingers actually itched to do it.

"They aren't married yet," he said like that was news to me.

"Her virtue is safe with my brother, don't worry." It wasn't a lie. Luca wouldn't dishonor Aria.

Umberto's lips thinned. I had a feeling that he wanted to start a fight as much as I did. Before things could get entertaining, the door to the bedroom opened and Aria walked out. She looked as if she'd seen a ghost. I gave Luca a look. Did he really have to scare the shit out of his fiancée a few days before their wedding?

"What are you doing here?" Umberto asked.

"You should pay better attention in the future and keep your breaks to a minimum," Luca told him.

"I was gone for only a few minutes and there were guards in front of the other doors."

Bored by their argument, I turned my attention back to the redhead.

Gianna put her hands on her hips, somehow pushing her chest out. She really had a body to die for. I wondered if Scuderi had already set her up with some loser from the Outfit. That would be a pity.

Gianna met my gaze. "What are you looking at?"

I let my eyes wander the length of her. "At your hot body."

"Then keep looking. Because that's all you ever get to do with my *hot body*."

"Stop it," Umberto warned.

Gianna really shouldn't have said that. I'd always enjoyed the hunt. While Luca didn't bother once a girl proved to be work, I'd always preferred going after a difficult conquest. It kept things interesting. Getting a girl into our beds had never been a problem for either of us. We were good-looking and rich, not to mention the kind of bad boy many bored society girls needed to spice up their boring lives, but there was no fun in always getting what you wanted without having to fight for it.

Gianna's narrowed eyes followed me when Luca, Romero, and I left the suite. I smiled to myself. The girl had fire.

Luca sighed. "Don't tell me you've set your sights on the redhead. She's a major pain in the ass."

"So what? She'd definitely make my life more interesting."

"What? Killing off Russians and having a new girl in your bed every other night isn't doing the deal for you?"

"I like to change things up now and then."

"You can't have her. She's off-limits. I won't tell Father you brought war with the Outfit down on us because you pawed at Scuderi's daughter. There's only one way you could have the redhead in your bed and that's if you marry her, and that's not going to happen."

"Why not?"

Luca paused. "Tell me you're joking."

I shrugged. I didn't really want to marry yet, or ever for that matter, but Father had been on my case for months. Every woman he'd suggested so far had been boring as hell.

Luca gripped my shoulder. "You won't ask Scuderi for his daughter's hand tonight."

"Is that an order?" I asked quietly. Luca would be my Capo very soon and he was above me in the hierarchy of the Famiglia but I wasn't good at following orders.

"No. A piece of advice." Luca smirked. "If I ordered you, you'd do it just to annoy me."

"I'm not a hotheaded teenage boy," I said, then grinned because Luca knew me too well.

"I just want you to take your time. You might find Gianna's bitchiness fascinating now, but I doubt that'll last more than a few days. I know you. The moment the hunt is over and you got what you wanted, you'll lose interest. But this time you'd be stuck with her forever."

"Don't worry. I have every intention of scoring tonight. That'll make me forget all about Gianna."

chapter 2

—Aria & Luca's wedding, GIANNA—

This wedding was a farce. Aria leaned away from Luca and clutched my hand the moment we sat down at the table. It was obvious how unhappy she was. She was trying so hard to hide it, but for me it was plain as day. Of course nobody gave a shit. It was pretty much standard that the bride was forced into marriage, so unhappiness was a given. Nobody ever asked what we wanted. Nobody ever cared. Not even the other women.

It was then that I made a promise I was determined to keep: I wasn't going to end up in a loveless marriage. I didn't care if it was my duty or if honor dictated it; nothing in this godforsaken world could make me marry for anything but love.

Matteo kept glancing my way from across the table, that annoying cocky grin on his face. He'd pretty much ogled me throughout the entire wedding. I had to admit that he didn't look too shabby in his light gray vest, white shirt, and dress pants. Somehow his tall muscled frame stood out even more dressed up like that. Of course, I'd have bitten my tongue off before admitting to anyone that I found Matteo's looks tolerable, especially when his personality wasn't anywhere close to being sufferable.

Aria clutched my hand under the table even tighter because of something Luca had said to her. She was oblivious to Matteo's flirting with me. Oblivious to anything but her distress.

I squeezed her hand but then the dance floor was opened and soon we were ripped apart as Luca led her to their first dance as a married couple. I quickly pushed to my feet, desperate to sneak away toward the bay where I could be alone, but Matteo cornered me at the edge of the dance floor, that same cocky grin on his striking face. Why did the bastard have to look so good?

His dark hair was intentionally messy and his eyes were so dark, they were almost black. It was impossible not to check him out. Of course, he was perfectly aware of the effect he had on most women and obviously expected me to fawn over him as well. Hell would freeze over before that happened.

He bowed without taking his eyes off me. "May I have this dance?"

My stomach did a stupid flip at the sight of his grin. He was more easygoing than most Made Men, but I had a feeling that was only a cover-up. Maybe he'd perfected the boy-next-door routine, but beneath it a predator was lying in wait, ready to pounce. I wasn't going to be his prey.

Father watched me from his spot at the table, so I had no choice but to nod in response to Matteo's question, or risk a huge scene. Not that I would have cared but I didn't want to add more stress for Aria. She was already on edge.

Matteo took my hand and rested his palm on my lower back, the warmth of his skin seeping through the thin fabric of my dress. My stomach lurched but I forced my face into a mask of boredom. I hated how my body seemed to react to Matteo. If I'd be allowed to interact with other guys, I'd probably be unimpressed by Matteo, but like Aria this dance was the most action I'd ever gotten.

I peered up at him. This close up I could see that his eyes were dark brown with an almost black outer ring. He had thick black lashes and the shadow of stubble ghosted his cheeks and chin. His smile widened and I turned my head away, focusing on the dancing guests around us. Everyone was laughing and smiling, enjoying themselves. From the outside it looked like a marvelous feast. It was easy to be taken in by the mansion's garden that was decorated to perfection. It was *so damn easy* to let the breeze drifting over to us from the ocean carry away reality. The unique atmosphere only a place in the Hamptons could offer could convince anyone that life was a dream.

I knew better.

Matteo pulled me even closer, pressing our bodies together so I could feel every inch of muscle as well as the weapons hidden beneath his vest. I squirmed, though part of me wanted to lean in, get closer, and claim his mouth for a kiss. That would have been the scandal of the wedding, no doubt.

Father would blow a gasket. That was almost enough to make me want to do it. Why should girls be forced to wait with their first kiss until they were married? It was ridiculous. I pitied Aria for having to experience her first kiss in front of the entire wedding party. That wouldn't happen to me. I didn't care whom I had to bribe to kiss me.

Matteo leaned down, a teasing smile curving his mouth. "You look gorgeous, Gianna. The pissed-off look goes really well with your dress."

Before I could stop myself, a laugh burst out of me. I tried to cover it up with a cough but Matteo didn't buy it judging from the look on his face. Damn it. I narrowed my eyes—in vain. I decided to ignore Matteo for the rest of our dance, hoping that my body would do the same, but then the bastard started moving his thumb back and forth on my back, and every nerve ending in me seemed to jerk to life.

I wanted to kiss him, and not just to spite my father and every other male in our world who thought it was okay to keep women on a leash. I wanted to kiss him because he smelled delicious, and that was exactly the reason why I needed to get away from him quickly.

Sadly, Matteo seemed intent to drive me crazy, because after our first dance he managed to steal two more dances from me, and to my utter annoyance my body didn't stop reacting to his closeness. I had a feeling he knew, and that was why he kept stroking my back ever so lightly, but I couldn't ask him to stop without admitting that it was bothering me, and somehow part of me didn't want him to stop.

It was almost midnight when people started to shout for Luca to bed Aria. She didn't manage to hide her panic. When she stood and took Luca's offered hand, her eyes met mine but then Luca was already leading her away, followed by a crowd of shouting men. Anger surged through me. I pushed to my feet, determined to follow and help her. Mother gripped my wrist, jerking me to a stop. "This isn't your business, Gianna. Sit down. Aria will do what's expected of her and so should you."

I glowered at her. Wasn't she supposed to protect us? Instead she watched without a flicker of compassion. I wrenched away from her, disgusted by her and everyone around us.

Father stood beside Salvatore Vitiello, who shouted something that sounded like "We want to see blood on the sheets, Luca!"

I almost tackled him. What a bastard. New York and its sick traditions. Despite Father's warning glare, I turned and followed after the men. Luca and Aria were almost at the house, and I had trouble fighting my way through the male guests to get to them. I wasn't even sure what I was going to do if I reached them. I could hardly pull Aria into our shared bedroom and lock the door. That wouldn't stop anyone, least of all Luca. That guy was a beast.

A few of the men made lewd comments in my direction but I ignored them, my eyes firmly focused on Aria's blonde head. I'd almost reached the front of the crowd when Aria disappeared into the master bedroom and Luca closed the door. My breath caught, worry and anger taking center stage in my body.

I was wavering between storming into the bedroom to kick Luca's ass and run as far away as possible so I didn't have to hear what was going on behind that door. Most of the male guests were on their way back outside to resume drinking, only Matteo, who was shouting disgusting suggestions through the door, and a few younger Made Men from New York were still around. I backed away, knowing there was nothing I could do for Aria, and hating it more than anything else. So often in the past Aria had protected me from Father, and now when she needed protection, I was unable to help her.

Instead of returning to the party, I decided to go to my bedroom. I wasn't in the mood to face my parents again. I'd only get into a huge fight with Father, and I really didn't need that on my plate today. Before I could head down the corridor toward my room, two guys stepped in my way. I didn't know their names. They weren't much older than me, maybe eighteen. One of them still sported some baby fat and acne. The other was taller and looked like more of a threat.

I tried to sidestep them but the taller guy blocked my way. "Piss off," I said, glaring at the two idiots.

"Don't be a killjoy, Red. I wonder if you are red down there too?" He pointed between my legs.

My lips curled in disgust. *As if I hadn't heard those words before.*

The acne guy snorted with laughter. "We could try to find out."

Suddenly Matteo was there. He gripped the tall guy in a headlock and held a sharp long knife to the guy's crotch. "Or," he said in an eerily calm voice. "We could try to find out how long it takes for you to bleed out like a pig after

I cut your dick off. How about that?"

I used the moment to ram my knee into acne guy's balls. He cried out and dropped to his knees. I probably shouldn't have enjoyed it as much as I did.

Matteo raised his dark eyebrows at me. "Wanna have a go at this one too?"

I didn't need to be told twice. Instead I landed a good kick and sent the second guy to his knees as well. Both guys looked up at Matteo with fear-widened eyes, ignoring me completely.

"Fuck off before I decide to cut your throats," Matteo said.

They scrambled off like dogs with their tails between their legs.

"Do you know them?" I asked.

Matteo sheathed his knife. He didn't look as drunk as he'd seemed at the party. Maybe it had all been for show. A quick glance around made me realize that we were alone in this part of the house, and from the way my heartbeat quickened and my stomach fluttered, I knew this really wasn't a good idea.

"They are the kids of two of our soldiers. They aren't even Made Men yet."

Inducting them into the mafia probably wouldn't turn them into nicer human beings. "I could have handled them myself," I said.

Matteo scanned my body again. "I know."

That wasn't the answer I had expected, and I wasn't entirely sure if he was pulling my leg or not. "It's funny how you can act like a knight in shining armor one second and the next you're encouraging your brother to sexually assault my sister."

"Luca doesn't need encouragement, believe me."

"You make me sick. All of this does." I turned and stalked away but Matteo caught up with me and barred my way with an arm against the wall.

"Your sister will be fine. Luca isn't cruel to women."

"Is that supposed to reassure me?"

Matteo shrugged. "I know my brother. Aria won't get hurt."

I searched his face. He seemed serious. I wanted to believe him but from what I'd witnessed, Luca was anything but a kind man. He was brutal and cruel and cold, and I wasn't sure if Matteo's definition of not being cruel to women matched my own.

"I really want to fucking kiss you," Matteo said in a rough voice, startling me.

My eyes widened. He didn't move, just stood in front of me with his arm propped up against the wall and his dar eyes boring into mine. We weren't engaged, thank God, so speaking to me like that was more than inappropriate. Father would have gone nuts if he'd heard. I should have been anxious, embarrassed at the very least, by his words, but instead I found myself wondering how it would be to kiss someone, to kiss Matteo. The girls in my class had all kissed and done far more already. Only Aria, the other girls from mob families, and I were sheltered from the outside world, always guarded by bodyguards. How would it be to kiss someone forbidden? To do something a good girl didn't do?

"Then why don't you?" I heard myself say. Alarm bells went off in my mind but I ignored them.

This was my choice. If we weren't who we were, if we hadn't been born into this screwed-up world, if Matteo wasn't a Made Man and a killer, maybe then I could have fallen for him. If we'd met as two normal people, then maybe we could have become something.

Matteo moved closer to me. For some reason I backed away until I bumped into the wall, but Matteo followed and soon I was trapped between cold stone and his body. "Because there are rules in our world and breaking them has consequences."

"You don't seem like a for rules." I wasn't sure why I was encouraging him. I didn't want his attention. I wanted out of this fucked-up world and its fucked-up people. Getting involved in any way with someone like him would make that impossible.

Matteo smiled darkly. "I'm not." He reached for my face and slowly raked his fingers through my hair. I shivered at the light touch. I didn't even like Matteo, right? He was annoying and arrogant and never knew when to shut up.

He's like you.

But my body wanted more. I grabbed his vest, my fingers crinkling the soft material. "Me neither. I don't want my first kiss to happen with my husband."

Matteo let out a quiet laugh and he was so close that I could feel it more than hear it. "This is a bad idea," he murmured, his lips less than an inch from mine, his eyes dark and devoid of the usual playfulness.

My insides seemed to burn with need. "I don't care."

And then Matteo kissed me, lightly at first as if he wasn't sure if I was being serious. I tugged at his vest, wanting him to stop being careful, and Matteo crushed his body to mine, his tongue slipping between my lips, tangling with mine, giving me no time to wonder what I was doing. He tasted of whiskey and something sweeter, like the most delicious whiskey truffle I could imagine. His body radiated heat and strength. His hand cupped the back of my neck as his mouth set my body alight with need.

God, no wonder Father didn't want us to be around men. Now that I knew how good kissing felt, I never wanted to stop doing it.

There was a gasp, and Matteo and I pulled apart. I was still dazed when my eyes settled on my sister Lily who stood frozen in the hallway, probably on her way to her room. Her eyes were wide. "Sorry!" she blurted, then took a few hesitant steps in our direction. "Does this mean you're going to marry?"

I snorted. "No, it doesn't. I won't marry him. This means nothing."

Matteo shot me a look, and I almost felt bad for my rude words, but it was the truth. I had no intention of marrying a Made Man, no matter how good he could kiss, or how much he could make me laugh. The men in our world were killers and torturers. They weren't good men, they weren't even decent men. They were bad, rotten to the core. Nothing could change that. Maybe they occasionally managed to imitate normal guys, especially Matteo had that act down to a T, but in the end it was only a mask.

Matteo turned to Lily. "Don't tell anyone what you saw, okay?"

I slipped away from him, needing to bring some distance between us. How could I have let him kiss me? Maybe I was lucky and he was more intoxicated than he let on. Maybe he wouldn't remember a thing tomorrow morning.

"Okay," Lily said with a shy smile.

Matteo gave me a knowing look before he walked past Lily and turned the corner. The moment he was gone, Lily rushed toward me. "You kissed him!"

"Shhh," I said as we walked down the hall.

"Can I sleep in your room tonight? I told Mother I could."

"Yeah, sure."

"How was it?" she asked in a hushed whisper. "The kiss, I mean."

At first I wanted to lie but then I opted for the truth. "Amazing."

Lily giggled and followed me into my room. "So are you going to kiss him again?"

I wanted to, but I knew it would be a majorly bad idea. I didn't want to give him any ideas. "No. I won't ever kiss Matteo again."

I should have known that wouldn't be the end of it.

The next day, a couple of hours before my family had to leave for Chicago, Matteo caught me alone in front of my bedroom. He didn't try to kiss me but he stood very close. It would have been easy to bridge the distance between us, to grab his shirt and pull him against me. Instead I put my guards in place and glared. "What do you want?"

Matteo clucked his tongue. "Last night when we were alone you didn't give me the cold shoulder."

"I'd hoped you were too drunk to remember."

"Sorry to disappoint you." If he didn't stop smiling that arrogant smile I'd wring his neck, or kiss him, I hadn't decided yet. Choice number one was the better option, no doubt.

"It was a one-time thing. It didn't mean anything. I still don't like you. I only did it because I wanted to do something forbidden."

His dark eyes lingered on my lips before they slid lower. "There are plenty of other forbidden things we could do," he murmured, stepping closer, too close, and enveloping me with his scent.

"No, thanks."

He rocked back on his heels, smile getting impossibly wide. "Why? Losing your courage? I could ask your father for your hand in marriage if you're tired of forbidden things."

"*Right*," I said sarcastically. "I will never marry you, that's a promise. And now that Aria's already trapped in New York, Father wouldn't send me away anyway."

Matteo shrugged. "If you say so."

His overconfidence made me snap. I jabbed my finger against his muscled chest. "You think you are irresistible, don't you? But you aren't. You and Luca and all the other men in the fucking mafia think you are oh-so-great. Let me tell you something: if you weren't fucking rich and didn't carry a fucking gun wherever you went, you wouldn't be better than anyone else out there."

"I'd still be good-looking and I could still kill most of the wimps out there with my bare hands. What about you, Gianna? What would you be without the protection of your family and your father's money?"

I sucked in a deep breath. Yes, what would I be without all that? Nothing. I'd never had to do anything by myself, never had been allowed to do so, but not for lack of wanting. "Free."

Matteo laughed. "You won't ever be free. None of us are. We are all caged in by the rules of our world."

That's why I want out of this world.

"Maybe. But a marriage to you won't ever be my cage." I stalked off, not giving him another chance for a comeback.

chapter 3

—MATTEO—

Maybe Gianna didn't understand it yet but marriage would be her cage no matter if she wanted it or not.

Last night after our kiss, I'd returned to the party to drink myself into a stupor when I'd come across my bastard of a father and Rocco Scuderi, talking about Gianna and his plans for her to marry some old geezer who was known for his hard hand with women. I hadn't said anything then because I knew Father. If he thought I wanted Gianna because I desired her, liked her or wanted to protect her from a worse fate, he'd never agree to set me up with her.

Now in the morning after the presentation of the sheets, I searched for Luca and found him on his way to the master bedroom with Aria at his side. "You two lovebirds will have to postpone your mating session. I need to have a word with you, Luca," I said.

Luca and Aria turned around to face me. Aria's cheeks turned bright red and she peered up at my brother with a mix of worry and embarrassment. He glared at me before lowering his gaze to his wife. "Go ahead. Check if the maids packed all your stuff. I'll be back soon." She quickly disappeared in the bedroom.

"The sheets were fake, weren't they? My big bad brother spared his little virgin bride."

Luca glowered as he stepped close to me. "Keep your fucking voice down."

"What happened? Did you have too much to drink and couldn't get it up?"

"Fuck off. As if alcohol ever stopped me," he said.

"Then what?"

Luca glared. "She started crying."

I chuckled. I reached for the knife holder around his forearm and pushed it up, revealing a small wound. Luca snatched his arm away.

"You cut yourself."

Luca looked like he was considering slicing me up into bite-sized pieces. Since I still needed his help, I decided to keep my taunting to a minimum.

"I knew it. I told Gianna last night that she didn't need to worry about Aria. You have a soft spot for damsels in distress."

"I don't—" He frowned. "You were alone with Gianna?"

I nodded, then led him away from the bedroom, in case Aria was trying to eavesdrop. She'd only tell her sister everything. "I kissed her, and she tastes even better than she looks."

"I can't fucking believe you got more action than me on my own fucking wedding night," Luca muttered.

"The ladies can't resist my charm."

He clamped his hand down on my shoulder. "This isn't a joking matter, Matteo. The Outfit won't find it funny if you go around deflowering their girls."

"I didn't deflower anyone. I kissed her."

"Yeah, as if that's ever the end of it."

"I want to deflower her. But I'm not an idiot."

"Really?" that's what Luca's expression said.

"I want to marry her."

Luca stopped abruptly. "Tell me you're kidding."

"I'm not. That's why I need your help. Father won't talk to Scuderi on my behalf if he thinks I want Gianna for any other reason than spite or revenge. You know him."

"So what do you want me to do?"

"Help me convince him that she hates me and insulted me and that I want to marry her to make her miserable."

"Isn't that the truth? The girl can't stand you, and you want her because of it. How is that any different from the story we're going to tell Father?"

"I don't want to make her miserable."

Luca looked doubtful. "The end result might be the same. That girl is going to drive you insane, you realize that, don't you? I'm really not sure if I want her in New York."

"You'll deal with it. And Aria will be happy to have her sister with her."

"You really think you thought that through, don't you?"

"I did, and Father will choose some bitch that'll make me miserable for me soon enough."

"So you rather choose your own bitch who'll make you miserable."

I shook off his hand. "Gianna isn't a bitch."

"You want to hit me because of her," Luca said with a twisted smile.

"I want to hit you for a lot of reasons."

Luca shook his head. "Come on. Let's find Father."

We headed down the corridor and down the stairs toward Father's office. He was on his way out of the room. I forced my face into a mask of fury. "I can't believe her fucking nerve."

"There's nothing you can do," Luca said to me, then he turned to Father. "The Scuderi redhead provoked Matteo."

Father raised his brows in mild interest. "How so?" He gestured for us to move into his office, then closed the door.

I pretended to be seething while Luca made up some ridiculous story that ended with Gianna telling me that her father would never give her to New York, and that nobody could convince him otherwise.

"She made it sound as if I was beneath her, as if we were beneath her. I want the bitch to pay. I don't care what she wants. I want her in my bed."

Excitement flashed in Father's eyes. The sadist actually believed that bullshit, because in his twisted, power-hungry, sadist mind, it made sense. "I suppose I can talk to Scuderi. He'll be glad to be rid of her. She's a handful." His smile widened. "You'll have to teach her manners, Matteo."

"Don't worry," I said. I'd teach her a lot of things.

Two days later my father and Scuderi came to an agreement and Gianna was mine. Now I just had to figure out a good time to tell her.

—GIANNA—

Sometimes at night when I relived our kiss, I wondered if maybe Matteo and I weren't such a bad idea, but then Aria called and told me about how she'd found Luca cheating on her, and that was the wake-up call I'd desperately needed. Made Men would always kill, always cheat, always ruin anything they touched. I wouldn't let anyone treat me like that. I wouldn't even give them the chance to try. No matter how much my body wanted to kiss Matteo again, I swore to myself that I would push him away. One kiss had already been too much. If I let him close again, he'd never leave me alone.

Of course when I visited New York a couple of weeks after Aria's wedding, Matteo was there in Luca's apartment to have dinner with us. The grin he gave me when Aria led me toward the table made my blood boil. Had he told anyone about our kiss? I hadn't even told Aria about it, and I'd always told Aria everything. This would be a long dinner.

The next day I convinced Aria to take me to a club dancing, desperate to forget Matteo. It was my first taste of freedom, and boy, did it taste good. Not as good as Matteo, an annoying voice reminded me, but it was soon blasted away by the beats filling the dance floor of the Sphere. It was an exhilarating experience to have strangers check me out, to have them want me. I'd never dressed this sexy before, had never been allowed to, and couldn't help but feel strangely empowered. I was dancing with a tall guy when he was suddenly shoved away from me by none other than Matteo *fucking* Vitiello.

"What the fuck are you doing?" he snarled.

"What the fuck are *you* doing? This is none of your business." My dance partner had found his balance again and stepped up to us but before he could say something Matteo punched him below the ribs, sending him to his knees, and then two bouncers were there and dragged the guy away.

I stood in stunned silence. "Have you lost your fucking mind?"

Matteo brought his face close to mine and gripped my upper arm. "You won't ever do this again. I won't let you mess around with other guys."

"I wasn't messing around, I was dancing." Then his words really sank in. "With *other* guys? So you think because we kissed once you can tell me what to do with my life? Newsflash: you don't own me, Matteo."

He smirked. "Oh, but I *do*." His dark eyes roamed over my skimpy outfit, lingering on my naked legs. "Every inch of you."

I shook off his grip. "You are insane. Get away from me." He followed Luca without another word, but left one of his stupid baboons-slash-bodyguards with me. I was so angry, I wanted to run after him and pummel him to dust.

Instead I went over to Aria who looked lost as she stood unmoving in the center of the dance floor. "That asshole," I muttered.

After a moment, her eyes settled on me. "Who?"

"Matteo. The guy has the nerve to tell me not to dance with other men. What is he? My owner? Fuck him." Aria looked as if her thoughts were miles away. "Are you okay?"

She nodded. "Yeah. Let's go to the bar." Luca's two lapdogs, Romero and Cesare, followed us and Aria lashed out at them. "Can you watch us from afar? You're driving me crazy."

Stunned, I watched as she rushed toward the bar and ordered drinks for us. Romero and Cesare were watching us with hawk eyes from afar. So much for feeling free and having fun. Anger at Matteo resurfaced again but I swallowed it. I wouldn't let him ruin the evening.

"You can go dancing," Aria said with a shaky smile, clinging to her drink like it was her lifeline.

"In a few minutes. You look pale."

"I'm okay."

She didn't look okay, and I wasn't sure why she didn't want to tell me what was bothering her. Although, I really had no right to complain. After all, I still hadn't told her about the kiss.

"I really need to go to the restroom," I said after several minutes of silence.

"I need to sit for a few more minutes."

I hesitated, wondering if it was a good idea to leave her, but it wasn't like she was alone. After all, Romero never let her out of his sight, thanks to Luca's possessiveness.

I made my way toward the back of the bar where the restrooms were, trying not to lose my shit on Cesare who was like an annoying shadow. When I returned to the bar a few minutes later, all hell had broken lose. Aria was swaying and Cesare had to hold her up while Romero had his knife buried in some sleezebag's leg. "You will follow us. If you try to run, you'll die," Romero growled.

"Aria?" I whispered, my heart pounding in my chest. She didn't seem to hear me.

"Take her drink. But don't drink," Cesare told me. I picked up the glass, too shaken to be annoyed by his patronizing tone.

We made our way to the back and then down into a basement. Aria's legs barely supported her. I stayed beside her the entire time. When we stepped into a sort of office, my eyes settled on Matteo who lounged in a chair. His gaze zoomed in on me before taking in the rest of the scene. He pushed to his feet. "What's going on?"

"Probably roofies," Romero said.

Roofies? I narrowed my eyes at the asshole who'd drugged my sister. I wanted to hurt him, but the expression on Matteo's face made it clear that I would get my wish. His eyes held a promise to me. I knew it was sick, but somehow this made me want to kiss him even more.

Something was so wrong with me.

Aria and I were sent away before Luca and Matteo started dealing with the bastard, and Romero led us out the back door toward an SUV. My heart clenched when I settled on the back seat with Aria's head on my lap. She was so helpless. I stroked her blonde hair as I listened to her rambling. The idea that someone wanted to hurt her scared the shit out of me. This was probably the first time that I was glad for our bodyguards. Without them that sick fuck would have kidnapped Aria and raped her. But I knew he'd get what he deserved, and I was oddly okay with it. I hated the mob and what it stood for, but right now I couldn't bring myself to feel bad for Aria's attacker. Maybe this was a sign of how much this life had shaped me, a sign of how messed up I was. I couldn't get the look on Matteo's face out of my head. That flicker of excitement as he pulled out his knife before Aria and I left the room. He and Luca were both monsters. I wasn't sure yet who was more dangerous of the two. But the worst thing was that part of me felt attracted to Matteo's monstrous side.

Almost one month had passed since I'd last seen Matteo. Somehow his words about owning me still wouldn't leave my mind. Every time I relived our kiss, I brought them to the forefront of my brain to let my anger wash away any kind of longing my body felt. The only reason why I even still remembered that stupid kiss was because things at home were so bad. I was constantly fighting with Father, most of the time about my habit of saying whatever crossed my mind, just like today. "I don't give a damn what's expected of me."

Mother shushed me, her eyes shock-wide, but I was beyond listening. If Father told me one more time that I should behave like a decent lady, I'd lose my shit. "Why is it so difficult to get into your head? I don't want to be a lady, definitely don't want to be a good little wife to some mob asshole someday. I'd rather cut my own throat than end up like that."

I saw it coming but didn't even try to avoid it. Father's palm hit my face. It was one of his lighter slaps, which usually wasn't a good sign. He hit hard when he had no words to break my spirits. If he went easy on me, I wouldn't like what he had to say. He gripped my shoulders hard until I met his gaze. "Then maybe you should go looking for a sharp knife, Gianna, because Vitiello and I decided to marry you off to his son Matteo."

My mouth fell open. "What?"

"You must have made quite an impression because he asked his father to make this arrangement."

"You can't do that!"

"I can. And it wasn't my idea. Matteo seemed very adamant about marrying you."

"That bastard."

Father's grip tightened and I winced. Lily only stared with huge blue eyes. She and Aria had only occasionally experienced Father's rougher side. He usually reserved his slaps and cruelness for me, the bad daughter. "This is exactly the reason why I'm glad to have you out of our territory. If I married you off to one of our soldiers, I'd have to punish one of our own for beating you to death for your insolence, but if Matteo Vitiello tortures some sense into you, I'll be off the hook because I can't risk war with New York."

I swallowed my hurt. I knew Father liked me least, and it wasn't as if I needed his approval or affection, but his words stung anyway. Mother, of course, didn't say anything, only stared down at her plate while folding and unfolding her stupid napkin. Lily's eyes were brimming with tears but she knew better than to open her mouth when Father was in a mood. She and Aria had always been better at self-preservation than me.

"When did you make the decision?" I asked firmly, trying to mask my feelings.

"Matteo and his father approached me right after Aria's wedding."

And suddenly I knew when Matteo had decided to marry me: when I'd told him the morning after our kiss that I would never marry him. The arrogant asshole couldn't take the hit to his pride. He was marrying me to prove a point: that he got whatever he wanted, that he had the power while I was a marionette in the hands of the mafia. "I won't marry him or anyone else. I don't care what you say. I don't care what the Vitiellos are saying. I don't *fucking* care."

Father shook me hard until my ears started ringing. "You will do as I say, girl, or I swear I will beat you until you forget your name."

I glared. I'd never hated anyone as much as I hated the man in front of me, and yet part of me, some hopeful, stupid, weak part loved him. "Why do you do this? It's not necessary. We already gave them Aria to make peace. Why do you force me to marry? Why can't you let me go to college and be happy?"

Father's lips curled in disgust. "Go to college? Are you really that stupid? You are going to be Matteo's wife. You are going to warm his bed and bear his children. End of story. Now go to your room before I lose my patience."

Lily sent me a pleading look. What had once been Aria's job was now Lily's: keeping me out of trouble. If it hadn't been for her, I would have continued the fight. I didn't care if Father beat me over and over again, it wouldn't change my mind.

I turned on my heel and ran up to my room where I grabbed my phone and flung myself on my bed. I speed-dialed Aria and after the second ring she answered. Hearing her voice, the tears I'd been holding back, slipped out. At least, our bastard of a father couldn't see them.

"Aria," I whispered. The tears were coming faster already.

"Gianna, what happened? What's going on? Are you hurt?"

"Father's giving me to Matteo." The words sounded so ridiculous. Nobody in the outside world would even understand them. I wasn't a piece of furniture that could be handed over to someone and yet that was my reality.

"What do you mean he's giving you to Matteo?"

"Salvatore Vitiello spoke to Father and told him that Matteo wanted to marry me. And Father agreed!"

"Did Father say why? I don't understand. I'm already in New York. He didn't need to marry you off to the Famiglia too."

"I don't know why. Maybe Father wants to punish me for saying what I think. He knows how much I despise our men, and how much I hate Matteo. He wants to see me suffer." That wasn't exactly the truth. I didn't really hate Matteo, at least not more than I hated every other Made Man. I hated what he stood for and what he did, hated that he had asked Father for my hand like my opinion didn't matter.

"Oh, Gianna. I'm so sorry. Maybe I can tell Luca and he can change Matteo's mind."

"Aria, don't be naïve. Luca knew all along. He's Matteo's brother and the future Capo. Something like that isn't decided without him being involved."

"When did they make the decision?"

After I was stupid enough to kiss him. "A few weeks ago, even before I came to visit." I couldn't tell her that it had happened at her wedding. Aria would only figure out a way to blame herself for my misery.

"I can't believe him! I'm going to kill him. He knows how much I love you. He knows I wouldn't have allowed it. I would have done anything to prevent the agreement."

Aria sounded remarkably like me in that moment, and while my heart swelled with love for her because of her willingness to protect me, I couldn't allow it. Maybe Aria didn't see it, but Luca was a monster and I didn't want her to get hurt, not for me, not when it was already too late. "Don't get in trouble because of me. It's too late anyway. New York and Chicago shook hands on it. It's a made deal, and Matteo won't let me out of his clutches."

And I knew it to be true. Even if he decided he didn't want me, he would never admit it. I'd always thought I could evade marriage, had always thought I could figure out a way to go to college, to find a life away from the mob world.

"I want to help you, but I don't know how," Aria said miserably.

"I love you, Aria. The only thing that stops me from cutting my wrists right now is the knowledge that my marriage to Matteo means I'll live in New York with you." I'd never considered suicide a valid option, had never felt miserable enough to do it, but sometimes it felt like the only choice I had left in my life, the only way to decide my own fate and to ruin Father's plans was actually when to end it. But I'd never actually go through with it. I couldn't hurt my siblings like that, and regardless of my hopeless future, I clung to life too much.

"Gianna, you are the strongest person I know. Promise me you won't do anything stupid. If you hurt yourself, I couldn't live with myself."

"You are much stronger than me, Aria. I have a big mouth and flashy bravado, but you are resilient. You married Luca, you live with a man like him. I don't think I could have done it. I don't think I can." I'd seen glimpses of Matteo's darkness in New York when he'd offered to kill Aria's attacker to make me happy, and afterwards in his eyes when he'd been covered in blood like Luca. There hadn't been regret or guilt in his gaze then. Sometimes I thought he was the more dangerous of the two because he was less in control. Sometimes I thought he hid how messed up he was with his outgoing personality.

"We'll figure it out, Gianna," Aria said.

I knew she couldn't do anything.

That evening Matteo fucking Vitiello actually dared to call my phone. I ignored him. There was no way in hell that I'd talk to him. Not after what he'd done. If he thought this was over, if he thought he'd won, then he had another thing coming.

chapter 4

—MATTEO—

I was ready for this fucking day to be over. First Father's funeral, and now hours of discussion with the Cavallaros and Scuderis about ways to keep the Russians at bay and to show them who was boss. It wasn't like I needed time to grieve. Luca and I hadn't harbored any feelings except for contempt and hatred for our father in a very long time but I wasn't a fan of funerals and everything they entailed. Especially seeing my stepmother cry her fake tears had grated on my fucking nerves. Did she really think anyone believed she actually missed her sadistic husband? She'd probably spit on his carcass when nobody was looking. It's what I wanted to do.

The only good thing about this whole ordeal had been Gianna who had to attend the funeral with her family. She'd ignored my calls ever since she'd found out about our marriage a week ago, but she couldn't avoid me forever. I was actually looking forward to our first private encounter. I loved when she was angry.

After the meeting, I was on my way to my motorcycle when I heard steps behind me. I turned, finding Luca running my way, the phone pressed against his ear and a thunderous look on his face.

Before I could ask him what had crawled up his ass, he lowered the phone and said, "Cesare called. The Russians are attacking the mansion. Romero is trying to get everyone to safety, but there are too many attackers."

"Where are Gianna and Aria?"

"I don't fucking know. We'll have to take a helicopter."

I followed Luca toward his car. He floored the gas the moment we both had sat down. We should have never let Aria and Gianna leave for the Hamptons without us. We'd thought they'd be safer there. We'd thought our enemies would attack in the city where so many members of the Outfit and the Famiglia had gathered to honor my father. We'd been fucking idiots.

Luca hit the steering wheel. "I'm going to hunt down every fucking Russian if they hurt Aria."

"I'll be at your side," I said. I didn't care how many Russians I'd have to cut into tiny pieces to get to Gianna. Damn it.

When we finally landed near our mansion in the Hamptons, Luca and I didn't speak. We both knew we might be too late. "They are fine," I said to Luca.

We got out of the helicopter and shot our way free until we reached the lobby of the mansion. I pulled my knife out of the throat of some asshole and straightened when one of the Russian bastards shouted from inside.

"We have your wife, Vitiello. If you want to see her in one piece you better stop fighting and drop your weapons."

Luca glanced my way. "Don't do anything stupid, Matteo."

"You aren't the only one with something to lose," I said grimly. "Gianna is in there too."

Luca gave a nod then slowly walked forward. I followed a few steps behind him. My eyes found Aria first. One of the Russian underbosses, a fucker named Vitali, was holding a knife against her throat. Luca would kill the bastard.

"So this is your wife, Vitiello?" Vitali asked, but I barely listened.

Gianna was sprawled out on the floor, a huge bruise on her forehead. I could tell that she was trembling, from fear or pain, I wasn't sure. Her blue eyes met mine. A huge Russian asshole towered over her. Bloodlust filled my body. I twisted my knives in my hands, trying to decide which part of the Russian's body I'd slice off first, probably the hand he'd used to hit her.

Gianna didn't take her eyes off me, like she knew I was going to make this all okay. I wouldn't let any of those fuckers hurt her now that I was here. And by God, I'd make them pay, make them regret the day they'd laid eyes on Gianna, make them regret the day they were fucking born.

"Let her go, Vitali," Luca snarled.

"I don't think so," Vitali said in that fucking annoying accent. "You took something that belongs to us, Vitiello, and now I have something that belongs to you. I want to know where it is." I wasn't sure what the Bratva bastard did because I kept my eyes on Gianna's captor and the assholes behind him but Luca took a threatening step forward, then stopped.

"Put your guns down or I'll cut her throat."

When pigs learn to fly, motherfucker.

There was a thud, then another. My eyes flew to Luca, who'd dropped his fucking guns to the floor. I couldn't believe it. He narrowed his eyes at me.

Was he serious? From the look on his face, he was. I put my knives down slowly. Gianna closed her eyes as if she thought everything was over. It wasn't over, far from it. Not before I'd killed every fucking asshole in the room and made them regret the day they were born.

"Your wife tastes delicious. I wonder if she tastes this delicious everywhere," Vitali said as he pulled Aria against him like he was going to kiss her. I could tell that Luca was seconds away from attacking.

The Russian asshole behind Gianna nudged her butt with his shoe and grinned. His foot would be the second thing I'd cut off, and I'd take my fucking time killing him.

Vitali licked Aria's chin. She looked like she was going to be sick. Then she reached into her back pocket and pulled a switchblade out. Where the hell had she found it? The moment she rammed it into Vitali's thigh, I fell to my knees, gripped my gun with my left hand and one of my knives with my right hand. I shot four times in quick succession. Two bullets tore through the calves of the asshole who'd kicked Gianna, the third broke every bone in his right hand, the fourth smashed the skull of another bastard. I flung the knife at the same time. It pierced the eye socket of Russian number three.

I stormed toward Gianna, slipped my arms under her body and carried her over to the side where she was shielded by a massive wooden sideboard. I knelt in front of her and shot another Russian, then another. Gianna's face was pressed up against my knee, and I put my palm down on the top of her head, stroking her unruly red hair.

A woman cried out. My eyes darted around until they settled on Luca who was cradling an unmoving Aria in his arms. I froze, my heart slamming against my chest.

"No!" Gianna cried hoarsely. She tried to sit up but her arms gave away and she fell against me. "Aria!"

I wrapped my arm around her and she stared up at me with terror-stricken eyes.

"Help Aria! Help her!" she whispered.

She tried to stand again. I helped her up, one arm around her waist, but didn't let her go to her sister. Luca looked like he would kill anyone who dared to approach. There was an expression on his face I'd never seen before. Leading a life of brutality, Luca and I had the potential to snap. But until now I hadn't thought there was anything on this planet that could actually bring Luca to the brink.

Gianna started crying. I touched her cheek. "Shh. Aria will be fine. Luca won't let her die."

For everyone's sake I hoped I was right. Gianna leaned against me, hands clutching my shirt. I peered down at her.

When Aria finally opened her eyes, Gianna let out a sob and pressed her face against my chest. I cupped her head, then brushed a kiss against it. She didn't react. She was probably in shock.

"What about Gianna, Lily, and Fabi?" Aria asked in a weak voice.

Gianna lifted her head but didn't let go of me. "Fine."

Luca lifted Aria into his arms and after some discussion carried her upstairs to one of the bedrooms. The doc was already on his way.

Gianna tried to stand on her own but swayed and had to grip my arm. Her eyes lost focus for a moment before they settled on me again. She didn't say anything, only stared up at me. I lightly brushed my fingertips over the bruise on her forehead. "Is this the only place you're hurt?"

She shrugged then winced. "My side hurts, and my ribs."

"Hey, Matteo, what about this asshole?" Romero asked, nudging the Russian who'd kicked Gianna.

"Is he the only survivor?"

"There is at least another one," Romero said.

"Good. But that one is mine. I'll question him."

"That's the guy who hit my head," Gianna said quietly.

"I know."

She searched my face but I wasn't sure what she was looking for. Her eyes fluttered shut for a moment but she quickly opened them again.

"You need to lie down," I said.

She didn't even try to protest, which was a bad sign. I tightened my hold on her and led her toward the staircase.

"Matteo?" Romero called.

I glanced over my shoulder at him and the other men. "I'll be back in a moment. Get rid of the bodies, and take the two living Russians down into the basement."

Romero nodded. "Okay." Then his eyes slid to Cesare's body on the ground. There was nothing we could do for him. I'd known him for a long time. He'd been a good, loyal soldier. The time to mourn him would come, but it wasn't now.

I helped Gianna up the stairs, and pretty much carried her down the corridor toward one of the guest bedrooms. I really wanted to take her to the room I slept in when we were in the mansion but I didn't want to have a fucking fight, not until Gianna was fit enough to be an equal contestant. She lay down on the bed, and closed her eyes with a groan.

I bent over her. "I want to take a look at your ribs. Don't punch me."

Her eyes fluttered open, and the hint of a smile tugged at her lips. I wondered if it was because she had a concussion or if she'd finally come to terms with our impending marriage.

I pushed her shirt up, revealing inch over inch of creamy skin, but before my mind could come up with any ideas, I found the first bruises. A big one on her waist and two slightly smaller ones over her rib cage. Gently, I pressed down on the bruise on her waist but she flinched away from my touch with a hiss.

"Fuck. That hurts."

I gritted my teeth. I couldn't wait to go down to the basement and have a word with the asshole who'd hurt her. I slid my hands higher, lightly tracing her ribs.

She shivered. "What are you doing?"

"I want to see if your ribs are cracked," I told her.

"You want to use your chance to grope me, admit it." Her attempt at humor was ruined by her shaky voice but I decided to play along. She didn't need to know that I was thinking of a way to prolong her attacker's suffering.

I smirked. "We'll be married in less than a year, then I can grope you whenever and wherever I want."

Her smile died and she turned away, closing her eyes. Maybe she hadn't come to terms with our marriage yet...

I straightened. "I need to go back down. I'll send the doc to you when he's done with your sister. You should catch some rest. Don't walk around the house."

She didn't open her eyes, didn't give any indication that she'd heard me at all.

I walked out, and closed the door. The doc was heading my way, one of his assistants, a young woman whose name I kept forgetting, a few steps behind him. "Where's Aria?" he asked in his raspy, chain-smoker voice.

I pointed toward the master bedroom. "When you're done with Aria, take a look at Gianna. I don't think she's seriously injured but I want to be sure."

He gave a curt nod, not even slowing. Nobody wanted to make Luca wait.

"Call me before you go in. I want to be there when you check on Gianna."

The doc was over sixty but that didn't mean I wanted him alone with Gianna, not after almost losing her.

He paused briefly, pale eyes settling on me. "She's yours?"

"Yes."

He nodded simply then he continued toward the master bedroom. I turned and headed downstairs.

When I stepped into the basement, the two Russian survivors were tied to chairs. Tito, one of our best enforcers, leaned against one wall, his arms crossed. Romero stood beside him. Another soldier, Nino, attached a drip to the asshole I was going to tear apart. The other Russian was in slightly better shape and didn't need a transfusion—yet. Once Tito got his hands on the poor bastard that would change too.

Tito straightened and inclined his head.

"I hope you didn't start yet," I said.

"We waited for you," Tito said.

"Does it look as if Tito started his work yet?" Nino asked eagerly. The kid had a sick fascination with torture.

"Good." I stalked toward Gianna's attacker. He glowered at me. "What's your name?" I asked.

"Fuck you," he said in heavily accented English.

I smiled at Tito, Romero, and Nino. Then I unsheathed my knife and held it out for the Russian bastard to admire. "You sure you don't want to tell me your name?"

He spit in front of my feet. "Where's that red-haired whore? Her pussy was calling for me."

Nino nudged Romero with an eager smile. Tito had pulled his own knife and was wiping it on his jeans.

"Tough words for a dead man," I said lightly.

"I won't tell you anything."

"That's what they all say." I stepped closer. "Let's see how tough you really are. Twenty minutes is the longest it ever took me to get someone's name."

I slammed my fist into his side, right over his left kidney. While he gasped for breath, I nodded at Tito to start his work on the other Russian bastard.

Twelve minutes later I'd learned that the man in front of me was called Boris and had been working for the Bratva in New York for six years, before that he'd been in Saint Petersburg. He was still reluctant to give me more than the basic information. I paused, staring down at his blood-covered face. "You sure you don't have an answer to my question?"

He coughed, blood dripping down onto his shirt. "Fuck you."

"I can do this all night, but I can promise you, it won't be pretty."

—GIANNA—

I grew tired of waiting for the doc to show up. I didn't feel very dizzy anymore, and I barely winced when I straightened. And to be honest, being alone freaked me out after what had happened today. I'd been sure we'd all die, and my body still wasn't convinced otherwise. My pulse was fast and occasionally I broke into a sweat. All because the mob had a bone to pick with the Bratva.

I walked out of my room, then hesitated in the corridor. My eyes darted to the end of the hallway where the master bedroom was. Luca and the doc were probably still taking care of Aria. They'd send me away if I tried to walk in, or worse lock me into the guest bedroom so I couldn't wander the house. I decided to go in search for Lily and Fabi instead. I yanked my phone out of my pocket and sent my sister a text.

Where R U?

Instead of replying, a door opened and Lily's dark blonde head poked out. Her face was puffy from crying and her eyes were huge and fearful. When her gaze settled on me, she ran in my direction and threw her arms around me.

"Where's Fabi?" I asked when I could breathe again. My ribs were throbbing fiercely from her hug but I didn't want her to know I was hurt. She looked terrified as it was.

"Asleep. They gave him some kind of sleeping pill because he was having a meltdown." She looked up at me. "I was so scared, Gianna. I thought we were all going to die, but Romero protected Fabi and me."

Her cheeks turned red. Her crush on Romero had been growing rapidly over the last few months. I didn't have it in me to tell her what kind of man he must be if Luca chose him as Aria's protector. Lily would realize soon enough that we were surrounded by the bad guys, not knights in shining armor.

"What about Aria? Romero only said she was fine before he left Fabi and me alone in that room and told me not to walk around the house because it was too dangerous."

"She was shot in the shoulder, but the doc is taking care of her. She'll be alright."

That's what I hoped. My eyes darted to the master bedroom again. I'd have to try to sneak in later when the doc and Luca were gone.

"Go back to your room, I'll be back soon." I turned to leave but Lily followed me like a lost puppy.

"Where are you going?" she asked.

"Downstairs. I want to see the damage."

"I'm coming with you."

I sighed. Aria would have told our sister "no," but it was hypocritical of me to tell Lily to behave when I'd rarely followed orders in my life. Lily wasn't a small kid anymore. "Okay, but be quiet and stay away from the men."

Lily rolled her eyes. "I'm not interested in them."

"I didn't say you were, but they might be interested in you."

I really didn't want to have to explain to Luca that I had to kill one of his men because they touched Lily. Of course, I'd first have to figure out a way to kill them. We headed downstairs. The entrance hall was a mess. Blood and broken glass littered the floor. At least the bodies were gone, but a trail of blood led outside to a pile of dead Russians. I really hoped they didn't treat Umberto's body like that. My chest tightened but I fought the sadness. Umberto had chosen this life. Death was part of the game.

I blocked Lily's view of the corpses and dragged her toward the living room, which wasn't in much better shape. The white couches would definitely have to be replaced. I didn't think any bleach in the world could get out the stains. Lily made a small distressed sound and I pulled her further along, already regretting that I had allowed her to come with me. A couple of men were taking a smoking break on the terrace, and glanced our way as we passed. They didn't seem bothered by the blood. I walked faster.

"Hey," Lily protested but I ignored her. If I'd been on my own, I wouldn't have cared but I didn't want to put my sister in danger.

We headed to the back of the house where the kitchen was, and almost bumped into another man. "Watch where you're going," he said, then paused and actually checked us out. I didn't know him and I had no interest of finding out more about him.

I pushed Lily past him. His eyes followed us all the way to the back of the corridor. When we turned the corner, we came face-to-face with a steel door, which was left ajar. A cry of pain carried out from below and made me shiver.

Lily clutched my arm, blue eyes wide. "What was that?"

I swallowed. I had a pretty good idea what was going on but I wasn't going to tell her that. "I don't know." I took a step closer to the door, then hesitated. I couldn't take Lily with me, but I couldn't leave her alone in the hallway when there were so many creepy fucks running around. I opened the door and peered down a long, dark staircase. Light spilled out from somewhere in the basement. Lily was almost pressed against my back, her breath hot against my neck.

"You don't want to go down there, right?" she whispered.

"Yes, but you will stay on the stairs."

Lily followed me a few steps down before I gave her a warning look. "Stay there. Promise me."

Another cry sounded from below.

Lily flinched. "Okay. I promise."

I wasn't sure if she meant it but she looked freaked out enough that I was willing to take the risk. I crept down the remaining steps, but halted on the last step, scared of what I might see. Exhaling, I stepped down and found myself in a huge basement. Bile shot up my throat. I wasn't stupid. I knew what the mob did to their enemies, especially if they wanted to get information out of them, but hearing stories and actually coming face-to-face with the horrendous reality of it were two very different things.

I braced my hand against the rough wall, my fingers curling around the hard edge. Two men were bound to chairs. Matteo and a tall, heavily muscled guy seemed to be in charge of pressing information out of them, while Romero stood back, but he must have had some part in their torture too because his hands were covered in blood, and so were his clothes. But it was nothing compared to the sight of Matteo. His white shirt was covered in blood, his rolled-up sleeves revealed blood-covered skin. There was red and red and red, so many different shades of it. But the worst, God the worst thing, was his face. There was no pity, no mercy, no nothing. There wasn't excitement or eagerness either, that was what I tried to cling to. At least he didn't get off on what he was doing. He didn't seem to feel anything judging from his expression.

I'd always known his easygoing, playful, flirty attitude was a mask to cover up the ugly truth, but again knowing and having that knowledge confirmed in such a brutal way were two very different pair of shoes. Maybe if I'd been more naïve I could have convinced myself that Matteo was doing this because he'd had to bury his father today, because he was grief-stricken and needed an outlet for the pain, but I knew better. This was common mob business. Grief had nothing to do with it.

One of the tied-up Russians was the man who'd hurt me and I knew that was why Matteo had chosen him as his victim.

I'd always wanted out of the world I'd been born in, this fucked-up brutal world I knew, but in this moment I made the decision to actually try to flee. No matter the cost, no matter what it took and what I had to do, I would escape this hell. How could anyone want to stay when they saw this?

I knew people got used to these things, but I didn't want to get used to them. I could already tell that I had less trouble with blood every time I saw it. How much longer until the sight of someone being tortured would do nothing to me? How much longer until the voice in my head that said the Russian bastard deserved it and would have done the same to me if given the chance wasn't a quiet whisper but a roaring shout?

Something brushed my arm and I jerked back, barely stifling a cry of surprise. Lily stood beside me, and then everything went very quickly. I opened my mouth to send her back up but at the same time her eyes settled on the scene in the center of the room, and I knew things would get very ugly. I'd heart Lily scream before but that had been nothing in comparison to the sound breaking free from her lips when she saw the blood and the men who'd lost it. I supposed it was close to the sound fluffy lambs made when they were being slaughtered.

I actually flinched away from Lily. Her eyes went wide, then dilated scarily, her face taking on an expression that scared the shit out of me. All eyes jerked toward us. Matteo released the Russian, narrowed his dark eyes at me, as if I was the one doing something wrong. Lily kept up her screaming, a high-pitched wail that made the hairs on my neck rise.

"Romero!" Matteo snarled, nodding toward my sister. "Take care of Liliana."

Romero advanced on us. Tall and imposing.

Lily had always fawned over him, but now even she couldn't see anything but the killer in him. His hands were red. Red from blood, and Lily completely lost her shit. I could only stare. I was unable to move. Somewhere in the back of my mind a voice was telling me to talk to my sister, to try to calm her, to do something, *anything*, but that voice was drowned out by the terrified static filling my head.

The steel door slammed against the wall above our heads and then Luca was suddenly there. "What the fuck is going on here?"

Nobody replied.

Romero spoke to my sister in a soothing voice. "Calm down, Lily. Everything is okay."

Really? The scene in front of us told a very different story. Nothing about this was okay.

Of course, Lily wasn't to be calmed. Romero gripped her arm and Luca went to help him, but she was fighting them like an animal. How could such a skinny girl fight off two men?

Romero slung his arms around her chest, trapping her arms against her sides, but that didn't stop Lily from kicking out at him and everything around her, and she still didn't stop screaming at the top of her lungs.

"Shut her up! Aria will hear," Luca growled. He tried to catch her legs but she lashed out and kicked his chin. He stumbled back, more from surprise than anything else. Of course they could have subdued her easily if they hadn't been so careful not to hurt her. I took a step in their direction, worried that they might give up the gentle approach soon, but the ground tilted under me and I had to grip the wall again.

"Lily," I said. "Lily, stop."

She didn't even hear me.

The tall, muscled guy took a few steps toward them as if he was going to interfere, but Matteo pushed him back. "No. Stay out of it."

I'd forgotten about Matteo, but while I had watched Lily, he'd managed to clean his hands. They were still pink but at least not smeared with blood. His eyes settled on me but I had to look away. I couldn't return his gaze right now. I had a feeling I wasn't far from pulling a stunt like Lily and going bat-shit crazy on them. The coppery scent of blood hung like fog in the air, clogged my throat and nose, seemed to sink into my skin, bury itself deep in my body together with the horrible images.

Lily managed to kick off the wall, causing Romero to stumble back, lose his balance and land on his back with Lily on top of him. He grunted and lost his hold on my sister. She pushed to her feet, a look like a hunted animal on her face. Her gaze passed right through me.

"Lily, calm down," I tried again.

She tried to storm past Matteo but he was too quick. He grabbed her wrist, and wrapped an arm around her waist. Then she was suddenly on her back and he was kneeling on her legs and had her hands pinned above her head. Luca headed toward them with a syringe in his hand. That was the final straw.

I stumbled toward them despite my wobbly legs. "Don't hurt her!" I hissed. "Don't you fucking dare hurting her!"

"I'm trying very hard not to hurt her, but she's making it difficult. Luca, now!" Matteo growled from his spot on top of my sister.

I blocked Luca's way. "What is that?" I pointed at the syringe.

"Something that will calm her down," Matteo said.

"Get out of the fucking way." Luca brushed past me, knelt beside my sister who was still struggling against Matteo's hold, and pushed the needle into her arm. It didn't take long for her to grow quiet and stop struggling. Matteo released her wrists and sat up. Lily whimpered before curling into herself and starting to cry silently.

"I hope you all burn in hell," I whispered harshly as I knelt beside her and stroked her hair. Matteo watched me with unreadable dark eyes. There were a few specks of blood on his throat; they seemed to be all I could see.

One of the Russians started to laugh. For a second I considered punching him in the face. I wasn't even sure how he was still capable of any sound the way he looked.

Matteo shot to his feet and got right into his face. "Shut the fuck up, or I swear I'll cut your dick into pieces while you watch."

"Romero, take Liliana into her room and tell the doc to check on her," Luca ordered, his voice already back to business.

Romero lifted Lily into his arms, and she actually pressed her face into his chest and sobbed. He was the last person she should seek out for comfort. He was one of the fucking reasons why she'd freaked out in the first place. Maybe she didn't even realize who held her.

I stood as well to follow after them. I wouldn't leave my sister alone with any of them. Luca gripped my wrist. "I want to have a word with you first."

"Let me go!" I snarled but he didn't budge.

Matteo grasped Luca's forearm. "Let her go."

Luca and he stared at each other for a moment, then I was finally free but now Matteo was blocking the stairs. I still couldn't look at his face. I glared at Luca instead. "I need to go to Lily. Maybe you didn't notice but she had a breakdown because of you sick fucks."

"She'll get over it," Luca said dismissively.

"Do you hear yourself? You make me sick. Lily won't ever get over what she saw today. She'll probably have fucking nightmares for years, only because of you."

Luca smiled coldly. "If you want to blame someone, blame yourself, because I have a feeling she was only down here because she followed you."

"Luca," Matteo said in warning. "It wasn't Gianna's fault."

It was my fault, at least partly, but I would never admit it in front of them. If it weren't for their sick business, nothing of this would have happened. I decided to switch to attack-mode. "I wonder what Aria will say when she finds out what happened."

Luca narrowed his eyes. "You won't tell her."

"Oh, I won't?" I asked. I had absolutely no intention of telling her. She didn't need the extra baggage, but Luca didn't need to know that. Matteo stepped between his brother and me, and touched my arms. I jerked back as if he'd burnt me. "Don't touch me ever again."

"I really don't get what you see in her," Luca said.

"Luca, stop provoking her," Matteo hissed, then he turned his dark eyes on me. "You can't tell Aria. It won't serve any purpose, only make her miserable."

"Maybe she'll decide to leave him." I nodded toward Luca.

"Aria won't ever leave me," Luca said quietly. "She took a fucking bullet for me today. I almost lost her. I won't ever lose her again. And I won't let you ruin things between us."

The worst thing was that I knew he was right when he said Aria wouldn't leave him, not even when I told her what I'd seen today. It wasn't as if she didn't know what kind of man Luca was and what kind of things his men did on his orders. He'd killed and tortured for her before, and she still loved him. Somehow she could forget the monster and only see the man when she was with Luca. I was pretty sure I couldn't do it. I could hardly meet Matteo's gaze.

"I won't tell her," I said eventually. "But not for you. I'm doing it for her. I want to see her happy." And for some fucked-up reason Luca was making her happy, happier than I'd ever seen her. For her sake, I would pretend.

Luca turned to Matteo. "Take her to her room and make sure she stays there until Scuderi comes to pick them up. I don't want her to make another scene."

I bit back a snarky comment. "I want to see Aria. She needs me."

I could tell that Luca wanted to tell me "no" but he surprised me when he said, "You can stay with her when I'm not around."

"It's not like I'm eager to be in a room with you."

"Come on, Gianna." Matteo gripped my arm and didn't even release me when I protested. He led me up the basement stairs, then along the long hallway and up the stairs. We didn't speak until we reached my room and I jerked free of his grip.

My eyes darted to his pink hands and blood-covered shirt. Matteo followed my gaze, grimacing. "I'll go change."

"Don't bother. I won't ever forget what I saw."

Matteo walked up to me and I stood my ground, despite my body's desire to flee. "You are clever, Gianna. Don't tell me you didn't know what we were doing behind closed doors. Believe me, the Outfit doesn't handle enemies with kid gloves either."

"I know. That's why I despise everything about the fucking mob. And you are right, I wasn't surprised about what I saw today. It only confirmed what I'd known all along."

"And what is that?"

"That you are a sick fuck and that I'd rather die than marry you."

Matteo pulled me against him, his dark eyes practically scorching me with their intensity. "Maybe you think you could live in the normal world, maybe you think you could date a normal guy, but you'd get bored, Gianna. Maybe you don't want to admit it, but it excites you to be with someone like me. If a normal guy tells you he'd kill and torture to protect you, he'd be lying, exaggerating at best, but I'm making a promise I can keep."

"Let me go," I gritted out.

He did, then gave me his fucking shark-smile and headed for the door. "I'll lock the door. Luca will unlock it when he takes you to Aria."

"So you're going back to torturing that guy?"

Matteo's gaze flickered with an emotion I couldn't place. "Maybe. I'm a sick fuck, remember?" He slipped out. "But maybe I'll let Luca have some fun with the Russians first." His gaze lingered on me for another moment before he closed the door and locked it. I reached for a vase on the sideboard and flung it at the door where it shattered and tumbled to the floor.

I squeezed my eyes shut, making a promise I was determined to keep. I would escape before my wedding to Matteo. I would leave this life behind and never return. I would try to live a decent, honest, ordinary life.

Afterward I felt calmer, even if I knew it would be close to impossible to escape from the mob. It would take a plan and help, but I still had ten months until my wedding. Plenty of time.

Later when Luca picked me up and took me to Aria, I didn't even provoke him. I ignored him, even when he warned me again not to tell Aria about the basement. He didn't have to worry. I couldn't burden Aria with the truth, not when she still had to live in this world and with Luca.

chapter 5

—GIANNA—

"You look so pretty," Lily said from her spot on my bed in the guest room of the Vitiello mansion in the Hamptons. At least, it wasn't the same room I'd had last time. I had to suppress a shiver when I thought of that day and all the blood I'd seen.

I glared at my reflection. Mother had chosen the dress for me because I'd refused to go shopping with her for my engagement party. It was a surprisingly nice dress, which didn't make me look like a tramp. I still shuddered when I remembered the slutty dress they'd chosen for Aria when she'd gotten engaged to Luca.

My dress was dark green, my favorite color. I was surprised Mother knew that much about me, or maybe Lily had helped secretly. The skirt was flared and reached my knees. Definitely modest. Maybe Father thought I was bad girl enough and didn't need a slutty outfit to emphasize that further.

"I don't know why they bother," I said. "They know I don't want to celebrate my engagement to Matteo. I don't want to marry him."

"It's tradition."

Lily was wringing her hands nervously in her lap. Pushing my own feelings aside, I walked toward her and sat down. She didn't even look up but her lower lip was trembling.

"Hey, are you okay?"

She gave a small shake of her head. "I know it's stupid but I'm kind of scared."

"Of Luca, Matteo, and Romero?"

"I'm sorry."

I wrapped my arm around her. "Why are you apologizing? It's perfectly natural for you to be afraid of them after what you saw in September."

She shuddered. "I can't get it out of my head. I dream about it almost every night."

Two months since that day, and almost every night she woke me with her screams before she slipped into my bed. "They would never hurt you, Lily. We are girls, they will always want to protect us from harm." It was laughable that I was singing their praises, but I would have done anything to calm Lily down.

"I know." She took a deep breath. "I hope I don't freak out like last time. Father would be so mad if I made a scene."

I kissed her cheek. "You won't. I'll be at your side. And Aria will be there too. Everything will be okay."

Someone knocked at the door but before I could reply, Fabi poked his head in, his eyes darting between Lily and me. "Are you having a girl talk?"

"Yes," Lily said at the same time as I said, "No."

Fabi narrowed his eyes and slipped into the room. He looked too cute in his tuxedo. "Father sent me to tell you everyone's waiting." He straightened his shoulders, his little chin lifting a little higher. Fabi had turned ten a couple of days ago and in a few years, he would already start his initiation process. I was glad that I probably wouldn't get the chance to see my sweet, good-natured brother become a killer.

"You ready?" I asked Lily, who nodded quickly but her eyes told a different story. I understood her only too well.

Fabi tugged at his collar, which looked tight even from afar. "Lily is supposed to come with me, so you can enter alone."

Lily stiffened beside me. She had clung to me when we'd first stepped foot into the mansion this morning. I wasn't sure why Luca and Matteo had insisted on celebrating in New York, and worse in the very place where Lily had seen Romero and Matteo torture a Russian, but it was too late now. So far we'd managed to avoid them all. I hadn't even seen Aria yet.

"No. I don't care what Father wants. Lily and I will go down together."

Fabi gnawed on his lip. "Father will be angry."

I stood, pulling Lily with me. "He'll get over it." He wouldn't make a scene in front of New York. He'd wait with his punishment until we were back in Chicago. Lily, Fabi, and I headed downstairs together and Lily's grip on my hand tightened with every step we took. As we passed the front hall her eyes darted to the back where the entrance to the basement was. She shivered. Voices were coming from the living room and we headed toward the door, our shoes clicking on the marble floor; a floor that had been slick with blood two months ago. I tried to forget what I'd seen that day. I needed to focus on today if I didn't want things to end badly.

It wasn't a big celebration, but the most important members of the New York Famiglia and the Outfit had been invited. I was determined to be on my best behavior today. I didn't want Father to think I was thinking of ways to escape and up the number of my bodyguards.

The moment we entered the living room, I knew I could kiss that plan goodbye. Lily let out a small sound in the back of her throat, her nails digging into my palm. Father was talking to Dante Cavallaro, Luca, and Matteo, while the other men, as well as Aria, my mother, and Matteo's stepmother, Nina Vitiello, stood around them. Father's eyes narrowed immediately when he saw me with Lily. Fabi quickly rushed toward him and Father scowled at him, probably giving Fabi a lecture under his breath.

Matteo's gaze captured me with its intensity. He was dressed in black pants and a white shirt.

"Gianna," Father said in a tight voice. "We've been waiting for you."

Everyone expected me to walk over to my father, so he could hand me over to Matteo, and I would have if Lily hadn't started shaking beside me at the sight of Matteo, Romero, and Luca.

Her eyes darted to me. There was a flicker of fear on her face. I didn't want Father, much less anyone else, to know that she was terrified. Father would be furious. Maybe he'd even hit her, and Lily really didn't need another bad experience. She'd been struggling enough in the last few months.

She was frozen beside me.

"Gianna, stop the nonsense and come over here," Father growled.

Aria came toward me. "What's wrong?"

Lily and I exchanged a look. So far we hadn't told Aria anything, but it would be hard to explain Lily's strange behavior.

"Long story," I said. "Can you take Lily's hand?"

But Father had had enough. He stalked toward me and grabbed my wrist in a crushing grip before he dragged me toward Matteo. "I've had enough of your insolence." I almost stumbled on my heels as I hurried after him.

Matteo pulled me against him, forcing Father to release me. The look on Matteo's face bore a remarkable resemblance to the one he'd had when the Russian had kicked me. I was glad to escape Father's wrath for now and didn't pull away from Matteo. Aria was hugging Lily to her side and both were whispering quietly. I hoped Aria could calm our sister down. I hated seeing Lily so distressed.

"I know what you did there," Matteo murmured in my ear once he'd put the engagement ring on my finger.

"And what would that be?"

"You helped your sister."

I slipped out from under his arm. "I wouldn't have had to help her if she wasn't terrified of you."

Matteo didn't look sorry. Maybe he wasn't capable of guilt. "I'll have a word with her."

"Stay away from her," I hissed, but he seemed to find my threatening tone funny, and I blew. My voice rose. I was beyond caring if the others would hear. "And while you're at it, stay away from me too. I don't want anything to do with your fucked-up world."

Unfortunately Father heard, and so did probably everyone else in the room, and while Matteo didn't seem to take my outburst to heart, Father's scowl promised punishment. I had a feeling Matteo would have stopped him, if I'd asked for his help, but I didn't want to be indebted to Matteo. I'd rather bear Father's beatings.

I couldn't stop staring at the yellow gold ring with the huge diamond in the center. Father had made it very clear what would happen if I took it off.

In our world it was like a cattle brand. Everyone would know whom I belonged to.

chapter 6

—GIANNA—

I hated having to involve Aria in any of this, but she was my last option. The biggest problem was actually asking her. I didn't trust the phones. I wouldn't put it past our father to rig them so he could keep an eye and ear on me. I had to ask her in person but as a punishment for my misstep at the engagement party I hadn't been allowed to see Aria since our family's Christmas party. But after weeks of begging, Lily and I finally managed to convince Father to let Lily and me fly to New York for Lily's birthday in April.

Lily was practically bouncing with excitement during our flight. I was still surprised how quickly she'd recovered from the horrible events of last September. I really hoped she wouldn't be set back by being back in New York. She'd been avoiding Matteo and Luca the last few times we'd seen them but this time we'd be staying at Luca's penthouse, so there was no way she could do it.

The moment we walked into the waiting hall buzzing with voices, I wanted to groan. Matteo stood beside Aria and Luca. I should have realized he would come. He seemed determined to ignore my antipathy. Sometimes I almost considered to give up on running away and to try to come to terms with my marriage to Matteo, but then there were the moments when he gave me that cocky grin like now, and then I wanted to run away as fast as my feet could carry me because I actually wanted to kiss him, despite what I'd seen him do in September.

Lily kept close to me. It was the only sign that she hadn't forgotten what had happened almost seven months ago. She didn't take my hand like she might have done a couple of years ago but her arm brushed mine as we walked toward Luca, Matteo, and Aria. "Are you okay?" I whispered.

She jumped, flushing. "Yeah." She squared her shoulders. "I'm fine." She almost managed to hide her nerves from me. Aria ran toward us when we'd almost reached them and threw her arms around both of us. "I missed you so much."

"We missed you too," I whispered, kissing her cheek.

Lily beamed at both of us.

Aria shook her head. "You're as tall as me now. I still remember when you didn't want to go anywhere without holding my hand."

Lily groaned. "Don't say anything like that when Romero is around. Where is he anyway?"

I rolled my eyes, and Aria laughed. "He's probably at his apartment." Lily must have managed to get over her anxiety around Romero at some point. Puppy love turned you blind.

"Come on," Aria said. "Let's go."

As expected, Lily turned shy again the moment we stood in front of the guys. My protective side made me want to step in front of her and shield her from everything, but I knew she'd be embarrassed if I did something like that. My gaze found Matteo's eyes; they were warm; they were a normal guy's eyes, and for an instant I wanted to believe the lie he was so good at telling, but I forced myself to break our staring contest.

"The birthday girl," Matteo said with a smile at Lily, arms crossed over his chest. He looked so approachable and harmless, and I knew he was doing it on purpose because of Lily. Despite my best intentions not to, I felt grateful, and at the same time couldn't help but wonder how he could be so kind and funny one moment, when he was capable of the horrible things I'd seen in September.

"Not yet," Lily said, biting her lip. "Unless you have an early present for me." I almost exploded with relief. I'd worried Lily would be as nervous as last time when she'd see Matteo, but he was a master manipulator and had her wrapped around his finger again.

"I like the way you think," Matteo said with a wink. He took her suitcase then held out his arm for her to take. She glanced between Matteo and me. "Won't you carry Gianna's luggage?"

"Luca can take care of it," Matteo said, eyes dancing with mirth as they settled on me. Why did he have to be so…tolerable? If I didn't know any better, I'd say he had a suspicion I was trying to figure out a way to run away from our impending marriage.

I narrowed my eyes at him before turning to Lily. "Go on."

She linked arms with Matteo and they walked ahead. Luca took my suitcase without a word before following after his brother and my younger sister. I fell back with Aria. "Maybe Father should have married Lily off to Matteo instead of me," I said, only half-joking. She seemed to have no trouble getting along with him.

"Matteo needs someone like you, someone who talks back to him. I don't think she could handle him."

I snorted. "But you think I can?"

Aria searched my face. "There's something you're not telling me."

"Later," I whispered, and she nodded with a glance toward Luca and Matteo.

I didn't get the chance to talk to Aria until much later that day, and only because Luca and Matteo had business to conduct in their dance club "Sphere." Romero was still there but Lily had convinced him to play Scrabble with her in the living room so he was occupied as I led Aria out onto the roof terrace despite the cold. Once we stood at the edge of the roof, she turned to me. "You're up to something, aren't you?"

I hesitated, suddenly feeling guilty for even considering to involve Aria. "I can't do this, Aria. I want out. Out of this world. Out of my arranged marriage. Just out."

Her face became still, blue eyes wide. "You want to run?"

The wind had picked up and tore at my hair, but I wasn't certain if that was the only reason why I shivered. "Yes."

"Are you sure?"

"Absolutely," I said, though sometimes doubt kept me awake at night. This was a huge step. "Ever since the Bratva attacked the mansion and I saw what Matteo is capable of, I knew I had to run."

"It's not just Matteo, you know that, right? He isn't any worse than any other Made Man."

"That makes it even worse. I know that pretty much all the men in our world are capable of horrible things, and one day even Fabi will be, and I hate it, hate every second I'm trapped in this messed-up world."

"I thought you and Matteo were getting along better. You didn't try to rip each other's head off today."

"He's trying to manipulate me. Didn't you see how easily he could make Lily forget her nervousness around him?"

Aria shrugged. "It could be worse. Most men wouldn't have forgiven you for giving him such a hard time, but he really seems to like you."

Did he? I was never sure with Matteo. He was too good at hiding his emotions, at choosing the mask he wanted to show to the world. "Are you on his side?" I asked with a bit more force than I'd intended.

"I'm not on his side. I'm just trying to show you an alternative to running away."

Stunned, I said, "Why? You know I've never wanted this life. Why are you trying to make me stay?"

Aria glared, gripping my wrist. "Because I don't want to lose you, Gianna!"

"You won't lose me."

"Yes, I will. Once you've run away, we can't ever see each other again, maybe not even talk unless we figure out a way to do it without risking the mob tracing you."

Of course, in the back of my mind, I'd known that would be the result of my escape, but I'd pushed it aside, not able to bear the thought. "I know," I whispered. "You could come with me."

Aria parted her lips in surprise and even before she spoke I knew her answer. "I can't."

I nodded, facing away from her and letting my gaze wander over New York. I blinked a few times. "Because you love Luca."

She put her hand on mine. "Yes, but that's not the only reason. I can't leave Fabi and Lily behind either, and I've made peace with this life. It's all I've ever known. I'm okay with it."

Guilt crashed down on me. "Do you think I'm abandoning them if I leave?"

"They'll understand. Not everyone is cut out for a life in this world. You've always wanted to live a normal life, and they'll still have me. You have to think of yourself. I just want you to be happy."

I wrapped my arms around her, burying my face in her hair. "I don't think I can be happy here."

"Because you don't want to marry a killer, because you can't live with what Matteo does."

"No," I said quietly. "Because I can see myself being okay with it."

Aria drew back, pale brows drawn together. "What's wrong with that?"

I wanted to laugh and cry at the same time because I had a feeling that Aria wouldn't have asked that question before Luca. "Are you okay with what Luca does? Don't you ever lie awake at night feeling guilty for being married to a man like him?"

"We come from a family of men like him." She stepped back, her arms dropping to her sides. "Do you want me to feel guilty?"

"No. But normal people would feel guilty. Can't you see how messed up we are? I don't want to be like that. I don't want to spend my life with a man who carves up his enemies."

Aria stared but didn't say anything. She looked so horribly sad and hurt that I wanted to kick myself hard for ever opening my stupid mouth.

"I'm sorry. I didn't want to make you feel bad. I just…" I trailed off, not sure how to explain my conflicted emotions to Aria. "I know I have to risk it. I have to try to get away from all this and live a life without all the violence and messed-up morals. I'll always regret it if I don't."

"You know you can't ever come back. There's no going back once you've run. Even if Matteo would forgive you for insulting him like that, the Outfit would be responsible for your punishment until your marriage. And running away from the mafia is betrayal."

"I know."

"The Outfit punishes betrayal with death. Because you aren't a Made Man they might decide to go easy on you and throw you into one of their whorehouses or marry you off to someone far worse than Matteo."

"I know."

Aria gripped my shoulders. "Do you really? Few people risk running from the mob and there's a reason for it. Most people get caught."

"Most people but not all of them."

"Have you ever heard of someone who escaped the mob successfully?"

"No, but I doubt anyone would tell us about them. Neither Father nor Matteo or Luca have any interest in putting ideas in our heads."

Aria sighed. "You are really determined to go through with this."

"Yes."

"Okay," she said. This was the perfect moment to ask her for help but I realized I couldn't do it, couldn't ask that of her.

Of course Aria being Aria didn't need to be asked.

"You can't do it alone. If you want any chance at succeeding you'll need my help."

I stared at my sister, my beautiful, brave sister. I'd often thought we were twins who'd been born apart by some cruel twist of fate. She was the one person I'd die for. And if she'd asked me to stay, told me she couldn't live without me, I wouldn't even have hesitated. I'd have stayed, would have married Matteo. For her. But Aria would never ask that of me. Aria was the one thing that reminded me that there was good in our world too, and I hoped she'd never let the darkness around us corrupt her. "No," I said firmly. "I can do it on my own."

But Aria ignored my comment.

"If I help you to run, I'll betray the Famiglia and by doing so my husband," she said with a distant look in her eyes.

I shook my head. "You are right. And I can't let you take that risk. I won't let you risk it."

She linked her fingers with mine. "No, I will help you. I'm your only choice. And if anyone can make it, then it's you. You never wanted to be part of all this."

"Aria, you said it yourself, what I'm doing is betrayal and the mob deals harshly with people who betray them. Luca isn't the forgiving type."

"Luca won't hurt me." There wasn't the hint of doubt in her voice. Sadly, I didn't share her conviction. I opened my mouth to object but she raised her hand.

"He won't. If Salvatore Vitiello were still alive, things would be different. I'd have been under his jurisdiction, but Luca is Capo and he won't punish me."

How could she trust that cruel bastard like that? What must it be like to love someone so much that you would put your life in their hands without hesitation? "Maybe his men won't leave him a choice. He's a new Capo and if he looks weak, his men might revolt. Luca won't risk his power, not even for you. The Famiglia comes first to Made Men."

I was talking to a wall from the impact I was making on Aria. "Trust me," she said simply.

"I trust you. It's Luca whom I don't trust."

"And if you think about it, I wouldn't really be betraying the Famiglia. You are still part of the Outfit until you marry Matteo. That means what I'm doing is a betrayal of the Outfit at most, but I'm not bound to them, so I can't betray them."

"Be that as it may. Luca might not see it that way. Even if you aren't betraying the Famiglia, you're still going behind Luca's back. Not to mention that Matteo will probably move heaven and earth to find me."

"True," Aria said slowly. "He'll hunt you."

"He'll eventually lose interest."

Aria looked doubtful. "Perhaps. But I wouldn't count on it. We have to make sure he can't find you."

Above us the sky was turning dark gray, the first signs of an impending rainstorm. If I were superstitious, I'd probably see it as a bad omen. "Aria, I shouldn't have come to you with this. You can't get involved."

Aria rolled her eyes. It was such a me-thing to do that I couldn't help but smile despite the severity of our conversation.

"Don't try to talk me out of it. I'd feel guilty if I didn't help you and you got caught," she said firmly.

"And I will feel guilty if you get in trouble for helping me."

"I'm helping you. End of story."

"How can I ever make it up to you?"

"Just be happy, Gianna. Live the life you want, that's all I want."

That was so typically Aria. If anyone deserved a life outside of this fucked-up world, it would be her. I pressed my lips together, fighting tears. "Shit."

Aria smiled. "Come on. We need to figure out when and how to get you away."

"I suppose it's a bit too late to give it a try during this visit?" I forced a smile, wanting to get rid of the heavy feeling in my chest.

"Yeah. But you'll definitely have to run when you are in New York. You'll never escape from Father's men."

Sadly, she was right. Father didn't let me out of his sight for a second. He didn't trust me. The only thing missing from my prison was leg irons. "But Romero is always around."

Aria and I both glanced toward the living room where Lily was laughing at something Romero must have said. She looked so happy. "I think we can get him off our back," Aria said.

"Next time Lily won't be around to distract him. I don't want her to know about this."

Aria nodded. "I'll figure something out. I tricked him once before. I can do it again. Luca trusts me. Romero doesn't follow me as much as he did in the beginning."

Guilt twisted my insides again but I ignored it. "I have to get a passport so I can leave the country. I'll never be safe in the States."

"You should go to Europe."

"I've always wanted to visit Sicily," I joked.

Aria cracked up. "Yeah, that sounds like a foolproof plan."

"I need money. Maybe I can find out where Father keeps his stack of cash."

"No, he'd notice. We'll have to take Luca's money. If we wait until the last minute before we take it, he won't notice until it's too late."

"Are you sure?" I asked.

Aria nodded but there was a flicker of hesitation in her eyes.

"Maybe we can get money from somewhere else. I could ask one of the credit sharks for a loan. It's not like I'll be around for them to get it back," I said quickly.

Aria shook her head at once. "All the credit sharks either belong to the Famiglia or to the Bratva. That would be the quickest way to get caught."

"I know I can't ask the Famiglia, but what about the Russian credit sharks? I don't have to announce to them who I am. I could pretend I was some random girl with financial troubles."

Aria seemed to consider that but then she shook her head. "It's too risky. Those guys are dangerous."

Memories I'd tried to bury resurfaced like a tidal wave. I'd been terrified when the Russians had attacked the mansion. I'd been sure we'd die a horrible death, sure we'd be raped and tortured. I really didn't want anything to do with the Bratva ever again but Aria didn't need to know how much the images of that day still bothered me. Most of the time I managed to lock them away, and once I was in Europe, away from this world, they'd hopefully disappear for good. "Aria, you are married to the man all those dangerous guys are scared of."

"And you are engaged to the man who cuts those dangerous guys up," she said. "But the Russians are worse than our men. They don't have any honor."

I wasn't sure if that was possible, but I wasn't in the mood for that argument. "Okay, so no loan sharks, but what about a forged passport? I'll have to get that from somewhere. Is there anyone we could bribe?"

Another gust of wind tore at us, raising goose bumps all over my body. Aria moved closer to me until we huddled together. "No one will go against Luca."

"Except for us," I said with a snort. "Tell me this isn't crazy."

"It's crazy, but we'll figure something out." She paused, scrutinizing me.

I raised my eyebrows. "What?"

She smiled. "I have an idea. You know how people always say we look alike?"

"Not if you look closely. I'm a couple of inches taller than you and then there's this." I lifted a strand of my hair.

"Yeah, but if we dye your hair blonde, nobody will doubt that you are me. Luca has a few forged passports with different names in the same place where he stashes the money, in case we ever need to leave the country fast. You could use one of them."

"Luca will be able to track them."

"Yes, but you'll already have landed in Europe by then. You can throw away the passport once you're there and travel around without a passport until you figure out a way to get a new one. They don't have border control in the EU, so you should be fine to cross over to other countries within Europe."

Hope kindled in my body. "That could actually work."

"It will."

We stared at each other. "So I'm really running away," I whispered.

"Yes," Aria said quietly.

"When?"

"Next time you visit, so we have time to really think every detail of our plan through."

I couldn't believe I was really going to do this, but now I wouldn't back out, even if part of me wondered if this was really what I wanted.

I was allowed to visit Aria again in May; pretending that I had finally come to terms with my marriage to Matteo had made my father more lenient with me.

Lying had once been hard for me but I was getting better at it.

I hugged Lily and Fabi before I left Chicago, knowing it might very well be the last time I saw them, but I didn't allow myself to linger on that thought. It would make things only more difficult. If I started to cry, someone might get suspicious.

When I arrived in New York, Aria picked me up from the airport with a new bodyguard. There was something bittersweet about our reunion. The new guy gave me a quick nod after Aria and I had pulled apart. "Who is he?" I whispered.

"That's Sandro. He's one of Matteo's men." So Matteo had already chosen a bodyguard for me, for a future life as his wife, someone who would cage me in whenever Matteo wasn't around to do it.

Once we were in the penthouse, my new bodyguard retreated to the kitchen under the pretense of giving us privacy. As if there was ever such a thing under his constant surveillance. Aria and I lingered near the sofa, out of earshot. "Does Luca still have Romero guard you all day?"

Aria shrugged. "I don't mind having Romero around, especially when Luca is busy. Sandro has taken Cesare's place mostly, but he's never watched me before. "

"You need to ask Luca to let you go to college or do something else before you go crazy over here. I want you to be happy too, Aria. I want to know that you'll be okay once I'm gone."

"Don't worry. And the last few weeks I've been pretty busy planning your escape," Aria said with a teasing smile but there was a hint of wistfulness in her voice.

We both glanced at Sandro who was making coffee. "Why is that Sandro guy really here?"

"Because of you."

"Because I'm the troublemaker?"

"No," Aria said with a laugh. "Because Matteo wants you to get to know the guy who'll be your bodyguard once you move to New York."

"Oh great, how thoughtful of him." Again a decision about my life that no one had bothered to discuss with me. With a nod toward Sandro, I asked, "How are we going to get rid of him?"

"I have a plan." Aria opened her bag and pointed at a small syringe. At my confused look, she explained, "I remembered how you'd told me that Luca found the tranquilizer he used on Lily in a drawer in the basement. Last time I was in the mansion, I sneaked down there and took what we needed."

My eyes widened. "You are a genius, Aria."

"Not really."

Our eyes darted toward our bodyguard once more. He was busy with his phone. "How are we going to inject him with the tranquilizer?" I asked. "He's tall and strong, and probably a skilled fighter."

Aria bit her lip. "We have to distract him. Maybe I can talk to him and you ram the needle into his thigh?"

"What if I break the needle by accident or if he smashes it?"

"I have a second syringe, but that's it, so we should try to get it right the first time."

Aria could be so badass if she tried. "Are you sure the dosage is right?"

"I don't want him to get hurt so I reduced the dosage they listed on the packaging."

"Okay. It still should be enough to knock him out for a while, right?"

Aria nodded. "We should probably tie him up. I found duct tape in the gun cupboard."

She knew where her husband kept his guns? "Luca must really trust you."

Aria didn't say anything and I felt bad for bringing him up. Did I have to remind her how she was risking her marriage for me?

"Come on," she said after a moment. "Let's do this. Matteo and Luca will be back in a few hours. We should be gone by then."

After another look toward Sandro who was still reading something on his phone, she quickly handed me the syringe. I hid it behind my back as we strolled toward Sandro who finally looked up from his phone and set it down on the counter.

"Would you like some coffee?" he asked with a nod toward his own cup. He was polite and his brown eyes were friendly. He didn't *look* very threatening, but I didn't let that fool me.

Aria leaned next to him against the counter and pressed a palm to her stomach.

Sandro frowned. "Are you okay?"

"I'm not feeling so good," she said, then her legs buckled. It was a bit over the top if you asked me, but Sandro must have acted without thinking because he reached for her. *My chance.*

My arm shot out and I rammed the syringe into the back of his thigh and injected the tranquilizer. Sandro hissed, let go of Aria and lashed out instinctively. He caught my arm and I was thrown against the kitchen island, my back colliding painfully. I swallowed a cry.

"What the fuck?" he gasped, eyes furious as they darted between Aria and me. He reached for his phone but Aria shoved it away. It flew off the counter, crashed to the ground and skidded over the marble. Sandro staggered toward it, his movements already less coordinated than usual. I quickly rushed toward the phone and kicked it away. "Where's the stupid tape?"

Aria nodded and rushed away.

Sandro glared at me. "What are you doing?" he growled. He advanced on me, his hand fumbling for the gun in his chest holster. Did he want to hold us at gunpoint?

He didn't get very far. His legs gave away and he fell to his knees. He shook his head like a dog then tried to stand again.

"Aria!" I screamed. What if this didn't work? What if our plan was over before it had really begun?

"I'm coming!" She ran toward me with the tape. "Grab his arms."

I tried to pull Sandro's arms behind his back, but he was too strong even in his dazed state. He shook me off.

"It's not enough tranquilizer!"

"I don't want to hurt him," Aria said panicky.

I tried to grip his arms again but he managed to stagger back to his feet, pushing me out of the way. Aria moved quickly and thrust the second syringe into his leg. This time he dropped to his knees almost instantly, then fell to his side. Aria and I made quick work out of tying him up then she touched his throat.

"Is he okay?" I asked.

"Yeah, it seems so. I hope we didn't give him too much."

"He's a tall guy. I'm sure he'll be fine." I got up. Aria did the same and then she rushed off again. A few minutes later she returned with a huge stack of dollar notes as well as two passports. For a moment I thought she'd decided to go with me and that was why there wasn't only one passport, then I realized how ridiculous that thought was.

"Here." She handed me everything. "That's about ten thousand dollars. That should get you by for a while, and two passports just in case. But you should really get rid of them once you're in Europe."

I stuffed everything into my bag then grabbed my suitcase.

"Ready?" Aria asked, hesitating.

"As ready as I'll ever be." She didn't return my smile, only glanced at Sandro again before setting her phone down on the counter. I did the same to prevent them from tracking us.

We took the elevator down and hailed a taxi. Traffic was on our side and we pulled up in front of the JFK airport after forty-five minutes.

After we'd entered the departure area, I headed straight to the ticket counter to buy a one-way ticket to Amsterdam while Aria stayed back; the photo in the passport looked more like her than me and if we stood beside each other nobody would have been fooled.

I gingerly slid the fake passport across the counter. The woman barely glanced at the photo, despite the fact that I didn't have blonde hair like the girl in it. She probably thought I'd dyed it red. Twenty minutes later, I walked over to Aria with the ticket to freedom in my hand. I'd have thought I'd feel more excited, instead nerves twisted my stomach so tightly I worried I'd throw up, but I couldn't let Aria see it.

"So how did it go?" she asked nervously.

I waved the ticket in response. "She didn't even ask about my hair."

"That's good, but once you're in Amsterdam, you need to change your appearance."

I smiled, touched by her concern and at the same time wondering if I was really doing the right thing. This could be the last time I ever saw Aria. I couldn't even imagine a year without her, much less the rest of my life. "Don't worry."

A small part of me wondered how Matteo would feel once he found out. I didn't think my disappearance would do more than bruise his pride. This wasn't about love, or even feelings.

Aria peered toward the main entrance again. "When does your flight leave?"

"In two hours. I should probably go through security."

"I will rent a car and drive it out of town as a red herring. Luca will think you and I ran away together. Maybe it'll buy you additional time. Once you're off the plane, go to a restroom and put on the wig, in case there's already someone looking for you at Schiphol airport."

Aria was talking fast but it didn't stop me from noticing the way her voice was shaking. She was trying to be strong for me.

I wrapped my arms around her. "Thank you so much for risking so much for me. I love you."

"Create the blog we talked about and post an update the moment you get the chance. I'll worry if I don't hear from you tomorrow at the latest," she said, her fingers digging into my shoulder blades. "Promise me you'll be happy, Gianna. Promise."

"I promise." Could you even promise something like that? My eyes burnt furiously but I fought the tears. This was hard enough without me turning into a blubbering mess. I pulled back, and ran a hand over my eyes.

Aria had lost her fight with tears. "If you ever want to come back, we'll figure something out."

"You said it yourself, there's no going back," I said, and finally the truth sank in. This was it. This was goodbye to the life I'd known, to my family, to my home, to everything. I took a step back from Aria, dropping my arms. She gave me an encouraging smile. I quickly turned around and hurried toward the security check. If I didn't leave Aria now, I'd lose my courage. Doubt was already eating away at my resolve, but this was my only chance. I had to take it. I needed to live my own life, needed to make my own decisions, needed to get away from the horrors of our world.

The security guard didn't stop me. Nobody did. Once I was through security, I risked another peek over my shoulder to where Aria stood. She raised her arm in a wave before she walked away quickly, wiping her eyes.

I watched her back disappear. My heart felt heavy, my throat tight. It wasn't too late yet. I could still go back. We could figure out some ridiculous explanation for drugging Sandro. Nothing was lost yet.

I peered down at my ticket to Amsterdam, my ticket to freedom, before I headed to the terminal where boarding would start soon.

As I waited, I kept checking my surroundings nervously, but nobody showed up. And why would they? Nobody suspected anything. When Sandro finally woke in a couple of hours and called Luca and Matteo, I'd be on the plane.

My heart was beating in my throat when I boarded the plane. It was my first time traveling in economy class. Father had always bought business or first-class tickets when we hadn't used a private jet. I was wedged between a stranger, who insisted on using my armrest, and the window. I barely dared breathing until we were finally up in the air, and even then I kept looking for a familiar face among the other passengers. It took a while before I finally settled back into my seat and relaxed. Now that there was no going back, a flicker of excitement mixed with my anxiety. This was my life and I was finally taking it into my own hands, finally taking back control from those who had ruled every aspect of my existence until now. I was going to be free.

—MATTEO—

Luca's phone rang. "Yes, Romero?" Silence. "Repeat that."

I was checking last month's earnings for our clubs in Manhattan but looked up at the strain in Luca's voice. His expression made me close the laptop. "What's going on?"

Luca pushed to his feet. "Romero found Sandro drugged and tied up on the floor of the penthouse. Aria and Gianna are gone."

I straightened. "You're fucking kidding."

"Do you think I would joke about something like that?" he snarled into my face.

I glared right back. "I thought Aria was in love with you."

For a moment Luca looked like he was going to punch me. Then he whirled around and stormed out of the basement of the Sphere. I hurried after him. "This is Gianna's fault. This girl is the root of every problem. Why couldn't you stay the fuck away from her like I told you?" he muttered.

If only I fucking *knew*. For some reason, I couldn't get her out my head. And now she'd run. From *me*.

"I'm sorry, boss," Sandro said again, half hunched on Luca's sofa, eyes bloodshot.

I wanted to fucking kill him for letting her get away. I should have never let her out of my sight. I got up and started pacing the room again, my eyes darting up to the bedroom door. Luca had disappeared with Aria behind it more than twenty minutes ago. *She* hadn't run away. That had all been for show. She'd helped my fiancée run, but she'd come back to Luca. She'd come back.

Normally I wouldn't doubt Luca's skill to get information out of anybody, but this was Aria, and Luca wouldn't hurt her. Not even for me, not even when she was the only one who could help me find my fiancée.

"I shouldn't have taken the morning off," Romero said from his spot on the armchair.

"One bodyguard should have been enough. I should have been enough. They were only girls," Sandro muttered.

I didn't say anything. I was too pissed. My pulse was pounding in my temples. I wanted to smash every fucking piece of furniture into tiny bits. The bedroom door finally opened and Luca came down the stairs. From the look on his face I knew I wouldn't like what he had to say.

"Don't tell me you couldn't get anything out of her," I snarled.

Luca scowled. "The only thing I know is that Gianna took a plane from JFK. Aria won't tell me anything, but our informants will let me know which plane Gianna took soon."

"Great," I muttered. "And then what? Aria knows Gianna's plan. They told each other everything. The only way to find Gianna is through your wife."

"She won't tell me anything."

I tried walking past him. "Then let me have a word with her."

Luca grasped my arm and pushed me back. "You will stay away from her, Matteo."

"*You* let her steal *your* money, *your* passports. You let her attack our men, let her make a fool out of you and betray you. You should want to punish her. You are Capo."

Luca's eyes flashed. I was walking on thin ice but I didn't give a fuck.

"Aria is my wife. It's none of your business how I deal with her. I told you that Gianna meant trouble but you didn't want to listen. You should have never asked for her hand," he growled.

My fingers longed to grip my knives. I turned my back on him and stalked out onto the roof garden. I needed to cool off before I lashed out at my own brother. Luca and I had fought occasionally when we were younger but it had never been for real. I had a feeling that a fight between us wouldn't end well today. We were both royally pissed and out for blood.

I braced my arms against the banister and let my eyes wander over New York. Gianna was slipping through my fingers. With every second that passed she was bringing more distance between herself and me. Once she landed wherever she was going, she wouldn't stop running until she was sure she was safe. She'd be alone, unprotected. What if something happened to her?

Steps crunched behind me and I tensed but didn't look over my shoulder. Luca stopped beside me. "I called Scuderi. He's furious and blames us of course."

"Of course," I said quietly.

"He's sending two of his men after Gianna."

"I will go with them."

"I figured you would. I told Scuderi as much. You will meet them in Amsterdam."

I turned. "Amsterdam?"

Luca nodded. "I got word that she took a plane to Schiphol."

"When do I leave?" I asked, the thrill of the impending hunt spreading in my veins.

"Four hours."

"I need to leave sooner."

"Impossible. I tried everything I could."

"Damn it. Gianna will be long gone when I arrive."

"You'll find her. You are the best hunter I know. She doesn't stand a chance."

I clapped his shoulder. "You let me go, even though you need me here."

"You aren't of much use to me if all you can think about is Gianna."

"It could take weeks," I said. "I won't return until I've caught her."

"I know. If Aria had run, I would have done the same."

I nodded. I wouldn't stop until Gianna was mine. I didn't care if I had to search the entire world, if I had to turn every single stone, if I had to squeeze information out of every fucking person in Amsterdam, I would find Gianna.

chapter 7

—GIANNA—

I barely got any sleep in the six hours it took the plane to reach Amsterdam. Worry for Aria had taken the place of worrying about getting caught. She was sure Luca wouldn't see her actions as betrayal, but what if she was wrong? God, what had I done? I shouldn't have involved her, shouldn't even have told her about my intention to run away.

When I finally got off the plane and had successfully passed through immigration, I slipped into the first restroom I found and locked myself into one of the small stalls. At the bottom of my bag was the wig Aria had given me. It was long and blonde. Nobody would be fooled by it close up, but it would only have to do until I dyed my hair later today.

Fear clogged my throat when I headed into the waiting area, half expecting someone from New York or the Outfit to wait for me, but that was impossible. Even if Matteo had figured out where I was by now, I was fairly sure that the Famiglia didn't have close relations to any crime syndicates in the Netherlands, and it would take some time for mobsters from Sicily to travel up all the way to Amsterdam. For now I was safe. At least, until the next plane from the East Coast landed in Schiphol, which would be the case in a few hours.

I quickly left the airport with my suitcase, overwhelmed by the sound of people speaking in languages I didn't understand. I knew a few words in Dutch but hadn't bothered learning the language; the Netherlands had never been intended as more than a stopover.

I hailed a taxi and let it take me to a non-descript middle-class hotel in the city where I booked their cheapest room. Despite feeling tired from jet lag and the flight, I only deposited my suitcase in the room before venturing out again to buy a few items I needed.

Two hours later I was back in my small hotel room with light brown hair dye, scissors, a couple of new outfits that helped me fit in better than my super expensive designer clothes, as well as a pre-paid cell phone and a small laptop. After I'd connected my laptop with the wireless internet of the hotel and set up the blog Aria and I had talked about, I wrote a short post, saying that a new journey had begun and that I'd safely arrived at my destination. It was all a bit cryptic and nobody would probably read my blog except for Aria. I resisted the urge to write something more personal, or worse use my new phone to call her. I wanted to hear her voice, wanted to know if she was okay, but I couldn't risk it. Even this blog was already risky. Instead I slipped into the bathroom and changed my hair.

Two hours later I stared at my new reflection. My hair was caramel brown and I'd cut it into a bob that reached my chin. Of course that wouldn't stop people from recognizing me from close up but unless I paid a surgeon to redo my face, which I had no intention of doing, a new haircut would have to be enough. I'd just have to move from city to city until I was sure that Matteo had moved on to another target and I was safe. That would probably take a while.

Matteo had told me numerous times that he wouldn't give me up and I had a feeling he meant it.

I wouldn't give him a chance to catch me. Tomorrow, I'd leave Amsterdam and head for Paris, and who knew where I'd be the day after that? This was a new beginning with endless options.

I stared up at the white ceiling of my hostel room. I'd been living in twenty different places in the last three months, never staying anywhere for more than a week at a time. Sometimes when I woke in the morning I wasn't sure where I was, sometimes I even thought I was back in Chicago, and sometimes I found myself longing for it. Not for my father and the rules of our world, but for Fabi and Lily and Aria, and sometimes even for Mother.

I sat up, groaning, and went through my usual morning habit of reminding myself of my current pseudonym and everything that encompassed her before I got out of bed. It was almost noon. I still hadn't figured out any kind of routine. Most days I spent exploring the city where I stayed while always checking my surroundings. This fear of being followed, of being hunted, would that ever stop? I doubted it. Whenever I saw men in dark suites, panic filled me. I'd lost count of the times I'd imagined I'd seen Matteo from the corner of my eyes.

I hadn't made any real friends yet, which wasn't all that surprising; I never stayed anywhere long enough to build a connection. Which was better anyway. I couldn't risk getting close to anyone yet, maybe never. That didn't mean I was alone. I always stayed in youth hostels wherever I went, and met people from all over the world. Of course I couldn't tell them anything about me, not even my name. Currently I was calling myself Liz, short for Elizabeth, and was spending my year before college abroad road-tripping through Europe. That was pretty much my cover story wherever I went, only my name changed.

Lying to everyone 24/7 made any kind of friendship hard. I opened my laptop and checked my blog, which I still updated almost every day, even though I hadn't gotten a comment from Aria in weeks. In thirty-one days to be exact. My eyes darted to my cell phone on the nightstand. As so often recently I felt the almost irresistible urge to call her and find out what was keeping her from visiting my blog. I had a feeling it was for my safety. In her last comment she'd warned me "not to waste time in one spot because there was too much to explore in Europe." I'd taken that as a hint that Matteo might be after me and had jumped from city to city in the last few weeks, never staying anywhere more than one or two days, but I was growing tired of running constantly. I'd lost weight, and most of my clothes hung off me like they belonged to someone else. I wanted to belong again, to find a place to call mine.

I got dressed and stuffed my clothes into my backpack. I'd gotten rid of my suitcase four weeks into my journey. It wasn't practical lugging a heavy suitcase wherever I went. I didn't need most of my old belongings anyway. When would I ever wear evening dresses and high-heeled Louboutins again? That life was over. I stared down at my shabby backpack, at my cheap sneakers and jeans, and for a moment longing for something I'd thought I'd never miss came up in me. When I'd decided to run away from the mob, I'd known I'd miss my siblings horribly, and so far not a single day had gone by that I hadn't considered returning to Chicago just to see them again, to talk to Aria again, to have a steady home again, but so far I'd managed not to miss the luxuries my former life had afforded me, at least not this insistently. So why was I suddenly missing the things I'd despised?

Everything I'd ever owned had been paid for with blood money, and even my flight up till this point had been financed that way. But I was scarily low on cash and would have to find a job in the next place I stayed, though that would mean staying longer than just a couple of days unless I tried my hand at pickpocketing, which wouldn't really be a big improvement over mob money, except that nobody got killed for it.

I swung my backpack over my shoulder and exited my small room. Fifteen minutes later, I'd checked out and left my alter ego "Liz, short for Elizabeth" behind. I'd become someone new for my next destination. Maybe a Megan. It was August but heavy clouds draped over Vienna as I headed toward the train station. I'd loved the regal buildings but it was time to move on from Austria. I'd been living in the same country for almost two weeks and was getting antsy.

After I'd boarded my train to Berlin, I checked my cell-phone, a stupid habit I still hadn't dropped. I never got a message from anyone. The date caught my eyes. August, 15th. The day I was supposed to marry Matteo.

Unwantedly the kiss we'd shared flashed in my mind and a small shiver ran down my back. I'd kissed three guys in the time since I'd arrived in Europe, all of them cute foreigners who weren't interested in anything lasting, just like me, but none of those kisses had come even close to what I'd felt while kissing Matteo. Maybe it was because he'd had more practice than any other guy. Matteo was a gigolo, there was no doubt about it.

But what worried me most was that I found myself comparing every guy I met to Matteo, and they always fell short. They weren't as good-looking, as interesting, they didn't have a six-pack, and most importantly being in their proximity didn't give me a thrill. It annoyed the hell out of me that despite being thousands of miles away from Matteo, he still held some power over me. I wished I'd never let him kiss me then I wouldn't have that problem.

I'd just have to find a nice guy who could make me forget Matteo and his annoyingly sexy and arrogant smile. Maybe my next destination, Berlin, would help with that.

I only stayed four weeks in Berlin before I decided to move on. Something hadn't felt right, or maybe I wasn't used to staying in a place for a longer period of time anymore. At least I'd worked as a waitress for the last three weeks and managed to earn some money. It wasn't much but enough to buy me my train ticket to Munich and food for the next couple of days. I didn't have anything left for a hotel room however, so that was a major problem.

I had spent too much at the beginning of my flight, never having learned to be economical. Money had never been an issue growing up. If there was one thing that women in the mob never had to forego, then it was money. I was a spoiled brat, that much I'd come to realize.

The moment I arrived in Munich I knew this could work. I loved everything about the city, but there was still the problem that I didn't have any money to pay for a room. I didn't want to spend the night on the streets. I wasn't sure how safe it would be. As I walked through the city center, I noticed a few people singing and playing instruments, and they seemed to make a fast buck with it. There was always a heap of Euro coins in the hats they'd put on the ground.

I could play the piano. Father had forced Aria, Lily, and me to take lessons from the moment we could talk but I had neither a piano nor a keyboard I could use to make music. I had a decent singing voice, definitely nothing to get excited about but at least it didn't make people want to hold their ears. Maybe it was worth a try.

A group of three girls with colorful hair was singing and playing the guitar at the next corner, and I headed for them. When they finally took a break, I approached them. I really hoped they spoke English. They looked to be my age. "Hey. I was wondering if you know of any places where I could do what you do and sing for people? I'm out of money and this is pretty much my only shot at paying for a room tonight."

The girls exchanged a look and I was half convinced they hadn't understood me when the girl with short blue hair said in an accent I couldn't decipher, "You need a permission. The authorities are pretty strict in Munich. They'll fine you if you make music or any kind of other art in the streets without permission."

"Damn. Is it easy to get a permission?"

The pink-haired girl shook her head. "No. They only hand out a few permissions and they make sure you can sing and actually play instruments before they allow you to make music here."

I sighed and slumped against the wall of the building. The three girls exchanged another look then whispered in a language that definitely wasn't German before they turned to me. "We're sharing a small apartment. If you want you can sleep on the couch in the living room until you find a job and can afford your own place."

My eyes widened. "Really?"

Blue-haired girl nodded with a smile. "You're a backpacker, right?"

"Yes. Traveling through Europe before college."

"We're all from Croatia, but we've been spending the last few months in Munich. You'll love it." Pink-haired girl stood. "So what's your name?"

I hesitated a moment before deciding who I wanted to be. "Gwen."

Maybe Munich would finally become a place I could stay and figure out what I'd do with the rest of my life.

What was meant to be for a few days only had turned into two months. I was still sharing an apartment with the three crazy girls from Croatia. We'd become friends and I paid rent for my spot on the sofa, albeit not much. Of course every part of my life was built on lie after lie, but sometimes I almost forgot that I wasn't who I pretended to be. I'd even found a job as a waitress in a café that catered mostly to tourists and my German had improved greatly.

Now that I'd finally found a place where I wanted to stay, I'd decided to give dating a real shot. When my flat mates introduced me to Sid, a fellow musician from Canada with long dreadlocks, I knew he was someone I could get used to, and maybe even make me forget that stupid kiss I'd shared with Matteo.

Sid was nothing like Matteo. He was nothing like men in the world I'd grown up in. He was a vegan, peace-loving idealist, and he never hesitated to convince others of his ideals. He could spend hours talking about the horrors of dairy farms and the dangers of the NRA. Sometimes I wondered what he'd say if he knew who I was.

This idealistic world-improver was his mask, I'd realized. Maybe everyone wore some kind of mask. What had been a novelty and endearing in the beginning, quickly started to annoy me. Still I couldn't break up with Sid because it would seem like the ultimate failure. If even someone like Sid couldn't stop me from thinking about Matteo, who could?

Sid's hand crept under my shirt then unhooked my bra. I made a sound of protest. We were in the living room of my shared apartment, so if one of my flat mates returned she'd get a show. His fingertips were rough from playing the guitar. He pushed me down until I lay flat on my back and he was half on top of me. His tongue seemed to take up too much space in my mouth and he tasted of stale smoke. Why had I thought a smoking guy was hot? Maybe in theory, but the taste and stink weren't something I was too excited about. He started unbuttoning my jeans and kept rubbing his bulge against my leg like a horny dog.

"I want you, Gwen," Sid rasped, already trying to shove my pants down my legs. Gwen. For the first time, the name didn't make me pause. Two months using the same name seemed to be the magic barrier for getting used to a new identity. Pity that I got the feeling I wouldn't use it for much longer. Munich was getting too comfortable, and Sid was simply getting too much. He was being too pushy.

"Not yet," I gritted out, trying to hide my boredom and annoyance. It wasn't his fault that I wasn't into our make-out sessions. We'd been going out for almost four weeks, so it wasn't really all that surprising that he wanted to sleep with me. And I wasn't even sure what the hell was stopping me. Sid wasn't a bad guy. He could be funny after he'd drunk a couple of beers or had a few drags of pot, and his guitar play and singing weren't even half bad. And yet I didn't want to commit to this relationship fully, didn't want to go another step. Before I'd run off from home, I'd thought I'd jump into bed with every guy I met once I was free of my bodyguards; to spite Matteo and my father, more than anything else, so what was stopping me?

"Come on, Gwen. I'll make it good for you," he said as he tried to shove his hand into my panties.

I clamped my legs shut and pushed his hand away. I didn't want him to touch me *there*. For some reason the idea that he'd be the first to do that made me sick. "I'm really not in the mood. And I'm getting my period," I said to stop him from bitching around anymore. It was a fucking lie. The stress of the last few months had pretty much stopped me from having much of a period at all.

But he didn't know that. I just wanted this make-out session to be over, so I could grab my laptop and figure out where to run off to next. Sid would find a new girl quickly. His cute Canadian accent, laid-back nature and dreadlocks were a huge hit among German girls.

He didn't even bother hiding his annoyance, which in turn really made me want to push him off and tell him it was over. "You're never in the mood," Sid grumbled. "Jerk me off at least."

Anger shot through me at his demand. When I didn't react, he grabbed my hand and pressed it against the bulge in his pants. Where was the peace-loving idealist now?

With a bang, the door flew open. Before either Sid or I could move, three men stalked in. Matteo was one of them. Oh holy shit.

chapter 8

—GIANNA—

Matteo was first to enter, his dark hair messy and wet from the rainstorm raging outside, his white shirt plastered to his upper body. In that moment, I almost felt silly for thinking I could ever forget him. He was more man than all the guys I'd met combined. His dark eyes settled on me, then on my hand, which was still pressed against Sid's crotch. There really was no question what he'd walked in on, and his face twisted with fury.

"What the fuck, dudes?" Sid shouted.

"Shut up, shut up," I wanted to scream. I didn't get the chance. Matteo crossed the room in a few steps, grabbed Sid by the arm and hauled him off me. Sid landed on the floor hard, face twisting with pain, then anger. Matteo towered over me, nostrils flaring, eyes almost black, and a look in them that made me want to hide. I met his gaze straight on. He wanted to scare me. My fear was something I'd never give him.

Sid stumbled to his feet and almost lost his fucking pants. He must have unzipped them at some point to make it "easier" for me. He headed for Matteo. I jumped to my feet, knowing I had to intervene before things got even worse.

"Get out of this apartment or I'll call the fucking cops," Sid said.

God, no.

Matteo sent me a look that made me realize just how dangerous this situation was. Not for me, but for someone who should have never gotten dragged into the fucking misery that was mob life.

"He doesn't mean it," I blurted.

Sid glared. "The fuck I do." For the moment, he seemed to have forgotten about his peace-loving ideals.

Matteo hadn't pulled his weapons yet. I wanted to convince myself that it was a good sign but a glimpse at the two men with him made my heart plummet into my shoes. They were both my father's men and they had already closed the door and were standing beside it with expressionless faces. A closed door was never a good thing. Nothing I could say would change their minds because they were acting on my father's orders. They would do what he'd told them. There was only one person who could help me now.

Sid got right into Matteo's face as if he wanted to punch him. Matteo didn't even twitch, only stared down at Sid with the scariest look I'd ever seen in anyone's eyes. Even without knowing who Matteo was, Sid must have sensed just how dangerous the man in front of him was. Sid took a step back, his eyes darting between Matteo and me. I jerked into motion and stepped between Matteo and him. "He doesn't know anything. Please, just let him leave."

My father's men laughed and one of them murmured something that sounded remarkably like "slut." Matteo's expression darkened even further. My father's men were watching him expectantly. I'd insulted Matteo by running away, and worse by being with another man. In our world there was only one thing a man in Matteo's position could do to protect his honor. I'd only ever seen Matteo with some variation of an arrogant smile on his face, but there was no trace of amusement now.

"I should probably go," Sid said suddenly, backing away. "This got nothing to do with me."

Coward. The moment the thought crossed my mind, I felt bad. Running was really the only sensible thing for him to do. He couldn't protect me from Matteo or my father's men, but that he wasn't even going to try was something I could and would never understand.

One of my father's men, Stan or something like that if I remembered him correctly, grabbed Sid by the arms. Sid started struggling like a madman, but it was obvious he'd never had a fight in his life. Stan laughed, ripped Sid's arms back sharply then rammed his knees into Sid's back. With a cry, Sid fell to his knees, only held upright by Stan's grip.

"Hey! Stop it," I shouted, wanting to rush toward them, but Matteo snatched my arm, jerking me to a stop. I whirled on him, on the verge of snarling into his face but stopped myself. He was Sid's only chance, regardless of how ridiculous that sounded.

"Please," I said, even though begging left a bitter taste in my mouth. Matteo's dark eyes didn't even flicker as he peered down at me. Expecting him to help me after what I'd done was preposterous. "Don't kill him. Just let him go. He's not a danger."

"You want me to spare the fucker who had his fucking hands all over you? You let that sucker have what's mine and want me to let him walk away? That's what you want from me?" Matteo asked in a dangerously quiet voice.

I swallowed down a nasty retort. I wasn't his, would never be. Nothing I had done with Sid was Matteo's business. Even if I had fucked Sid, that still wouldn't have been his fucking business. Even if I'd fucked every single guy

I'd met that still wouldn't have been his business. I needed to tell him that I hadn't slept with Sid. Maybe it would placate him if he knew I hadn't given everything away. His ego would love that there was still something he could take from me. Pride kept my lips sealed.

"We should head out. Someone might have heard when we kicked the door in. Let's get rid of this asshole and move on," Stan said, knocking his knee into Sid's back again. Sid's eyes were huge as they flitted back and forth between us.

"Silence," Matteo said sharply and Stan snapped his lips shut.

I reached for Matteo's arm, my fingers digging into the damp material of his dress shirt, feeling the hard muscles beneath. I had to swallow my fucking pride if I wanted to save Sid's life. "Matteo, it's not—"

My words were cut short by the sonic crack of a suppressed gunshot. I froze, eyes flying to the source of the noise. The other Made Man was pointing a Glock with a silencer at the spot where Sid's head had been moments before. He was slumped forward, head hanging limply and blood dripping to the ground. Stan let go of Sid's arms. The body toppled over and landed on the ground with a resounding thud. I stared and stared. Slowly my hand slid down Matteo's arm.

"Did I give you the fucking order to kill him?" Matteo snarled.

"This was Outfit business. As long as she isn't married to you, she falls under our jurisdiction and so did the asshole here." Stan kicked Sid's lifeless form. I flinched. Inside a beast was raging, wanting to claw Stan's fucking eyes out, wanting to kill them all, but I was paralyzed.

Blood spread out around Sid's head, soaking his dreadlocks. My stomach constricted. I'd seen that much blood only three times before. The first time when Luca cut off Raffaele's finger; the second time on Luca's shirt after he'd dealt with the guy who'd drugged Aria; and the third time when the Russians had attacked us. It didn't get easier as some people said, as even *I* had suspected. I had a feeling it never would.

Stan nodded toward me. "What about other witnesses? You don't live here alone."

I blinked, terror gripping me so hard I could barely breathe. I couldn't let them kill my flat mates as well. The girls had been nothing but kind to me. They didn't deserve that. My eyes found Matteo. His gaze searched my face before he turned to my father's men. "We're done here."

Stan looked like he wanted to protest but the other guy nudged his shoulder. With a glare at me, Stan opened the door and checked the corridor. "Clear. Let's go."

I turned to Sid's body again. Matteo wrapped an arm around my waist. I didn't look his way. I couldn't avert my eyes from Sid as if my attention was the only thing that anchored him to life. He was long gone. Pieces of his brain dotted the red sea on the ground.

Matteo steered me toward the door, then down the corridor. Stan was in front of us, while the other man made up the rear. Surrounded. I was surrounded. I should have tried to run away. The odds had always been against me. It had never stopped me before. Maybe this was my last chance to escape. Once back in the States, I'd be trapped. Giving up wasn't in my nature. I'd always fought my own battles, but so far only I had to pay the price for my courage. Tonight, an innocent, someone who'd never been sullied by the darkness of my world had paid with his life for my dreams, for my wish for freedom, for my selfishness. I'd thought I could evade fate, could outrun a world of blood, but had inadvertently dragged innocents into that world.

Could I live with that?

I wasn't sure.

Maybe it was in our nature to bring misery and death to everyone around us. Maybe that was why it was best for us to stay among ourselves. Hadn't Aria said something along those lines a long time ago?

Aria. I'd finally see her again. That was the good news I was clinging to right now. She'd get me through this. She always did.

Matteo's grip on my wrist was painful. His eyes held a clear message, now that he'd caught me, he would never let me get away again.

Everything seemed to happen behind a fog. I was pushed into the back of a car and Matteo slipped into the back seat beside me then we drove off with squealing tires. I watched the place I'd called home for the last two months disappear. I pressed my forehead against the cold window. I hardly dared to blink. Every time I closed my eyes, crimson flashed behind my eyelids. Sid was dead because of me.

I could hear Matteo talking to someone on the phone in the background but I couldn't focus. Everything was over. He'd take me back to my father now, and I had no doubt that I couldn't expect any kind of mercy. I had betrayed not only the Outfit but also New York, had made my father and Matteo lose face. I would be punished. I glanced at Matteo who was glaring at the back of the front seat. I quickly fastened my bra again and put it back in place. Of course Matteo noticed.

I could tell he was furious. I wondered what kind of punishment he had in mind for me. I'd been on the run for six months. He couldn't possibly want me for any other reason than revenge. I knew the rules. I wasn't worthy of marriage anymore. Matteo probably already had a new fiancée and once he'd dealt with me, he'd move on with his life. If he'd wanted to kill me, he would have done so already. That didn't mean Father wouldn't do it the moment I set foot on

Chicago ground.

We pulled up in front of an airport hotel, and Matteo turned to me, his eyes holding a clear warning. "We'll spend the next few hours until our flight here. If you try to ask anyone for help, this will end in a bloodbath, understood?"

I nodded. Then Matteo pulled me out of the car with him and led me inside. Nobody paid us any attention as we headed toward the elevators and rode up to the fourth floor.

Matteo led me through the long hallway until we arrived in front of a simple white door.

Stan and the other Outfit man stopped too. "She should come into our room with Carmine and me. She's still part of the Outfit," Stan said, his eyes sliding over my body. I knew what he and the other guy would do to me if I came into a room with them.

"She's mine. I won't let her out of my eyes again. Now fuck off. Gianna and I have matters to discuss," Matteo growled. He slid the keycard into the slot and opened the door.

Stan and Carmine exchanged a look but didn't protest. Then Stan sent me a cruel smile. "Teach her some manners."

Matteo dragged me into the room, kicked the door shut and fixed me with a terrifying expression. "Oh, I will."

chapter 9

—GIANNA—

Matteo flung me onto the bed. Then he was on top of me. He pressed my arms into the mattress above my head, his knees beside my thighs. His eyes were almost black with fury. Did he want me to beg for mercy? Ask him for forgiveness? Then he had a long wait coming.

"You let someone have what's mine," he growled, his eyes scorching my body with their possessiveness. He leaned down as if he was going to kiss me. Our noses almost brushed but he only scowled. "Your father gave me his permission to do with you as I please. He doesn't care if you live or die. He doesn't care what I do to you. I think he'd even approve of me punishing you harshly."

I wasn't surprised. Father had already barely tolerated me before I'd brought shame to our family by running away. Now he probably hated me like the devil. I almost wanted Matteo to hurt me. I deserved it for getting Sid killed. I knew Matteo would have no trouble hurting me. I'd seen what he was capable of. Maybe physical pain would finally drown out the anguish I felt deep inside

—MATTEO—

Gianna didn't say a fucking thing as if she couldn't care less what I did to her.

I tightened my hold on her wrists to see if she would finally show some of that fire I was used to from her, but despite a small wince she didn't react.

I hated what she'd done to her hair. It was light brown, no longer the fiery red I loved. At least, she hadn't cut it off.

My eyes were drawn to the sliver of naked stomach that peeked out where her shirt had ridden up. The thought that someone else had touched her there, had touched her everywhere made me want to tear everything down.

She was supposed to be mine. *Mine alone.*

For a moment, the fury was so blinding I wanted to hurt her, wanted to show her that she belonged to me, wanted to fuck her so hard that she forgot everything else. I gripped her waist, my fingers brushing over her soft skin. Mine. Only mine from now on. Her father had told me I could use her as I saw fit before I took her back to him. Nobody would blink an eye if I took from her what had been mine for the taking in the first place. She tensed under my touch but still didn't say anything. Her eyes were resigned. No hint of her usual temper.

She didn't fight me, didn't do anything. She reminded me of a ragdoll. She probably waited for me to do what everyone expected me to do, to fuck her even if she was unwilling, to hurt her until she begged me for forgiveness. And I could have done it but I didn't want to. Despite what she'd done and how bad she'd made me look, I still wanted her, and not just her body.

"Being submissive isn't like you," I said quietly. Her pulse sped under my fingertips. It was the only sign that she wasn't as indifferent as her expression made me want to believe. Maybe she didn't care what happened to her because she was heartbroken over the bastard I'd found her with.

The idea sent a new spike of wrath through me and I quickly released her before I lost control. I slid off her and sat on the edge of the mattress, trying to ignore the look of surprise and shock crossing her face. I glared at the floor, clenching and unclenching my hands. If Carmine hadn't killed the fucker, I would probably have done it. I still wanted to do it, wanted to slice the part of his brain out that harbored the memory of Gianna's body under him.

Gianna sat up slowly, carefully as if she thought I might attack if she moved too fast. "Aren't you going to rape and torture me?"

I almost laughed. That's what everyone expected. Most men in our world even thought she deserved it. I turned to her, my gaze tracing her beautiful face. Even more beautiful than my memory had made me believe, even now when she was pale and her eyes were puffy from tears.

"Did you think I would?" I asked in a surprisingly calm voice. Some of my anger was suddenly gone now that she was watching me with her wide blue eyes.

"Yes. My father's men definitely thought you would. Didn't you see their expressions? They probably hope that you'll give them a go at me once you're done with me."

Of course, they'd told me so numerous times while we'd been on the hunt. I knew what they thought was happening right now. Fuck, part of me wished they were right. I wasn't a good guy. "I don't give a fuck about your father's men, and I don't give a fuck about your father. And if they lay a single finger on you, I'm going to kill them. They won't hurt you, nobody will."

Her brows crinkled. "Once I'm back in Chicago, Father will punish me."

Did she really think I'd hand her over to her asshole of a father? I hadn't hunted her for sixth months only to give her up. I smirked. "You aren't going back to Chicago, Gianna. You are coming to New York with me."

Hope and relief crossed her face. "To Aria? Is she alright? Did she get in trouble because she helped me?"

Somehow her response annoyed me. "Aria is fine," I said, before I stood and walked toward the window. I kept my back to her when I asked, "That guy, did you love him?"

I wasn't sure what I'd do if she said "yes." I couldn't hurt that fucker anymore, and I didn't want to hurt her, so what could I do? Kill someone else, preferably the two assholes from the Outfit who'd been grating on my nerves for too long, and maybe while I was at it, I'd kill her fucking father the next time I saw him.

"Sid?" she asked in a shaky voice, and I almost lost it right then. I scowled at her over my shoulder. Her eyes were actually moist with fucking tears.

"I don't care what his name was," I growled.

Fuck, I wanted to kill that guy so badly. I'd have paid a billion dollars if there were a way to resurrect the asshole, only so I could kill him again. Slowly, painfully.

"His name was Sid," she said stubbornly, a familiar glint returning to her eyes.

She still hadn't answered my question. "Did you love him?"

"No," she said without hesitation. "I barely knew him." I would have rejoiced if she hadn't started biting her lower lip like she was fighting tears. She looked fucking sad and then a tear slid out of her left eye. She blinked a few times.

"If you didn't love him, then why are you crying?"

She glared. Glared, as if she was the one with reason to be angry. "You really don't know?"

"I'm a Made Man, Gianna. I've seen many people die, have killed many myself." And right now I wanted to kill again more than anything else in the world.

"Sid didn't deserve to die. He died because of me. He never did anything wrong."

What the fuck? Really? "He touched the wrong girl. He died for touching what wasn't his to touch."

Gianna shook her head. "You wanted to kill him yourself, didn't you? That's why you stopped Stan? Not because you wanted to spare Sid's life."

Did that really come as a surprise to her? For someone who was convinced I and every other member of the mob were monsters, she seemed oddly surprised by my desire to kill the asshole who'd pawed at my fiancée.

Before I could reply, my phone rang. Luca's name flashed on my screen. I had only sent him a short text while I was in the car. He'd tried calling me but, except for a quick talk to the pilot of our private jet, I hadn't been in the mood to speak to anyone, but knowing Luca he wouldn't give up. Stifling a groan, I picked up, turning away from Gianna again.

"A text with 'I got her,' that's all I get from you?" he said angrily.

"I was busy."

I could hear Aria's high voice in the background, but thankfully Luca didn't put her on. I really wasn't in the mood to talk to a hysterical woman, least of all the woman who'd helped my fiancée escape in the first place. It was early morning in New York, couldn't Luca have let his wife sleep in for once?

"With what?" He paused. "No, don't tell me. I don't want to fucking know."

"Did he hurt her?" Aria asked loud enough for me to hear.

I didn't say anything.

Luca lowered his voice. "Is she alive?"

"Fuck you."

"I take that as a yes."

Aria was still speaking in the background.

"Tell your wife that her sister is fine."

"Gianna is fine," Luca said in a muffled voice, then to me. "When will you be back?"

"The flight leaves in less than two hours."

"You're flying directly to Chicago to meet Scuderi. Right?"

"He already called you, didn't he?" I said. Stan and Carmine had definitely sent their boss a message after we'd caught Gianna. That meant, of course, that he knew about Sid too.

"Of course, he did. His daughter has been on the run for six months. This is big news."

"Don't tell me he's happy to have her back."

"No, at least not for the same reason Aria is. He wants to see her punished. She made him lose face and you too. From what I heard you caught her with another guy. You realize the news will spread like wildfire. Scuderi is eager to make a public show out of punishing Gianna. He expects you to help him with it."

I gritted my teeth. "I don't give a fuck. I'm not taking her to Chicago. If he wants to talk to her, he can come to New York."

"You want to protect her after what she did?"

"Yes."

"Matteo, this is Outfit business. She isn't your wife, and nobody expects you to marry her after she went around fucking with half of Europe."

"Careful," I hissed.

"Damn it. Can't you just get over her? Fuck her, it's not like it matters anymore, and then hand her back to her father."

"Is Aria still around to hear you talk about her sister like that?" I asked.

"No. I need to think about the Famiglia. Gianna brought this upon herself. You have to take her to Chicago, Matteo. I won't risk war over her."

"Fuck you, Luca. You are my fucking brother. Shouldn't you be on my fucking side?"

"Not when you've lost your fucking mind."

"Fuck you."

Luca sighed on the other end. "Listen, I'm not saying that you should abandon her. Take her to Chicago and pretend you're delivering her to her father. Then make a deal with him. She's still promised to you, so he won't refuse you. He'll probably be glad to have her off his hands. Aria and I will be flying over there too. I'm emailing our pilot right this moment. You won't have to deal with this alone."

"Okay, I'm taking her to Chicago. But I'm not leaving without her, no matter what Scuderi says. She's mine."

"Alright, but I doubt there will be any problems. And believe me, I have no interest in letting Gianna get hurt by her father. Aria loves her sister, and I want Aria to be happy, so I won't let Scuderi kill or hurt her. We will bring her back to New York with us, even as your wife if that's really what you want."

"You'll go against Scuderi if he disagrees for some reason?"

"I will. For you and for Aria."

"Swear it."

Luca sighed again. "I swear it. You and Aria are going to be the death of me."

I almost smiled but hung up. When I turned back around to Gianna, she was watching me with an anxious expression, which she tried to mask the moment I looked at her but she didn't quite manage. Sometimes in the last few months I'd been sure I wouldn't find her, that she was too clever; I was glad that I'd been wrong. "Tradition dictates that I hand you over to the Outfit and your father."

Fear flashed across her face. Gianna wasn't stupid; she knew what might happen to her if her father got his will. I wasn't sure if Dante Cavallaro would intervene, and I didn't give a fuck. Protectiveness washed over me. They had no right to decide about her fate. This was my chance to show her that she'd been wrong to run away, that I was the right guy for her. For a long time she stared at me, her face unguarded and vulnerable. This was a side of her I'd only seen twice before: when Aria had been drugged and when Gianna had been in the hands of the Russians. I was still angry at her, still fucking furious, especially because I knew she'd run away again if I gave her the chance, but part of me was simply glad to have her back.

"I will take you to Chicago, but I won't leave your side, Gianna. I won't give you the chance to run from me again."

—GIANNA—

After what had happened today, I wasn't sure I'd ever risk another escape.

Matteo's phone rang again and he cursed. I was glad for the distraction. The intensity of his gaze had spoken to a part of me I'd tried to fight ever since the kiss. I lay back down, but the moment I closed my eyes, images of Sid's body flashed through my mind. Even if Matteo hadn't killed him, that didn't mean it wasn't his fault. He'd have done the same if Carmine hadn't acted first.

I must have dozed off because I jerked violently when something touched my arm. My eyes flew open and I found Matteo hovering over me. He straightened with a wry smile. "Sid's death doesn't seem to bother you too much if you can fall asleep like that."

I sat up, glaring, knowing he was being cruel on purpose, but at the same time wondering if it was true. Was I that callous? Was I more like Matteo than I wanted to admit? No. I had dreamed about Sid's death, and my chest felt like it was in a vise when I thought about him.

"We need to get going. Our flight leaves soon." Matteo grasped my wrist to pull me to my feet but I wrenched it away, suddenly angry. Matteo reached for me again, jerked me to my feet and against his body. "Careful, Gianna. Less than two hours ago I saw you messing around with another guy. I pride myself for my control but there is a limit to what I will take from you."

I swallowed my words and let Matteo lead me out of the room. Stan and Carmine were already waiting in the corridor. Their eyes scanned me from head to toe then Stan said, "She's still surprisingly unscathed. If my fiancée had gone around fucking other men, I'd have beaten her to a bloody pulp."

"Do I look like I care about your fucking opinion?" Matteo asked dangerously. I chanced a look at him, wondering why exactly he wasn't doing what Stan had suggested. I decided to keep my mouth shut for now. Self-preservation wasn't my strong suite, but I wasn't completely suicidal, even if death might be preferable to what Father had in mind for me.

Twenty minutes later we boarded the private jet of the Outfit and I took a seat next to the window. Matteo sat across from me but he didn't make conversation. Nobody tried to speak to me throughout the entire flight. I had a feeling Matteo was using the time to calm down. Occasionally I'd catch him watching me but I couldn't read the look in his eyes. When I rose halfway through the flight to go to the toilet, Matteo stood as well.

I swallowed a comment and walked toward the toilet in the rear. When Matteo didn't back off even as I opened the door, I couldn't hold back any more. Self-preservation be damned. "Are you going to watch me pee? It's not like I can escape by jumping off the plane."

"I wouldn't put it past you to try and kick a hole into the wall of the plane to kill us all."

Was he being serious? The corner of his mouth twitched but then his expression hardened again. For a moment our eyes were locked, then I quickly stepped into the small toilet and closed the door. Matteo didn't stop me but I knew he'd be waiting for me and probably listen for strange noises.

I leaned against the wall and closed my eyes. Fear and sadness raged in my body, and it was getting increasingly difficult not to break down into a sobbing mess. I almost wished Matteo had manhandled me. Why did he have to act like a decent human being?

"What are you doing? Don't force me to kick in that fucking door," Matteo muttered.

Not even caring that he would hear me, I took care of business before I stepped back out two minutes later. Matteo's eyes wandered over me as if he was looking for a sign that I was up to something. I would have laughed if I thought I could.

We returned to our seats and resumed our silence.

My stomach was in knots when we landed in Chicago. I hadn't gotten a minute of sleep while we were in the air. The knowledge that I would have to face Father soon kept me wide awake. Only yesterday, I'd eaten pizza with my flat mates and made plans for a trip to Croatia in the summer, and now my life was once again out of my control. Even worse, I might very well face harsh punishment from the Outfit. Matteo really had no reason to protect me from Father's wrath. And even if he tried, why would Luca allow him to risk a conflict with the Outfit over me? I was less than vermin in their eyes.

The private jet came to a stop and Matteo got to his feet and motioned for me to do the same. My legs shook as I followed him toward the door, which was already gliding open. Cold air blasted against my face. Snow dusted the landing strip and the surrounding buildings. It was around 4 p.m., but I felt as if it was the middle of the night. Matteo grabbed my wrist, giving me a warning look. "Don't run. Don't do anything stupid. Your father's men are looking for a chance to hurt you. I'd kill them of course but that won't help you."

Was he actually worried about me? Matteo was an enigma. I wasn't sure why he was so interested in me. I had a feeling it was his pride. He couldn't accept that I didn't want him, so he'd force me to marry him even if I didn't want it, even if *he* didn't want me anymore. If he really cared about me, he would let me go. No, this was a power play. Emotions had nothing to do with it.

"Don't worry. I want to see Aria."

He shook his head. "This isn't the right moment for your snark to return. Your father won't appreciate it."

Then why was he almost smiling if he thought it was such a bad idea? The door was fully down and Matteo led me down the few stairs, his fingers around my wrist unwavering. I felt like a toddler who did her first steps. Annoyance battled with worry in my body, but before I could decide if I wanted to risk a retort I spotted a familiar blonde head. Aria. She stood beside Luca, and when she saw me she started running.

I peered up at Matteo pleadingly but he didn't let me go and kept leading me toward Aria in unhurried steps. When my sister had almost reached us, he released me and I rushed toward Aria. We collided almost painfully. I crushed Aria against me, hugging her as tightly as possible and she did the same in return. "Oh, Gianna, I was so scared for you. I'm so glad you're here." She was crying and my own face was wet with tears. God, I'd missed her.

After a moment, she pulled back, her eyes doing a quick scan, lingering on my new hair color. "Are you okay? Did they hurt you?"

I brushed a few strands of her blonde locks away from her face, suddenly feeling like breaking down sobbing. Regret weighed heavy on my mind. I should have never run. Seeing Aria's worried face was another reminder. If I'd stayed, if I'd married Matteo, then Sid would still be alive, and Aria wouldn't have had to worry for months. Why did I have to want the freedom to make my own decisions?

"Gianna?" Aria lowered her voice. "Did Matteo do something?"

"Matteo didn't do anything," Matteo said in a hard voice, making Aria and me both jump.

"I didn't ask you," Aria said quietly. My eyes darted between them. I had a feeling they weren't on good terms. Also because of me. Luca arrived beside us and clapped his brother's shoulder. "Good to see you again."

I hadn't even considered that Matteo had been gone from home for a long time because he'd been after me. Luca barely glanced my way, not that I cared.

"I'm fine," I told Aria who seemed reluctant to believe me.

"The boss is waiting," Stan barked. "Let's go. It's not like the whore deserves a big welcome."

Aria gasped. I stiffened but managed not to show my shock. I didn't give a damn what Stan thought of me. But Matteo was the fastest to react. He pulled a knife and hurtled it at Stan who cried out when the blade nicked his ear.

"Next time my blade will split your fucking skull if you don't keep your mouth shut," he said.

Stan rested his hand on the gun in his holster but didn't pull it. Blood was dripping from his cut ear down onto his shirt. There was murder in his eyes. Carmine stood very still, but he hadn't pulled his gun either. When I turned to Luca, I knew why. He had both of his guns aimed at my father's men and behind him Romero whom I hadn't even seen before was doing the same.

"We don't want this to end badly, do we?" Luca asked in a very low voice. "Your boss wouldn't appreciate it."

Carmine nodded and relaxed his stance but Stan looked like he didn't care if my father punished him as long as he got to kill Matteo first. For several moments neither of us moved, then Luca put his guns back into their holsters. "Let's go."

Carmine picked up the knife Matteo had thrown and handed it back to Matteo, who didn't take his eyes off Stan.

"She'll drive in a car with us," Stan said.

Matteo's lips pulled into a cold smile. "This is the last warning you get. Stop pissing me off or I'll carve a smile into your throat."

Carmine grabbed Stan's arm and pulled him toward a black Outfit car while the rest of us headed toward two BMWs.

Aria moved to sit in the back with me, but Luca held her back. "No. I want Matteo to keep an eye on your sister." Aria gave me an apologetic smile before she sat shotgun beside Luca.

Matteo gave me a knowing look when he settled beside me on the back seat. "You'd probably jump out of the moving car if I gave you the chance."

I huffed. "I'm not completely crazy. Do you think I'd risk running around Chicago unprotected when my father's men are obviously out to hurt me?"

"So you trust me to protect you but still don't want to marry me."

Surprise shot through me. "You still want to go through with the marriage?"

"You could probably ram a knife into his back and he'd still want to go through with it," Luca said from the front. "He's a stubborn fucker."

"I didn't hunt you for six months only to let you go."

I searched his face, but I couldn't look past his arrogant mask. He wouldn't let me. "Maybe you shouldn't have wasted so much time hunting me." Then I'd still be in Munich, and Sid would still be alive. But I had to admit that part of me had missed my former life. Not all of it, mind you, but definitely my siblings and maybe even some other aspects that I didn't want to admit to myself yet.

Matteo didn't say anything but his lips tightened. The rest of the drive passed in tense silence.

I tried to hide my nerves as we pulled up in front of my old home. What would Father do to me?

chapter 10

—MATTEO—

The Outfit car came to a stop in front of the Scuderi villa and Luca parked the rental BMW right behind it. Luca and Aria exited the car immediately and I pushed the door open to follow them but paused when I realized Gianna hadn't even unbuckled her belt yet. She was staring intently down at her hands resting in her lap. Annoyance flared up in me. Couldn't she ever go the easy route? Did she have to be so damn stubborn?

"I'm not in the mood to argue with you, Gianna. You really shouldn't let your father wait right now. He's pissed as it is. Get out of the car or I'll carry you."

I waited for a clever comeback. Instead she reached to unbuckle herself. Her hands were shaking and suddenly I realized what was going on. Gianna wasn't stalling to annoy me. She was nervous about being back here. Her fingers struggled with the seat belt. I pushed them away and did it for her. Her eyes shot up, brows drawn together as she searched my face. She looked fucking anxious. She didn't even push my hands away, which were still resting on her thigh.

"We need to get out," I said again, this time without the previous annoyance.

She nodded slowly, her eyes darting toward the window. I could see Luca and Aria watching us, and behind them Stan and Carmine were waiting. Romero lingered next to our second car, scanning the surroundings. I didn't think this was a trap, but you could never know with the fucking Outfit. Things hadn't exactly been peachy between us in the last few months.

"I'm scared," she said quietly, then laughed harshly. "Isn't it messed up that I'm scared of my own father?"

"Your father is Consigliere and a huge asshole. There are plenty of reasons to be scared of him."

She was still staring at her lap. "He hates me. He wouldn't even hesitate to put a bullet through my head after what I did."

He'd have to go through me, and I had no doubt that I could take him down with one arm tied to my back. I hooked a finger under her chin and turned her face around to me until her blue eyes met mine. "I won't allow it."

For a moment she softened and her eyes darted to my lips but then Gianna became her usual self and pulled back. I almost groaned. She opened the door and slid out. When I caught up with her, there was no sign of fear on her face. She held her head high and sent Scuderi's men the most scathing look I'd ever seen from her. That was the Gianna I knew. The only indication that she wasn't as relaxed as she pretended was that she didn't argue when I rested my hand on the small of her back as I led her toward the front door. I couldn't wait to run my hands over every inch of her body, to finally claim her. Images of Sid with his paws on her slipped into my mind again and I had to resist the urge to hit something.

Luca raised his eyebrows, impatience written all over his face. "What took you so long for fuck's sake?"

I ignored him because the door opened in that moment and Scuderi appeared in the doorframe, a scowl on his face. Gianna shrank against me. I didn't think she even noticed because her face remained perfectly unimpressed.

Scuderi talked to his men briefly before sending them away and turning to Luca. They shook hands and then he hugged Aria. He hadn't spared Gianna a single look so far. It annoyed the hell out of me. His cold eyes zoomed in on me and I sneered at him. I hated everything about that man, even his stupid face and slicked-back hair. He looked like the worst cliché of a mobster.

"I see you found her," he said.

"I always get what I want."

He still didn't even glance Gianna's way but his expression turned cruel. "What you wanted was a reputable Italian girl. What you get are the ruins of God knows how many men."

Gianna stiffened under my hand, her eyes widening a fraction before she regained control over her face, but her father wasn't done yet. No wonder he and my father had gotten along so well.

"I can't see why you even bothered wasting your time on her. My men could have caught her without you."

His men would have done a lot of things with Gianna. Luca narrowed his eyes at me in warning. Could he tell how much I wanted to bury my knife in Scuderi's ugly mug? I glared back at Scuderi, wanting to wipe that superior grin off his face.

"I think we should go inside to discuss matters," Luca said, using his Capo voice. It usually grated on my nerves when he did that, but this time it was probably for the best. I had a feeling that my knife would accidentally find its way into Scuderi's eyeball if I had to bear his stupid expression another second.

Scuderi nodded and opened the door further. Gianna was practically pressed up against my side as we walked past him. Protectiveness burned through my veins. Maybe she didn't realize it but that she sought my closeness when she was scared was all the confirmation I needed for her feelings for me, even if she wasn't aware of them yet.

"How can you even touch her after what she's done? After what you saw her doing. I'd be disgusted," Scuderi said as he closed the door. He obviously didn't expect a reply because he turned to Luca. "If my wife had done something like that, I would have killed her, and I have a feeling you would have done the same, Luca."

Aria shot Luca a shocked look but he was busy staring Scuderi down. "I'm not here to discuss what-ifs with you. I want to have this settled once and for all. You promised us something and I expect you to deliver."

"What I promised isn't available anymore." Scuderi nodded toward Gianna. "But if you want damaged goods, I'm sure we can come to an agreement. Dante is waiting in the living room for us. This is foremost Outfit business, and Dante will have the last word on the matter."

Luca met my gaze, warning clear in his eyes. "Then let's go. I have better things to do than chitchat with you. And I'm sure we can come to an understanding that will benefit all of us."

I didn't give a damn about Dante or Scuderi. I was taking Gianna back to New York with me, even if I had to gut every single Outfit asshole in the process.

Gianna

I was trying very hard to keep a neutral expression but it was incredibly hard. To my embarrassment, Matteo's hand on my back really helped me focus. His expression on the other hand only fueled my own anxiety. He looked like a man out for blood. I chanced a look at Luca and my father, who weren't bothering to dish out pleasantries either.

Things had taken a definite turn for the worse since I'd left. If Luca was acting barely civil toward my father, relations between the Outfit and New York couldn't be good right now.

Aria gently touched my arm, eyes full of worry. I forced a smile, but it must have been off because she only frowned in return. Damn it. Matteo nudged me forward. Father and Luca were already heading toward the living room, but at the sound of hurried footsteps I froze, my eyes darting to the staircase. Lily and Fabi were storming toward me, their faces alight with happiness. Tears sprang into my eyes as my little brother tackled me, burying his head against my sternum. God, he'd grown since I'd last seen him. How was that even possible? I'd been gone for only six months. And then Lily threw her arms around me as well. "We missed you so much," she whispered tearfully. Fabi's hold on me was making breathing difficult but I didn't care.

I hugged them back just as tightly. While I'd been on the run, I'd barely dared thinking about my family because it had felt like a chasm was ripped into my chest every time I did.

"Didn't I tell you to keep them upstairs?" Father hissed, causing me to look up and find Mother coming down the staircase hastily.

"I'm sorry. They were too quick," she said in a meek voice. Her eyes flitted over to me briefly before she returned her gaze to Father without a word to me.

I swallowed. So this was it? Because I hadn't done what they wanted I was dead to them? I'd known Father would condemn me but I'd hoped at least Mother would be happy to have me back.

"Lily, Fabi, back to your rooms."

"But, Father, we haven't seen Gianna in forever," Fabi grumbled. Father crossed the distance between us in two quick strides and wrenched my brother and sister away before shoving them toward Mother. "Upstairs now."

Fabi jutted his chin out, and even Lily didn't move. Father's face was turning red in anger. "It's okay," I told them. "We can talk later."

"No, you can't. I won't have you around them. You are no longer my daughter, and I don't want your rottenness to rub off on Liliana," Father said, eyes hard.

I wasn't even sure what to say to that. He didn't want me to see my own sister and brother anymore.

"That's bullshit," Matteo said.

"Matteo," Luca warned. He was already gripping Aria's wrist to keep her from interfering. "This isn't our business."

Father glared. "That's right. This is my family, and Gianna is still subject to my rule, don't you ever forget that."

"I thought I wasn't your daughter anymore, so why do I have to listen to a word you say?"

Matteo gripped my waist tightly. What? He could provoke my father but I wasn't allowed to?

"Careful," Father said. "You are still part of the Outfit."

"We shouldn't let Dante wait any longer," Luca said.

This time we actually moved into the living room without incident. Dante Cavallaro was waiting in front of the window, talking on the phone. He hung up and turned to us. I had to suppress a shiver when his cold eyes settled on me. The iceman indeed. Suddenly I was really scared. This was serious.

I couldn't remember the last time I'd felt so horribly helpless.

"Luca, Matteo, Aria," Dante Cavallaro said in his emotionless voice. "Gianna."

I jumped in surprise. I'd figured he'd pretend I was beneath a greeting like my father had done. "Sir," I said, bowing my head slightly. I hated doing it but I knew what was good for me.

"You realize that what you did was betrayal?" Dante asked.

I wasn't sure what to say. If I agreed I'd be screwed, and if I didn't I'd infuriate the man who could decide to have me killed.

"Gianna is my fiancée, and if she hadn't run she'd be my wife by now. I think it should fall upon my brother as Capo of New York to determine if she deserves punishment."

My eyes flew from Matteo to Luca whose hard eyes sent another shiver down my back.

"That's ridiculous," Father muttered.

Dante didn't look offended though. "I take it you still want to go through with the wedding?"

"Yes," Matteo said without hesitation.

Nobody bothered to ask what I wanted of course, but I knew better than to open my mouth. Not when things could end really badly for me.

Dante gestured Father closer and they talked quietly for a moment. Father didn't look pleased in the least.

"I won't make this an official Outfit matter. I won't stop you from going through with the wedding. If you don't, however, I won't have a choice but to punish you," Dante said to me. He nodded toward Matteo before turning to my father once again. "I'll hand this over to you since Gianna is your family, and I hope at the end of this day there'll be an agreement that allows us to work together peacefully." With that he stepped back and motioned for Father to take over.

"Can you really afford to welcome someone like Gianna to New York? As a new Capo your people expect you to protect traditions and treat traitors without mercy," Father said to Luca.

"My men accept my decisions," Luca said, but there was a hint of warning in his voice. "Whatever that decision will be."

Suddenly I wondered if Luca would really burden himself with me. It wasn't like I wanted to become part of the Famiglia, but if the choice was between staying in my father's territory and living in New York with Aria, then I knew what I'd choose.

Looking like he was on the verge of pulling his knives, Matteo walked over to Luca to discuss something quietly and Aria used the moment to join me. I gave her a grateful smile.

"My brother will take your daughter off your hands, despite her transgressions. I think that's a very generous offer on our part. You should be glad that you don't have to look for a new husband for her."

Father scoffed. "As if I'd find someone. I wouldn't waste my precious time like that."

My blood was boiling, not only because of Father's words, but Luca's offer didn't sit well with me either. They acted like I was a piece of scum. Listening to them made me realize I had been right to run. This world was majorly messed up.

"So what do you say?" Luca asked, lips tight.

Father glanced at his boss but Dante seemed intent to stay out of it. He looked like he couldn't care less about the result.

"I hope you don't intend to have a wedding celebration. I want this matter to be dealt with as quietly as possible. She has caused me and the Outfit enough embarrassment already. I won't give her a chance to shame us further," Father said eventually.

I gritted my teeth so hard I was surprised my jaw didn't snap.

Matteo shook his head. "I don't need a wedding party. I prefer getting drunk without the old spinsters of the family around anyway."

A laugh tickled the back of my throat but I swallowed it. Matteo shot me a look as if he wanted to see if I found him as funny as he obviously found himself. Everything he did was calculated. That was something I could never forget. Matteo masked his deadliness with humor and smiles, but I wouldn't let that fool me. Not now, not ever, especially not when it was obvious he thought he was being generous by taking me back.

"The old spinsters wouldn't have come anyway. Nobody wants to be associated with someone like her," Father said with a glare in my general direction.

Aria's grip on my wrist was steely as if she still didn't trust me not to viciously attack our father.

"There will be a church service as is tradition," Luca said. "There's no need for guests beyond the closest family."

"Tradition," Father huffed. "Gianna spat on our traditions. The presentation of the sheets your Famiglia is so adamant about will have to be cancelled. And a white dress is out of the question too. I won't have her make a mockery out of our values."

Luca nodded. "That's reasonable."

Aria gave her husband an incredulous look, but I wasn't surprised that I wouldn't be allowed to dress in white. As if I gave a damn. For all I cared I would marry naked. I didn't want any of this. And I didn't give a fuck about their stupid traditions. They acted like they were doing me a favor, as if I was a criminal on death row who was handed a pardon on a silver platter. I'd done nothing wrong, nothing compared to what each of the men in this room had done.

"She's probably let every man in Europe have her, and you still want her?" Father asked again. I knew he was doing it to shame me and hurt me, and I hated it that he wasn't entirely unsuccessful.

I stared at the man who was my father, and felt nothing. I'd always known he didn't like me much, but I'd never realized how much he despised me. I sunk my nails into the soft flesh of my palms.

Matteo stood tall with that twisted smile on his face. "I hunted her for six months. If I didn't want her, do you really think I would have wasted so much time on her? I've got better things to do."

If I heard that one more time, I'd completely lose it.

"I thought you were looking for revenge, but my men told me you didn't lay a finger on her." Father directed a hard look at me. "Then again, you probably didn't want to get your hands dirty. I don't think a simple shower is going to wash my daughter clean again."

Aria gripped my wrist even tighter, and I halted. I hadn't even realized I'd taken a step toward our father to do…I wasn't even sure what I would have done. Hit him? Maybe. His words and expression made me actually feel dirty, and I hated that he had that power over me. At the same time I'd have rather thrown myself off the roof of this house than admitted that I hadn't slept with any guy while I was on the run. That was a secret I'd protect with all my might.

"Who says I'm not still out for revenge?" Matteo asked in a dangerous voice. His dark eyes met mine. The bastard. So the concerned looks in the car had been all for show? He knew I didn't want to marry him. He knew this was a punishment for me. Who knew what else he had in mind for me once I was in his clutches?

"I won't marry anyone," I snapped. "This is my life."

Father looked livid as he stomped toward me and slapped me hard across the face. My ears rang and the taste of copper filled my mouth. A long time and many slaps ago, I would have cried.

"You will do as I say. You soiled our name and my honor enough as it is. I won't tolerate your insolence a day longer," he growled, his face bright red.

"What if I don't?"

My wrist was almost numb from Aria's crushing grip. She'd managed to position herself halfway between Father and me, despite Luca's obvious disapproval but he was busy holding Matteo's shirt in an iron grip.

I tried to tug Aria back but never took my eyes off Father. Aria was still trying to protect me but this was a battle she couldn't fight for me.

Father's hand was still raised, ready to hit me again. What would he do if I hit him back? I wished I were brave enough to find out.

"For your betrayal nobody would blink an eye if I gave you to one of the Outfit's sex clubs, so we can make use out of your promiscuity."

Despite my best intentions, shock widened my eyes. Dante frowned but I wasn't sure if that was a good sign or not.

Matteo's eyes were burning with so much hatred that the hairs on the back of my neck rose. Luca was still gripping his shoulder, stopping him from what? I wasn't really sure. "That won't happen. Gianna will become my wife. Today," Matteo said.

"What? I—" I blurted but Father's slap silenced me again. It was harder than before and his ring caught my lower lip. Pain burst through my face and warm liquid trickled down my chin.

"That's enough," Aria said, and suddenly Luca was pulling her back and Matteo was gripping my arm tightly and leading me out of the room and down the hall toward the bathroom. I wasn't sure if it was the shock of what had happened or the speed in which Matteo dragged me away, but I didn't fight him, only stumbled along, not even bothering to stop blood from dripping onto my shirt from my split lip. Matteo shoved me into the bathroom, then entered after me and locked the door.

I stared at my image in the mirror. Blood covered my chin and more blood dripped from the cut in my lower lip and onto my shirt. My lip was already swelling, but I was happy to find my eyes dry, no sign of a single tear. Matteo appeared behind me, towering over me, his dark eyes scanning my messed-up face. Without his trademark shark-grin and the arrogant amusement, he looked almost tolerable.

"You don't know when to shut up, do you?" he murmured. His lips turned into a smirk, but it looked somehow wrong. There was something unsettling in his eyes. The look in them reminded me of the one I'd seen when he'd dealt with the Russian captives in the basement.

"Neither do you," I said then winced at the pain shooting through my lip.

"True," he said in a strange voice. Before I had time to react, he gripped my hips, turned me around and hoisted me onto the washstand. "That's why we are perfect for each other."

Back was the arrogant smile. The bastard stepped between my legs.

"What are you doing?" I hissed, sliding back from the edge of the washstand to bring more distance between us while pushing against his chest.

He didn't budge, too strong for me. The smile got bigger. He grabbed my chin and tilted my head up. "I want to take a look at your lip."

"I don't need your help now. Maybe you should have stopped my father from busting my lip in the first place." The taste of blood, sweet and coppery, made my stomach turn and reminded me of darker images.

"Yes. I should have," he said darkly, his thumb lightly touching my wound as he parted my lips. "If Luca hadn't held me back, I would have plunged my knife into your father's fucking back, consequences be damned. Maybe I still will."

He released my lip and pulled a long curved knife from the holster below his jacket before twisting it in his hand with a calculating look on his face. Then his eyes flickered up to me. "Do you want me to kill him?"

God, yes. I shivered at the sound of Matteo's voice. I knew it was wrong, but after what Father had said today, I wanted to see him begging for mercy and I knew Matteo was capable of bringing anyone to their knees, and it excited me. That was exactly why I'd wanted out of this life. I had the potential for cruelty, and this life was the reason for it. "That would mean war between Chicago and New York," I said simply.

"Seeing your father bleed to death at my feet would be worth the risk. You *are* worth it."

I wasn't sure if he was joking or not, but this was getting too…serious. I wanted to kiss him for his words, but it was wrong. Matteo was wrong. Everything was. Not too long ago I'd watched Sid getting killed and I knew it might just as well have been Matteo who'd pulled the trigger. I couldn't let him mess with my mind. He was too good at it.

I shoved his shoulder again. "I need to take care of my lip. If you have nothing better to do than to stand around, get out of my way."

He still didn't budge and he was simply too strong to move him. His muscles flexed under his shirt, making me wonder how he would look without it. *Wrong. So wrong.*

He set his knife down on the counter beside me.

"You shouldn't leave sharp objects in my reach when I'm pissed."

"I think I'll take the risk," he said, bracing his palms to both sides of my thighs, leaving me no choice but to lean back to bring some distance between us.

"Stop it," I growled because he smelled too nice and I felt my body wanting to move closer then winced again. I brought my hand up and felt my lower lip. It seemed to have swollen even more and it still hadn't stopped bleeding.

Matteo pulled my hand away. "You'll make it worse. It needs stitches. Should I call for a doctor?"

"No," I said quickly. I didn't want any more people to find out, and most of all I didn't want my bastard of a father to find out he'd managed to split my lip. "I'll do it myself."

Matteo raised his eyebrows. He took a step back and did a quick scan of the cupboards before he came up with a medical kit. He threaded a needle and handed it to me. I shifted on the washstand to see myself in the mirror then brought the needle up to my lip. I'd never stitched anyone up, least of all myself. I hated needles. I even had to close my eyes when I got a shot. Matteo was watching me and I didn't want to look like a wimp to him, so I nudged my lip with the tip of the needle, jumped from pain and pulled back again.

"Fuck. That hurts like hell." I flushed then glared at Matteo. "Go on. Laugh."

Matteo snatched the needle out of my hand. "This isn't going to work."

"I know," I muttered. "Can you do it?"

"It'll be painful. I don't have anything against the pain."

"Have you ever stitched yourself up?"

"A few times."

"Then I can handle you stitching me up. Just do it."

He handed me Tylenol. "Pop a few of them. They won't help with the immediate pain but they'll be good later."

"Vodka works too."

"I guess you found out in your months as a fugitive," he said with a grin that bordered on scary. He hadn't asked too many questions yet. Not even about other guys besides Sid. Maybe he didn't want to know, and I wouldn't tell him anyway. It was bad enough that one innocent had lost his life because of me. I wouldn't tell him the names of the other guys I'd kissed so he'd kill them too. Death was too harsh a punishment for a kiss, for anything really, but that wasn't something a man like Matteo would agree on.

"Among other things," I said because I never knew when to shut my mouth. And what better moment to choose for provoking someone than before they were going to poke you with a sharp needle.

"I bet," he said, the scary smile getting a bit scarier. Matteo cupped my chin. "Try to hold still."

I braced myself as he touched the needle to my lip. Despite my taunting, Matteo was careful when he stitched me up. It still hurt like hell every time the needle pierced my skin and my eyes filled with stupid tears. I fought them for as long as possible but eventually a few trailed down my cheeks. Matteo didn't comment for which I was glad. For him this was probably nothing. When he set the needle down after what felt like forever but had probably been less than five minutes, I quickly wiped the tears off my cheeks, embarrassed that I'd shown weakness in front of him like that.

"It'll swell even more. Tomorrow morning you'll have a fat lip," Matteo said.

I checked my reflection. My lip had already swollen considerably since I'd last seen it, or maybe that was my imagination. I pulled down my lower lip to check the stitches. You couldn't see them from the outside. At least I wouldn't have an ugly scar. "You can't possibly want to marry me looking like this." I pointed at my face. "We should postpone the wedding."

Matteo shook his head with a small laugh. "No chance in hell. You won't slip out of my hands again, Gianna. We will marry today. Nothing will stop me."

chapter 11

—GIANNA—

After my lip was taken care of, Aria and I were allowed to go to my old room while the men discussed how to proceed with the wedding. Two bodyguards were ordered to keep watch on me. One waited in front of the door, the other below my window, in case I decided to climb out of it. The moment the door of my room closed I leaned against it and let out a shaky sigh.

Aria touched my cheek. "How's your lip?"

"Okay. Matteo stitched it up for me."

"I'm so glad he decided to marry you."

My eyebrows shot up. "Not you too, Aria."

Aria pulled me toward the bed and made me sit down. "Father would have given you to one of his soldiers as punishment, Gianna. And you can be sure he would have chosen the least appealing option. Someone really nasty. He's really mad at you. Matteo isn't a bad choice. He must care for you if he went to such great lengths to find you."

"He's a proud man. Pride made him pursue me, nothing else."

"Maybe," she said uncertainly. She picked up a brush from the nightstand. Everything was still as I'd left it six months ago. I was surprised Father hadn't burnt all of my things. I was so tired I could barely keep my eyes open. It was almost seven in the evening. It would have been past midnight in Germany. I couldn't believe how much had happened since I'd woken in Munich this morning.

"Was it worth it?" Aria asked softly as she combed my hair. I couldn't remember the last time she'd done it. Her fingers felt good on my scalp and I had to resist the urge to burry my face against her stomach and cry.

I met her compassionate gaze, and for some reason her understanding infuriated me. "Was the chance at freedom worth pissing off Father and being called a whore and slut? Yes, absolutely. But was my silly wish for something more worth the life of an innocent guy? Then fuck no. My entire existence isn't worth that much. Sid paid the ultimate price for my selfishness. There is nothing I can do to redeem myself." Tears sprang into my eyes.

"Luca told me," Aria said. "I'm so sorry."

I brushed the tears off my face. "Maybe I should let Father marry me off to one of his sadist soldiers. It would serve me right."

"Don't say that, Gianna. You deserve happiness as much as anyone. You couldn't have known what would happen. It's not your fault that they killed Sid."

"How can you even say that? Of course it's my fault. I knew who was hunting me. I knew what Matteo and Father's men were capable off. I knew I was putting anyone whom I let close at risk. That's why I never dated any guys in all the other places I stayed. I flirted and kissed, but then I moved on. Your words from long ago always echoed in my mind. That being with another guy when you're engaged to a man like Luca would mean that guy's death."

"I wasn't talking about you. That's been a long time ago."

"But Matteo is just like Luca and I knew that. I knew that he'd kill any guy he would find with me, but I still went out with Sid. I might as well have pulled the trigger myself!"

"No. You didn't think he'd catch you. You wanted to feel at home and start a new life like you deserved after being on the run for so long. You felt safe and wanted to give love a chance. That's okay."

"No. No, it isn't. You don't get it, Aria. It wasn't even about love. I didn't even really have a crush on Sid. I didn't even like him all that much at the end because he could be a jerk, and that makes it even worse. I risked too much for sloppy kisses and awkward groping, and Sid died because of it."

"Please don't blame yourself. Blame Father and his men. Blame Matteo. I don't care, but don't blame yourself."

"Oh, I'm blaming all of them, don't worry, but that doesn't change that, without me, Sid would still be playing his crappy guitar and flirting with Munich girls."

"You can't change the past, Gianna, but you can make the best of your future."

I couldn't help but smile. "I missed your optimism." I rested my head in her lap and closed my eyes. "I missed you so much."

She stroked my hair. "I missed you too. I'm so happy that you'll live in New York with me."

"First I have to marry Matteo. How am I going to be a wife, Aria?"

"He and Luca work a lot. You won't have to see him very often."

"But still. I'll have to sleep with him and share a bed with him and try to be civil to him for God knows how long. It's not like he'll give me another chance to run."

"You're thinking about running again?" she asked in a small voice.

"I don't know. Maybe."

"Maybe it won't be as bad as you think. Matteo can be funny and he's good-looking, so on a physical level at least it shouldn't be too bad. I'm sure he's a good lover considering how many girls he's had in the past."

I cringed. "Right. If we return to New York tonight, he'll probably expect to sleep with me."

Aria searched my face. "Are you worried he'll let his anger out on you for sleeping with other guys before him?"

"I never did."

Aria blinked. "You never did what?"

"I never slept with any guy. I would have if I'd had a bit more time to get to know a guy but that was never the case."

"Why didn't you say anything? Father treated you horribly. Maybe he would forgive you if you told him the truth." She moved as if she wanted to head downstairs to tell him herself, but I pulled her back down on the bed.

"Don't," I said firmly. "I don't want anyone to know. I don't care if they call me a slut. I don't want to give them the satisfaction of knowing."

Aria gave me a look that made it clear she thought I'd lost my mind. "You have to tell Matteo at least. You have to."

"Why? So he can pride himself on being my first? Fuck no. He's already acting like he's my savior. It'll be only worse if he finds out."

"No, you have to tell him so he can be careful."

I snorted. "I don't need him to be careful. I don't want him to know."

"Gianna, if your first time is anything like mine you'll be thanking your lucky stars if Matteo is careful, trust me."

"I'll survive." But Aria's words were starting to make me nervous.

"That's ridiculous. If he thinks you're experienced, he might take you without much preparation. That'll really hurt."

I shook my head. "Aria, please. I've made my decision. I don't want Matteo to know. It's none of his business."

"What if he finds out anyway? There would have been no way I could have hidden it from Luca."

"I'm good at hiding pain. Maybe I'll bite into a pillow."

Aria laughed. "That sounds like the stupidest idea I've ever heard."

Someone knocked. I quickly sat up, my stomach in knots. What if Father and Dante had changed their minds and I was to stay in Chicago?

When the door opened and Mother walked in, I exhaled. She didn't smile and didn't try to come closer. She was the image of a perfect Italian wife, always properly dressed, always submissive and polite, and incredibly skilled at hiding bruises whenever Father lost it and slapped her. She was everything I never wanted to become. If Matteo ever slapped me, I'd hit him back, no matter the consequences.

"The priest is on his way. He'll be here in fifteen minutes. We need to get you ready for the ceremony," she said matter-of-factly.

My eyes widened. "So soon?"

Mother nodded. "The Vitiellos want to return to New York as soon as possible, which is probably for the best."

I rose from the bed, then slowly walked toward Mother. "Father will be glad to see me gone."

"What about you?" I wanted to ask but didn't dare to.

Mother lifted her hand and brushed my cheek for the barest moment before taking a step back. "You shouldn't have run. You ruined your reputation."

"I don't care about my reputation."

"But you should." She turned to my wardrobe and opened it. "Now let's see if there's a dress you can wear for the ceremony. Of course I wish I could have seen you walk down the aisle in a beautiful white wedding dress." She sighed. Was she trying to make me feel guilty? Because it was working.

Aria moved to my side and squeezed my shoulder before helping Mother look for a dress. Eventually she chose a backless cream-colored floor-length fitted gown that I'd worn for New Years. Aria helped me with my makeup, though it didn't hide my fat lip.

"I'll see if the priest has arrived," Mother said, before hesitating in the doorway with a wistful expression. She opened her mouth but then turned and closed the door.

I tried not to take it to heart. I'd known my parents and most of the people in my world would condemn me for what I'd done, so why was it hurting so much?

"Do you think Lily and Fabi will be allowed to watch the ceremony?" I asked in an embarrassingly hopeful voice.

"Let me talk to Father. I'm sure I can convince him," Aria said.

I didn't protest as she walked out. If someone could convince Father, then it was Aria. I faced the mirror. My eyes were sad and tired. I didn't look like the blushing happy bride. Not that anyone expected me to. This wasn't even a real wedding. Despite my best intentions, regret gripped me once again. How could my life have become such a mess? All I'd ever wanted was to be free to make my own decisions. Maybe I would have married Matteo if he'd ever bothered to ask me instead of ordering me to do it. And now I wouldn't ever get a real wedding or a beautiful dress. I'd always thought I didn't care about these things but now that they were lost to me I felt saddened.

Aria returned. "It's time. The priest is waiting in the living room. Fabi and Lily are there too."

I mustered a smile. "Then let's get married."

—MATTEO—

Even without a wedding gown, Gianna was a fucking sight to behold. The dress hugged her curves; curves I'd take my time exploring when we were back in New York. I couldn't wait to lay claim to every inch of her body. I'd make her forget everything that was before me.

Gianna met my gaze as if she knew what I was thinking. And I really didn't bother to hide my want for her. I'd fuck her tonight, no matter how tired and jet-lagged I was. I'd waited too long for this. Gianna stopped beside me and I took her hand. The priest was looking down his nose at her. I couldn't wait to leave Chicago behind. Not that people in New York would look upon Gianna more kindly, but at least they were too scared of me to show their disdain openly.

Gianna's hand was cold in mine and she avoided my eyes as the priest spoke the wedding vows. When it was her turn to say "I do" I half expected her to say "no" and I really wasn't sure what I would have done then but she didn't. Gianna was a clever girl; she'd hide her hatred for our bond until she was a safe distance away from Chicago and her bastard of a father.

When it was finally time to slip on the wedding ring, she actually shivered. Somehow that annoyed the crap out of me. She should be grateful I wanted her as much as I did. Her stupid actions could have cost her everything. She could at least pretend to be grateful.

"You may kiss the bride," the priest intoned.

I didn't hesitate. I cupped her face and pressed my lips against hers. Gianna stiffened, making my blood boil even more. When I pulled back, she met my gaze head-on. She was really intent on provoking me. If she liked to play with fire, fine. I didn't mind getting burned. I'd walk through flames for her.

Less than sixty minutes later we were back in the air on our way to New York. My body was humming with desire as I watched Gianna in her sexy dress. She and Aria huddled together in the last row on the plane.

Luca sank down beside me and handed me a glass of Scotch. I swallowed it in one gulp. "An espresso would be better. I need to be awake."

Luca followed my gaze toward the girls. "You intend to have your wedding night once you're home."

"Damn right."

"From what I know about Gianna, she probably won't make it easy for you. What are you going to do if she fights you?"

I hadn't considered that. In every fantasy I'd had about Gianna, she'd been a willing participant. I wanted her to scream my name in pleasure, wanted to make her wet. Would she really refuse me? "She won't," I said with more conviction than I felt.

Luca's eyes were practically x-raying me. "Nobody would blame you if you took what you wanted against her will. It's not like she hasn't already done the deed."

My hands curled to fists but instead of following my first impulse and punching Luca, I counted to ten in my mind. Luca often said things like that to gauge someone's reaction. I didn't think he was being serious. Maybe before Aria I would have doubted him more.

His eyes took in my balled fists then scanned my face before smirking. "You are like an open book to me."

"Shut up," I muttered. My eyes found Aria and Gianna once more. They seemed to have an argument, an unusual sight. I'd never seen the two not getting along.

"What's that about?" I asked after a moment.

"How should I know?"

"You and Aria are practically soulmates, haven't you mastered the art of reading each other's mind yet?"

Luca gave me the finger. "I know your wife will make your life hell, so I'll cut you some slack."

"How considerate of you." I wondered how life would be with Gianna. Today she'd been mostly subdued, except for a few occasions but I had a feeling she'd recover quickly and return to her old snarky self. I hated seeing her quiet side, especially when it meant she was sad about that fucker Sid. I tried to forget the bastard but somehow he'd anchored himself in my brain. And then I couldn't stop thinking about him with Gianna. How many more guys had seen her naked? Had been in her? I really needed to find out their names and kill them all.

When we finally landed in New York, I was back to being royally pissed again. I barely glanced at Gianna as we took my Porsche Cayenne back to our apartment building. Every time I caught a glimpse down her shirt to the soft swell of her breasts, I almost lost my shit. I needed to get a grip on myself. It didn't matter what Gianna had done before today. Now she was mine, and if I didn't put a stop to my rising wrath, I'd only do something that I'd regret later on.

—GIANNA—

Matteo had a strange look on his face whenever he glanced my way. I couldn't really put my finger on it, but somehow it made me nervous. Of course I pretended I didn't notice anything.

Aria had tried to talk me into telling Matteo the truth throughout the entire duration of our flight, and even now that we were pulling into the underground garage of the apartment building, she was still giving me meaningful looks. I was worried that she'd take it into her own hands to share my secret with Matteo, but she knew I'd see it as a breach of my confidence and so I hoped she'd hold herself back.

Matteo took my hand when I got out of the car and practically dragged me toward the elevator. Aria and Luca had trouble keeping up with our pace. I had a feeling I knew why Matteo was so eager to reach his apartment. We all piled into the elevator. It started moving and Matteo's dark eyes watched me in the mirror, something hungry and furious gleaming in their depth. The hunger was inexplicable to me. I looked a mess. Shadows under my eyes, fat lip, pale skin.

Maybe I should have felt more anxious, but I only wanted to get this over with. Maybe Matteo would even lose interest in me once he'd had me, though part of me wondered if I'd really be happy if Matteo suddenly started ignoring me.

The elevator stopped with a bling and the sleek doors glided open. Without another word, Matteo pulled me into his apartment. I threw a glance over my shoulder and caught sight of Aria's worried expression moments before the closing elevator doors hid her from my view. Matteo led me toward a door to our right. I barely had time to take in the modern furniture and stunning view of New York before we rushed into the bedroom and Matteo flung the door shut. The desire in his eyes made it clear that he wouldn't take no for an answer tonight.

chapter 12

—GIANNA—

Nobody had ever looked at me like that, like I was the only source of water in a time of drought. And by God, I enjoyed it. Part of me at least, the other part, the stubborn part, wanted to hang onto my anger and sadness and indignation, and not give a damn about Matteo's desire for me.

In the last twenty-four hours my dreams had been crushed and an innocent life had been taken. I felt like it was my duty to fight this marriage, and the tingling that flooded my body whenever Matteo touched me. I owed it to Sid, and to my own self-respect. I'd fought too hard and long to be free.

Before I could make up my mind about what I was going to do, Matteo jerked me against him and claimed my mouth in a fierce kiss that made me gasp, then tense. His tongue slipped between my lips, and without wanting to I opened up for him, parted my lips, wrestled his tongue with mine. My hands found their way into his hair, tugging, raking, wanting him closer and at the same time wanting to shove him away.

Matteo gripped my butt and hoisted me up. My legs wound themselves around his waist, but our lips never parted. My body was aflame with lust. No kiss before had even come close to this. Matteo started walking, carrying me toward his bed.

Fight him, Gianna. Fight this. You owe it to Sid.

But I was sick of fighting for today, sick of my emotions. Today I only wanted to feel, let my body take control, forget everything for a few hours at least. There would be plenty of time for resistance later in this marriage.

Matteo threw me down on the bed and the air left my lungs in a rush, but I didn't get much time to recover because suddenly he was on top of me and his lips were back. His hand slipped under my shirt, fingertips gracing my stomach, then the sensitive skin over my ribs. He cupped my breast through my bra and I arched against him. He pulled away, and I barely managed to suppress a sound of protest. He seemed to know it though. He smiled in that arrogant way as he pushed my shirt up over my head and unhooked my bra. My nipples hardened and his smile widened even more.

Annoyance shot through me. He seemed so damn sure of himself, certain of his victory over me. He had another think coming.

"What would you do if I told you 'no'?" I asked in a challenging tone.

I'd expected fury or annoyance in return.

"You won't," he said without a hint of doubt in his voice. I glared but he didn't give me the time for a nasty retort. He lowered his head over my breasts and sucked one erect nipple into his mouth. A moan slipped out before I could stop myself and Matteo didn't allow me any time to gather myself, to raise my defenses. His mouth was relentless. The sensations rippling through my body were almost too much. How could he make me feel like that? His tongue circled my nipple before moving on to the other, leaving a wet trail between my breasts. I shivered. Matteo's eyes were glued to my face. He wanted to see me surrender to him, wanted to enjoy this victory to the very last. I resisted the urge to close my eyes. He would have seen it as another victory. I wouldn't give him that as well. He gently bit down on my nipple and I moaned, even louder than the first time.

With a self-satisfied grin, he moved lower, dipping his tongue into my belly button. I squealed like an idiot girl and tried to squirm away from him, but his hands came down on my hips, holding fast, as his tongue found every ticklish place on my stomach and hips. I was laughing so hard, tears were pooling in my eyes. I had expected him to be rougher after what he'd witnessed, had almost wished for it, but this playful side? That scared me because he seemed likeable, even loveable. I pushed at his forehead. "Stop it!" I gasped between laughter.

"What's the magic word?" he murmured against a particularly ticklish place right above my hip bone.

"Fuck you," I said sweetly. I braced myself but it didn't stop the squeals and laughs when Matteo traced his tongue over my hip bone. I was on the verge of begging when suddenly he stopped his assault. He unbuttoned my pants and pulled them down. His eyes traveled over my legs, and his hands followed the same path, barely brushing my skin. His motions were almost reverent; I didn't get it. Disgust and fury, those I would have understood.

When he kissed me through my panties, I became very still. I knew what he wanted to do. Nobody had ever done that. It felt very personal, as if I had to bare myself to him in more than just the physical sense, and I couldn't do it, wouldn't do it, no matter how much my body craved the experience. Matteo gripped my panties and slid them down my legs. He sat back for a moment, admiring me. "I'd wondered if you were a redhead."

I rolled my eyes, despite the flush spreading in my cheeks. "Isn't that what every man wonders?"

I realized a moment too late that mentioning other men wasn't the best idea in my current situation.

"How did you explain that to the other guys you've been with? Brown on top and red down below?" His voice and eyes had become harder, *dangerous.*

Nobody's ever seen me like this. The words lay on the tip of my tongue. "I thought you wanted to fuck me. I'm not in the mood for chitchat."

Matteo shook his head. "Oh, I will fuck you, don't worry." He crashed his lips down on mine and I kissed him back just as fiercely. "Feel, don't think" became my mantra. His hands roamed my body until they found their way between my legs. I forced myself to relax despite my nerves. When his fingers brushed over my folds, I gasped against his lips. The sensations were delicious. His thumb found my bundle of nerves and started rubbing. Two of his fingers slid back and forth the length of my slit while his thumb pressed down on my clit. Maybe my mind didn't want Matteo, but my body was so eager for him it was ridiculous.

My toes curled as he drove me higher with his fingers. I gripped his neck, bringing him even closer, wrangling his tongue with mine, as my orgasm crashed down on me. My nails dug into his skin but that seemed to turn him on even more judging from the growl deep in his chest. Suddenly two of his fingers moved lower and brushed my opening. Fear spiked. Clamping my legs together, I shoved at his chest and wrenched my lips away from his.

"Stop with the foreplay," I said breathlessly. What if he could feel something with his fingers? I doubted his cock would be as sensitive as his fingertips.

The hint of a frown crossed Matteo's expression but then he slid off the bed with a wicked grin. He stood tall in front of the bed. The bulge in his pants was unmistakable. He didn't give me much time to wonder what lay below the fabric. His hands made quick work out of unbuttoning his shirt and then he slid it off his strong shoulders and let it drop to the ground. This was the first time I saw him without a shirt. I'd caught glimpses of his six-pack through his white shirt before but it couldn't compare to seeing him bare-chested. My core tightened with desire. Even if Matteo's personality grated on my nerves, my body definitely reacted to his looks. His hands moved on to his pants, and in one swift motion he dropped both his pants and his boxers on the ground. When he straightened, it took all my acting skills to mask my embarrassment and nerves at the sight of him fully erect.

I really should have listened to Aria, but even as the thought crossed my mind I knew I was too proud to tell Matteo the truth. My eyes took their time taking in every inch of him, not even caring that he smirked at my obvious admiration.

And, boy, was he gorgeous. Everything about him was, his chiseled chest and six-pack, even his cock. I hated him for it. Hated how my body reacted to him so quickly and easily when it had never reacted to Sid or the other guys I'd made out with. He advanced on the bed, every move lithe and calculated. Every move aimed to show off his muscles and strength. God, I wished it wasn't making an impression on me. He put one knee on the bed, fixing me with a gaze that made me shiver.

"Stop playing around," I hissed because my nerves were getting the better of me and that was the last thing I needed.

And he did as I asked. He moved onto the bed and climbed between my legs, grabbing my hips with a dark smile. "I'm going to make you forget every fucking guy you've ever been with."

I glared, and was about to give him a nasty comeback, when he pulled at my hips sharply and slammed into me in one hard thrust. I arched up with a cry as pain shot through me. Damn it. Aria hadn't been kidding. This was fucking painful. So much for keeping it a secret. I sucked in a few quick breaths through my nose, my eyes clenched shut. "Oh fuck," I gasped out when I could speak again. This was much worse than I'd thought. I opened my eyes slowly, dreading what I would see. I should have bitten into a fucking pillow, or even my stupid tongue.

Matteo had frozen above me as he stared down at me in surprise. "Gianna?"

My face turned hot. "Shut up," I muttered. I loosened my fingers, which had clawed at the bedsheet.

Matteo's eyes were soft. "Why didn't you tell me?"

I decided to play dumb. Maybe I could convince him this wasn't what it looked like. "Tell you what?"

A sly grin twisted his lips, and I wanted nothing more than to wipe it off his face. Of course he didn't buy my lie. He wasn't an idiot. He was a master manipulator and I obviously had a lot to learn before I could trick him.

"That I'm your first," he said. Did he have to sound so. . .relieved and proud?

If I hadn't been worried that getting his cock out of me would hurt as much as getting it inside had, I would have shoved him away. Lying beneath him made a fair argument difficult.

I narrowed my eyes. "I thought we were going to fuck? I'm tired of talking to you."

Matteo braced himself on his hands, bringing us closer. I tensed at the twinge the movement caused.

"First I want you to answer my question. Why? You could have spared yourself a lot of pain, if you'd told me," he said calmly. He looked like this was the easiest thing in the world for him, being buried deep inside of me, and having a chat.

When it became clear that he would wait until I gave him what he wanted, I said, "Because I didn't want you to know."

His grin got even cockier. "Because you didn't want to admit that you waited for me."

"I didn't wait for you. Now stop talking and fuck me, damn it." This was getting too personal, and I hated how vulnerable I was, naked inside and out. How was I supposed to stop feeling if Matteo kept asking me things I didn't want to think about?

Matteo didn't take his eyes off me. They were dark and possessive, and seemed to stare right through me. If it hadn't felt like a defeat, I would have looked away. He pulled out slowly before sliding back in and I tensed from the pain. My body was a horrible traitor. At least, I managed to hold back a gasp this time. Matteo moved slowly and carefully, his muscles flexing with every thrust.

I hated that he was being considerate. I hated that he wasn't acting like a total asshole, hated that hating him wasn't as easy as I'd thought. If he wasn't an asshole, then somehow Sid's death was even more my fault, because my running away was unnecessary and selfish and unfounded.

I gripped his shoulders. "Stop holding back."

Matteo's brows drew together but he still didn't move faster.

I dug my fingers into his skin and jerked my hips despite the soreness between my legs. "Stop holding back!"

This time he listened. His eyes flashed and then he slammed into me harder and faster. I closed my eyes as I held onto his shoulders. I probably left marks with my nails. I didn't care and Matteo didn't seem to mind if his quick breathing was any indication.

The pain felt good, gave me something to focus on beyond the crushing guilt. But there wasn't only pain. Soon the stretched feeling turned into an exquisite pressure, a low hum of pleasure I'd never felt before. Matteo lowered himself, changing the angle in which he pushed into me, hitting an amazing spot deep inside me. Matteo's mouth found my throat and then he bit down on my skin lightly. A moan slipped out of my lips. My eyes shot open, meeting Matteo's intense gaze. I couldn't look away. I wanted to pull him closer and push him away at the same time, wanted to hide and open up to him, wanted and not wanted. "Are you going to come?" Matteo rasped.

I shook my head "no," not trusting my voice. Maybe I could have come. It felt increasingly good, but I needed to bring space between Matteo and me, needed time to get a handle on my emotions before they overwhelmed me. I was confused and tired and sad.

Matteo raised himself on his arms again and sped up even more, slamming into me over and over again, and then he tensed above me, his face twisting with pleasure, and damn he looked magnificent, like something even Michelangelo couldn't have created better. Matteo's movements became jerky and then he stilled, eyes closed, a few strands of dark hair stuck to his forehead.

My fingers itched to brush them away, to touch his lips and jaw. Instead I dropped my hands from his shoulders and rested them on the bed beside me where they couldn't do something stupid, something I'd regret later.

Matteo's eyes peeled open slowly and I sucked in a quiet breath. Why couldn't he stop looking at me like that? He didn't smile, only pierced me with his dark gaze.

I pushed against his chest. "You're getting heavy. Get off."

The corners of his mouth twitched, then he slowly pulled out and plopped down on the bed beside me and reached for me as if he was going to embrace me. Panicking, I sat up and slid off the bed. If he hugged me now, if he acted like we were a real couple, one that cared about each other, I'd lose my shit. I headed for the bathroom, not bothering to cover myself. Matteo had seen all of me already, and I wouldn't give him the satisfaction of thinking I was embarrassed to be naked in front of him.

I didn't hear him coming after me but suddenly Matteo grabbed my hand, stopping me from disappearing into the safety of the bathroom. Our eyes met. His were almost…regretful. "I shouldn't have gone so hard on you, but you know how to push my fucking buttons, Gianna. Did I hurt you?"

Concern, there it was again. Damn it. Why couldn't he stop acting like he was a normal guy? Did he really think that would make me forget who and what he really was? "Don't pretend you didn't like it."

"I don't. I loved every fucking second of it. I've waited a long time for this moment. I've spent almost every waking moment of my search for you imagining having your hot body under me. But in my imagination you were moaning my name and having multiple orgasms. You definitely weren't in pain."

That arrogant bastard. "Keep imagining that. It won't happen."

Matteo braced himself against the doorframe, trapping me between his arms. "Your body reacted to me, Gianna, even if you don't want to admit it. Next time you will come when I fuck you, trust me."

"What makes you think my body was reacting to you? Maybe I was imagining I was with someone else. The mind is a powerful tool." I tried to slip away under his arm but he pushed me against the doorframe. "Maybe I was imagining it was Sid and not you fucking me."

Matteo didn't even blink. He didn't believe a word I was saying. Damn it!

"If you'd really wanted Sid to be your first, you would have let him fuck you. So why didn't you?"

"Because you killed him!"

Matteo smiled. "We both know that's not the reason why, but let's just pretend it were true. Then I'm glad he's dead. That wimp didn't deserve the privilege."

I couldn't believe him. "You asshole. I knew you'd get a kick out of it, that's why I didn't tell you."

Matteo leaned close until there was less than an inch between our lips. "But I know and I won't ever forget. You are mine now, Gianna, and I fucking love that I caught you before you found a loser to pop your cherry."

I tried to slap him but he caught my wrist and actually kissed my palm with a self-satisfied grin. I wrenched my hand away from him. A myriad of insults flitted through my mind, too many to choose only one.

Matteo nodded toward the bed. "Maybe I should tell everyone that we can have a presentation of the sheets after all."

My eyes grew wide. That was the last thing I wanted, and Matteo knew it. He was taunting me. I pushed past him and this time he let me, and rushed toward the bed. There was a small pink smudge on the sheet. Men had it so much easier. Women had really been screwed over when it came to anatomy. We got our period, we couldn't pee standing up, we had to squeeze something the size of a melon out of our vagina and our first time sucked majorly. "You wouldn't dare," I said.

Matteo crossed his arms over his chest. He was still gloriously naked and was getting a boner again. The bastard was turned on by our fight. "You shouldn't tempt me."

I shrugged. "Even if you showed the sheets to your family, nobody would believe you anyway. They think I'm a slut, remember? They'd probably think you faked the stain with your own blood like Luca did on his wedding night." I tensed. This was a secret I was supposed to keep. Nobody knew. Why couldn't I ever keep my stupid mouth shut?

chapter 13

—MATTEO—

Gianna's eyes widened when she let Aria and Luca's little secret slip. Did she actually think I didn't know? Luca and I would die for each other. He knew he could trust me with every secret, even one that revealed he wasn't quite the cruel bastard he and everyone else thought he was. Somehow by some stroke of luck our sadist of a father had made the right decision when he'd chosen Aria for Luca. I didn't think he'd known how well those two would get along, or he wouldn't have agreed to the match. He'd always strived on the misery of others. "Don't worry. Luca told me. Your sister has warmed his cold heart. You Scuderi women have a talent for it."

Gianna relaxed. No matter how tough she thought she was, her body gave her away. She wasn't very good at hiding her emotions, which would make it easier for me. Her gaze returned to the stain on the sheets. Seeing it actually gave me a sick kick, so had the fine smear of blood on my cock. I wasn't like some men in our world who would have refused to marry Gianna because she might have messed around with other guys during her flight. Not that I didn't hate the thought that any guy had ever laid a fucking finger on her beautiful body, but I wanted Gianna too much to care, and I found the whole obsession with purity in our world ridiculous anyway. The best sex I'd had in my life definitely had been with women who knew what they were doing, but I had a feeling Gianna was a quick learner. Still after the initial shock when Gianna had cried out in pain, I'd felt a rush of possessiveness and fucking joy.

Gianna glanced at me, suspicion tightening her kissable lips. Her hair covered her pale skin like a veil and I couldn't resist brushing the strands from her shoulder, marveling at their silkiness. Only Gianna's skin was even smoother. I didn't think I'd ever get enough of touching her. My fingers found her pulse before I started stroking her throat lightly. For a moment Gianna held her breath and actually leaned into my touch before she seemed to catch herself. She took a step back so I had no choice but to drop my hand. I had to stifle a smile. She was so very predictable. At least, in her reactions to me. Sometimes in the past she'd managed to surprise me, which wasn't something other people managed often.

Gianna narrowed her eyes at me. If she knew how hot she looked when she was angry, she'd smile more often. I was already hard again and wanted nothing more than to fuck Gianna. Her eyes flitted down to my cock and she huffed. Shaking her head, she brushed past me and disappeared in the bathroom before slamming the door shut with an audible bang.

I released a small laugh before heading back to the bed, dropping on my back and crossing my arms behind my head. I couldn't keep the grin off my face. After months of frustration, I had been rewarded, even more than I'd hoped for. I waited for the sound of running water but silence reigned in the bathroom. I sat up, suspicion filling me. There wasn't any way Gianna could escape from the bathroom, but what if she decided to end her life rather than spend it with me?

Gianna seemed to love life too much for such an action, but I wasn't sure she wouldn't do it to spite me. I moved toward the bathroom door, ready to tear it down when it opened. Gianna stepped out, her eyebrows shooting up when she spotted me right in front of her. Her eyes weren't puffy, so at east she hadn't been crying, which was a relief.

Her nose crinkled. "What? Don't tell me you've been spying on me while I was in the bathroom?"

I crossed my arms over my chest with a smirk. I definitely wouldn't tell her what I'd thought. "We both know you need supervision."

With a sigh, she walked past me and climbed under the covers. After a quick scan of the bathroom, which looked the same as it had before, I joined Gianna. She had her back turned to me, and the blankets pulled up to her chin. I pressed myself against her back, my arm sliding around her naked waist. Having her naked body so close to mine was giving me all kinds of ideas and my cock was digging insistently against her butt. I couldn't wait to take her like this, to have her in front of me on all fours, to have her riding me. I wanted to fuck her in a thousand different ways.

"Don't even think about it," Gianna said quietly, warningly. "I'm tired and I don't owe you more than one go on our wedding night."

I laughed against her neck before pressing a kiss to her soft skin. "You are such a romantic, Gianna. Your words always warm my heart."

"Oh shut up," she muttered.

I tightened my hold on her. She didn't try to pull away, which surprised me, and again raised my suspicions, but I blamed her demureness on the long day both of us had had. It had been more than twenty-four hours since I'd slept.

Still, I fought off sleep until I heard Gianna's breathing deepening and her body softening against me. I didn't trust Gianna, not after what she'd done. I wasn't sure if I'd ever trust her completely. I knew she'd run the moment I let her out of my sight. I wouldn't give her another chance to evade me. I didn't care what I had to do to keep her in New York.

Luca had thought I'd lose interest in her once I'd fucked her. Part of me had hoped for it, but I could already tell that it wasn't the case. I still wanted her, probably more than before.

I was completely and utterly screwed.

—GIANNA—

The next morning I woke to Matteo moving around in the bedroom. I didn't give any indication that I was awake, instead I listened to his sounds. I didn't want to face him. He'd be smug about last night, definitely intolerable. Before a long shower and a strong coffee I wasn't in the mood for that particular kind of confrontation. When his steps finally moved away and the door clicked shut, I exhaled and opened my eyes. The skyline of New York was hung with heavy clouds. Maybe I could simply stay in bed, but I had a feeling Matteo might try to join me if I did. My traitorous body tingled with excitement at the idea of having his hands on me again, maybe even allowing him to go down on me for real.

I quickly sat up, slid out of bed and hurried into the bathroom to splash cold water into my face. I winced at the burning in my lip. I peered at myself in the mirror. My lower lip was swollen dramatically and the skin below it was bruised. I looked like I'd been in a fight, which wasn't that far from the truth. I opened my mouth to take a look at the stitches. Disgusted, I quickly snapped it shut again. The events from yesterday flashed through my mind.

I hadn't even had nightmares about what happened to Sid. I still felt horrible for his cruel death, but my dreams had been empty, a black void of nothingness. Maybe I did belong into this world after all.

My eyes slid down to a spot on the side of my neck where Matteo had left a hickey. The bastard had marked me like I was his property, and to him that was probably the case. I touched the bruise.

Grimacing, I turned away from my reflection, and took a quick shower. When I returned to the bedroom, I found my bags on the floor. Matteo must have carried them in while I was getting ready. Sneaky bastard. How could he move so quietly?

I quickly put my clothes into the drawers that Matteo must have cleared for me. Somehow it annoyed me that he'd made space for me as if he'd known all along that I'd eventually move in. He must have done it long ago. There hadn't been any time last night or this morning. Putting away the clothes that I hadn't worn in six months also made me realize that I desperately needed to go shopping. My old clothes felt like a relic from an old life. In our rush to leave my apartment in Munich, I hadn't been able to grab any of my new clothes.

Afterward, fully dressed I headed out of the bedroom, pausing briefly to listen for Matteo. It was silent in the apartment and as I walked through the living room toward the open kitchen I didn't encounter anyone, not even a bodyguard. Suspicion flared in me. Matteo would never leave me unsupervised after what I'd done. My eyes scanned the ceiling, the corners and every other possible place for security cameras, but I found none. I hesitated in the middle of the kitchen for a moment, eyes darting to the massive coffee maker. Screw it. I needed caffeine. If Matteo wasn't there, for which I was grateful, I'd pretend this was my home.

And I didn't even need to pretend. This was my home now, or it was supposed to be. Of course it didn't feel like it. It had been a long time since any place had felt like home. In the last few months of my living there, even my parents' house hadn't felt like one anymore. There was no use thinking about it now. I'd never forgive Father for how he'd treated me, nor Mother because she'd let him. Maybe I was dead to them, but they were dead to me too.

My finger hovered in front of the button that would turn the coffee maker on. This eerie silence was driving me crazy. Scolding myself for my ridiculous caution, I finally pushed it. I grabbed a cup and selected a cappuccino. I wasn't on the run anymore. The worst had already happened.

With a satisfying fizz, the hot liquid shot out. The moment it was done, I cradled the cup and took a long sip, feeling how the warmth and familiar taste cleared my mind further. I leaned against the counter, letting my eyes wander through the apartment. I actually liked the puristic design, the sleek black leather couches, black hardwood furniture and white walls. I wondered if Luca and Matteo had hired the same interior designer because their furniture was so similar. I could see myself looking for art pieces that would fit in, could see myself shop for pillows that would bring some color in, could see myself decorating a large tree for Christmas. I walked around the counter, perched on the stool and turned my back on the place I could so easily see myself living in.

This wasn't what I wanted. Or at least something I hadn't wanted six months ago, something I shouldn't want, not after risking so much to escape it. I closed my eyes and inhaled the comforting scent of my coffee. I needed to see Aria again, but was I even allowed to go one floor up to her penthouse? The idea that I had to ask Matteo and maybe even Luca for permission whenever I wanted to see my sister drove me up the walls. It was a good reminder of why I'd run in the first place, something I could never allow myself to forget.

A warm breath ghosted over my neck, followed by a low, "Good morning."

I cried out in surprise and sent my coffee cup flying off the kitchen bar. It broke into dozens of sharp pieces and spilled coffee everywhere. My head whirled around and I found myself face-to-face with a smirking Matteo.

"Fuck. Why the hell are you creeping up on me like that? You scared the hell out of me," I hissed.

He shook his head with an amused expression. "All those nasty words pouring out of your sweet mouth, is that really appropriate?"

He was making fun of me. His eyes took their sweet-ass time wandering over my curves, lingering on the hickey before moving a bit lower again. And the worst thing was the way my body was reacting to his closeness, his scent, his muscled chest. Thankfully, my face didn't feel hot, so maybe I hadn't blushed.

"Since when do you care about being appropriate?" I muttered. I slipped past Matteo and knelt beside the broken remains of my cup. I hoped Matteo didn't suspect what his proximity was doing to me. I picked up the pieces but Matteo came to my help. I wasn't sure if he was doing it to be nice or if he knew about his effect on me and was trying to play with me. From what I knew about him, I guessed the latter. I was trying not to look his way as he squatted beside me. He was giving me a good view of his perfectly shaped ass. Goddammit, why did he have to look like that?

Without warning, he brushed his finger over my swollen lip. "I really should have killed your father."

His touch was so gentle, it made me want to nuzzle my face against his neck and have a good cry. "Do you have a mop?" I asked casually.

He shrugged, dropping his hand. "I've seen Marianna run around with one on occasion."

I rolled my eyes. Of course he had no clue. He probably had never even done his own laundry. "Do you at least know where Marianna keeps the cleaning stuff?"

His gaze lingered on my cleavage. With a sigh, I rose to my feet and stalked off in search of a storeroom. When I finally returned to the mess in the kitchen, mop in hand, Matteo was talking on the phone. He was leaning against the counter, legs casually crossed.

I tried to listen to the conversation as I wiped the floor. I had a feeling it was about me.

"Come over now. I want this done ASAP."

With that he hung up, and turned back to me. I leaned the mop against the wall, then asked, "Who was this? A new bodyguard you hired to keep an eye on me?"

"Something like that. I'm going to put an ankle bracelet on you."

"What? Have you lost your mind?"

"On the contrary, but we both know you'll use the next chance you get to escape again, so until I can trust you to stay with me, you'll have to wear the bracelet."

I stared, completely stunned and so angry I was worried my head would explode. "So you admit I'm your prisoner. You're treating me like one after all."

Matteo advanced on me. "Without the bracelet I would have to lock you into this apartment, but with it, you can spend time with Aria, walk around New York, and live an almost normal life."

"I guess you want me to thank you for your kindness?"

The asshole actually chuckled. "No. Knowing you I didn't expect you to like the idea."

"Nobody would like that idea! And you don't know me, Matteo."

He moved very close and without warning he slipped his hand under my shirt, pushed aside my bra and twisted my nipple. At once, my core tightened with need. "I know that you love it when I do this with your perfect little nipple," he growled.

I wanted to deny it, but the way his thumb and forefinger teased me, I couldn't find the words. Matteo's dark eyes bore into me as he leaned very close. "I know you are wet. I know your pussy wants me even if you won't admit it."

He dropped to his knees and shoved down my tights and panties.

"What—"

I didn't get farther. He leaned forward and kissed my heated flesh. I sucked in a startled breath. Matteo freed one of my legs from my tights and panties before he lifted it and draped it over his shoulder. His eyes found mine as his tongue parted my lower lips and licked slowly. I shivered, pressing my mouth together from fear of making an embarrassing sound.

Matteo pulled back a couple of inches. "See, I knew it. Wet for me," he said in a rough voice. He pressed a few kisses against me before suckling lightly. My eyes wanted to roll back in my head from the sensation.

"Has anyone ever done this to you?" he asked fiercely.

I couldn't even find the power to lie. I merely shook my head "no."

"Good." He rewarded me with a mind-blowing kiss, his tongue tracing my opening, then darting back up to my clit.

"Oh God," I whispered.

Matteo released my throbbing labia. "You taste perfect, Gianna." He parted me and brushed a kiss over my clit. "Do you want me to stop?"

I gritted my teeth. I had never wanted anything less. It took all my self-control not to grab him and shove his face against me.

"The silent treatment?" Matteo asked in a teasing voice before he nudged me with his tongue, sending spears of pleasure through me before he captured my clit between his lips and suckled lightly.

I gasped and gripped the counter behind me, needing something to support me. My head fell back as Matteo did the most amazing thing with his tongue. With slow strokes he brought me closer and closer to the edge. I could tell this time it would be even more intense than yesterday. Without intending to, my hand gripped Matteo's head and my fingers tangled in his dark hair. Matteo rewarded me with a flick of his tongue against my clit.

"Yes," I whispered. I didn't even care anymore that I was admitting how good this felt. My entire body screamed for release. I was so close, my legs started shaking, my breathing quickened. And then the bell rang. I jerked in surprise and my eyes flew to the elevator. Nobody could come up without Matteo granting them access.

Matteo pulled back from what he was doing. My fingers on his head tightened. "Don't stop," I demanded. I couldn't hide the need in my voice.

Matteo straightened and wiped his mouth with an annoyingly cocky grin. He leaned in to kiss me but I turned my head so his lips brushed my cheek.

"Patience, Gianna. I've had six months to practice patience, now it's your turn, but don't worry, I'll eat you out later. You taste too good to resist," he murmured before stepping back and heading toward the elevator. "You should get dressed. We don't want to give Sandro a show."

I couldn't believe him. I quickly scrambled to put my panties and tights back on, before I washed my hands and straightened my skirt. My blood was boiling with fury. Matteo smirked as he pressed the button that allowed the elevator to stop on our floor.

This wasn't the end of it. Two could play this game.

chapter 14

—MATTEO—

Gianna was trying to kill me with her eyes. Not that I wasn't used to that look from her by now, but I had to admit it was still turning me on. I wished Sandro had waited a few minutes longer to show up, even if his early appearance gave me the chance to teach Gianna a lesson. Unfortunately I was punishing myself as much as Gianna with my little lesson. She'd tasted fucking perfect. I couldn't wait to lick her again, to have her screaming my name and rake her fingers through my hair. I was already getting a fucking boner again. Fuck this.

The elevator doors slid open and Sandro stepped in, holding up a black case. "Morning, boss. Hope I didn't interrupt anything," he said, his eyes sliding past me to Gianna. Despite his mess-up six months ago, he was still a good soldier. The best one next to Romero.

"You didn't," I said with a grin at Gianna, whose eyes narrowed even further. It was a good thing that Sandro didn't look anywhere near my crotch area because there was no way I could have hidden the bulge. Not that I fucking cared. "Let's do this now," I said eventually.

Gianna crossed her arms over her chest, somehow managing to push her breasts up in a delicious way. Was she doing it on purpose? She didn't move as we walked toward her. She looked like she couldn't care less but I knew her better than that. She was probably trying to figure out a way to make me pay for teasing her, not to mention for the ankle bracelet. But she'd brought this upon herself.

Sandro watched Gianna suspiciously as we stopped beside her. I couldn't blame him. His pride had taken quite a bruising when she and Aria had drugged him and tied him up. He was too clever to show his dislike though.

I pointed toward the barstool. "You need to take off your tights and sit down."

"Thanks for the heads-up. You could have mentioned the tights thing before and spared me a whole lot of trouble," she muttered. Fuck, her glare made me want to bend her over the kitchen counter and fuck her brains out.

Sandro pretended he was busy with the ankle bracelet in the case as I leaned close to Gianna. "But I loved watching you put on your sexy tights, and I'll love watching you take them off again."

Gianna almost tore her tights down this time before she perched on the stool, her long lean legs crossed. She pressed her lips together in anger, then flinched from pain. Fury for her father burst through my rising lust. Damn Luca and his determination to keep peace with the Outfit.

Sandro hesitated, ankle bracelet in hand, and darted an inquiring look my way.

I'd never put an ankle bracelet on anyone, so even if I fucking hated the thought of Sandro touching Gianna's leg, it was the logical choice. I nodded. "Go on."

"Extend your left leg."

Gianna sent me a scathing look but she raised her leg without protest.

Maybe she'd decided it was the better option than being locked into the apartment all the time, or maybe she was coming up with torturous things to do to me as retribution. I had a feeling I might enjoy whatever she had in mind, even if that wasn't her intention.

Sandro bent over Gianna's leg and started fastening the small black monitor around her ankle. I leaned against the kitchen bar next to Gianna. She didn't glance my way.

"Will this monitor my alcohol intake as well?" she asked Sandro. He raised his eyes to her, then me.

"I don't care if you're getting drunk as long as you do it in New York," I said. Her blue eyes fixed me with another scowl before she turned back to Sandro, who was checking the bracelet for its functionality.

With a nod, he straightened. "All done. You can trace her with your laptop, phone or any other internet-ready device."

"Great," Gianna muttered.

"Thanks, Sandro."

"Do you need anything else?"

I shook my head. "Not today. Romero is upstairs. You can return to your other tasks."

Sandro gave Gianna a curt nod before he turned around and headed for the elevator. After I'd let him out, I returned to Gianna.

"So how long am I going to have to wear this thing?" she asked, lifting her leg to take a closer look at the small black device around her ankle. I hated seeing her with that thing. It seemed wrong to shackle her like that, but Luca had suggested the bracelet and it was a neat solution. Gianna was too volatile for her own good.

"Until I decide I can trust you enough not to do something stupid."

"So forever." She dropped her leg back down.

I chuckled. "No. I like your gorgeous legs better without the ankle monitor, believe me. I'll relieve you of that thing as soon as possible." I traced my fingers over her bare knee, then higher until I reached the edge of her jeans skirt. She swatted my hand away and hopped off the barstool.

"Hands off," she said sweetly.

I raised my eyebrows. "I thought you wanted to continue where we left off before?" I really wanted to fucking continue where we left off.

She walked past me toward the coffee maker, swaying her hips in a way that turned me hard again. "I'm good," she said with a shrug. "All I need is a cup of coffee." She grabbed a new cup and put it under the coffee maker before peering over her shoulder at me. "What about you? Is there anything you need?" Her eyes wandered down my body toward my hard-on. I could tell that she was fighting a smile.

Oh, fuck. She really knew how to give me bedroom eyes. And obviously she thought she could play my game better than I did. "I'm good too."

She brought her cup to her mouth, took a sip, then ran her tongue slowly over her upper lip.

I stifled a groan. I had to meet Luca to discuss what I'd missed in the last few months while I'd been hunting Gianna, but I really wished I could watch her all day and maybe convince her to run her tongue over my cock. I strolled toward her and twisted a strand of her hair around my forefinger. "I hate your new color. I liked you better red."

Gianna pulled back and set her cup down with a clang. "Well, looking good wasn't my main concern while I was on the run. Maybe you didn't notice but a notorious mobster was hunting me."

I grinned. "Notorious?"

She rolled her eyes. "If you are fishing for compliments, then you're talking to the wrong person."

I didn't tell her to dye her hair back to her natural color, even though I wanted to. I knew she wouldn't do it if I tried to push her. Maybe admitting that I liked her red hair was already enough to make her want to stay a brunette forever. "I'm meeting with Luca. You can spend the day with Aria upstairs if you want."

Her eyes widened. "I'm allowed to spend the day with Aria?" After a moment, her mouth twisted and she added, "Not that I should need your permission to see my sister..."

"You and Aria haven't seen each other in a long time, I suppose you have a lot to talk about." I wondered if Gianna would tell Aria about last night and what exactly she would say. Normally I'd ask her what she'd enjoyed but I knew Gianna wouldn't give me an honest answer. Women had never complained about my sexual skills, but I wanted to hear it from Gianna. Maybe Luca was right and I was a vain asshole.

"Can we go up now?" Gianna asked, excitement lighting up her face. It was the first real emotion she'd shown me all morning.

"What about a kiss to convince me?"

She surprised me by grabbing my shirt, jerking me toward her and pressing her lips to mine. Her sexy body leaned up against me and her tongue slipped into my mouth. I didn't need any more encouragement. I grabbed her ass cheeks, squeezed, relishing in her gasp as our tongues danced with each other. I pushed my hard cock against her. She needed to know what she was doing to me. Fuck. I was so fucking hard, it was a wonder that I hadn't come in my pants yet like an idiotic teenage boy.

Without warning she drew back and I growled in response, my grasp on her ass tightening, but she pushed my arms down and stepped out of reach. "You wanted a kiss, you got your kiss. Now let's go to Aria."

That vixen. I knew by her rapid breathing and flushed cheeks that she was as affected by our kissing as me, but she seemed determined to suppress her lust. I'd simply have to up my game, show her what a mind-blowing orgasm really meant. After that, she'd hopefully be putty in my hands.

I walked toward the elevator as if I didn't give a damn. I had more than enough experience at hiding my emotions, so I had no trouble masking my arousal. I pressed the button that made the elevator doors slide open and motioned for Gianna to walk in. She frowned but then she headed into the elevator and leaned against the wall.

Hiding my smile, I joined her and jabbed the button that would take us up. It took several moments before Luca approved our going up. Before he'd married Aria, I had been allowed to take the elevator up without his approval, but since then he'd installed the manual override again. Not that I blamed him. I didn't want him or Aria barging in when Gianna and I were desecrating every available space of the apartment either. The elevator started moving and within a few seconds stopped again.

Aria was already waiting in front of the doors when they slid open. She barely spared me a glance before she pulled her sister into a hug and dragged her away toward the living area.

Luca stood with his arms crossed against the wall. "No kiss goodbye for you from your lovely wife?" he asked wryly.

Aria and Gianna had settled on the sofa, and were whispering among themselves. Romero raised his hand in greeting from his spot in the kitchen. He'd keep watch over Aria and Gianna while Luca and I were busy in Sphere. He knew what the two girls had done to Sandro, so he wouldn't let his guard down, and even if he did, the ankle bracelet would alert me of Gianna's whereabouts.

"Aria doesn't really look too sad to see you gone either," I said when Luca joined me in the elevator.

He smirked. "We already said goodbye twice this morning. What about you? How was your wedding night?"

I couldn't stop the grin. "Better than yours."

Luca's eyebrows rose in silent doubt. "So did she put out?"

"She did," I said. "And I was her first."

"Did she tell you that?" Luca asked doubtfully.

"No, she didn't. She was furious that I found out. But there was no way she could have hidden it."

"Good for you," Luca said, clapping my shoulder. "So are you still into her or have you come to your senses now that your cock isn't ruling your thinking anymore?"

I gave him the finger. "What makes you think my cock isn't still in charge?"

Luca sighed. "Suit yourself, but don't come bitching to me when she starts to annoy you." The elevator stopped and opened to the underground garage. "Now let's focus on business. You've wasted enough time. I need your full attention now."

"Don't worry," I said, but I had a feeling it wouldn't be easy to get Gianna out of my head. The image of her naked body beneath me had burned itself into my brain and I wasn't too keen on letting it go.

—GIANNA—

Aria dragged me toward the sofa, away from Luca and Matteo. We sat down and Aria reached for my fat lip with a frown. "I can't believe Father hit you so hard."

"He's done it before," I muttered.

Romero was watching us from the kitchen. I really wondered how he could stand being trapped in this penthouse with Aria all day. I doubted many soldiers had vied for the job.

After a moment, Aria leaned toward me, whispering. "Are you okay? How was last night?"

I glanced in the direction of Luca and Matteo but they had already disappeared in the elevator and were off to God knew where.

"Gianna?"

"I'm fine," I said, sending my sister a comforting smile. She looked like she hadn't slept much last night. Had worry for me kept her awake?

"And? How was it? Did you sleep with Matteo?"

I laughed. Aria reminded me of myself after Aria's wedding night. I had been so terribly worried for her. "Don't sound so anxious. I'm really fine." I was oddly fine. Maybe even too fine. It had been too easy finding my way back to my old life, as if the life I'd tried to lead in the last few months had never really fit. This morning I hadn't wondered where I was, hadn't had to remind myself of my current pseudonym. I was me again.

"You don't look fine. Please tell me what happened. I drove Luca crazy with my anxiety last night."

That made me smile. Everything that soured Luca's mood did. "I slept with Matteo." My mind returned to the feeling of him inside me, of his intense gaze, his strong body, his touch, and my core tightened again. I wasn't sure how I could stop my body from being so eager for Matteo's attention but I knew I had to figure out a way if I ever wanted to hold some sort of power in this marriage.

"You look like you didn't mind," Aria said with a teasing smile.

"Like you said, Matteo is good-looking, and he knows what he's doing, so it wasn't bad."

"Did he notice that you hadn't slept with anyone before?"

"Yeah. You were right. It hurt like hell. He was so damn smug about it. I really wish he hadn't figured it out. I feel like he's got more power over me now that he knows."

Aria shook her head. "You need to stop thinking like that. You and Matteo need to find a way to get along now that you're married. It's a good thing that he knows the truth."

"Matteo doesn't exactly make it easy for me either. He's always so arrogant. And he's the one who started with the games. And do you know what else he did?" I lifted my leg with the stupid ankle bracelet. I still couldn't believe Matteo had actually put that thing on my body, like I was a dog who needed a collar. Of course from his standpoint it was probably the normal thing to do. He was a controlling, possessive, power-hungry killer after all, but that didn't mean I liked it.

Aria grimaced. "I know. Luca mentioned it to me this morning. It was his idea." She paused with an apologetic expression. "I tried to talk him out of it, but he said he won't risk any more conflicts with the Outfit by letting you roam free."

"As if Father or anyone else in the Outfit would care if I ran off again. I'm not their problem anymore, remember?" I wiggled my fingers, showing off my wedding ring.

"Luca and Matteo would look weak if you managed to get away again, and that would weaken their position. Things between New York and Chicago haven't exactly been going smoothly in the last few months."

"Because of me?"

"Not just because of you," Aria said. "Luca and Dante don't get along very well. They are both alphas who aren't used to working with equals."

"I don't suppose you know of a way how to get rid of this thing?" I tipped my finger against my black shackle.

"No. Is it very uncomfortable?"

I shrugged. "Not really, but I hate it. And I can kiss short skirts and dresses goodbye unless I want everyone to think I'm a criminal."

Aria touched my arm lightly. "I'm sure Matteo will take it off soon."

"I doubt that." If I were him, I wouldn't trust me anytime soon. Probably never.

Aria's eyes darted to my hair again. She'd been doing it since she'd first seen me with the new color.

I smoothed a hand over my hair. "You hate it, right?"

"I'm not used to it. Maybe it'll grow on me. But I miss your red hair."

"Me too," I said. "Matteo hates my brown hair as well."

"Don't tell me you're going to stay a brunette because you want to annoy him?" Aria asked with a knowing look.

I wasn't that childish. Maybe six months ago that would have been my reaction but being on the run had helped me grow up. I wouldn't keep my hair in a color I didn't like to annoy Matteo. There were other ways I could make his life harder and I hoped to explore as many of them as possible. "I'll change it back to my natural hair color as soon as I get the chance. Do you think Matteo will freak out if we leave the apartment in search for a hairdresser?"

"Probably. You've been married for less than a day. Maybe you should try to stay on your best behavior for today at least."

"I'll do my best," I said sarcastically.

Aria got up. "It's almost lunchtime. Let's grab something to eat and I'll give my hairdresser a call and ask her to come over to do your hair, okay?"

I pushed to my feet. "Perfect. I'm starving." I followed Aria toward the kitchen area. Romero put his phone down on the counter, eyes and posture alert as we approached. Sandro had probably warned him of us. That reminded me of something I'd wanted to ask Aria ever since I'd run off. I waited until she'd finished her call with her hairdresser and fixed us a salad before I bridged the topic.

"Did you get into a lot of trouble with Luca for helping me?" I asked quietly. I didn't want Romero to overhear us. He seemed busy enough talking on his phone, probably to Matteo or Luca who were checking up on us.

Aria's face tightened. "He was angry at first, but he's forgiven me. I think he realized that I would never leave him."

She and Luca seemed happy enough but sometimes outward appearances were deceiving, and I wasn't entirely sure if Aria was telling the truth. She wouldn't say something that might make me feel guilty.

"You sure?"

"Isn't that my line?" she asked teasingly.

I grinned. "You taught me a thing or two."

"Good to know."

"There's something else I've been wondering about," I said quietly. "How did Matteo find me?"

"Luca didn't really talk to me about the search. He knew I'd warn you. Do you think it could have been the blog? I think Luca checked my laptop. I tried to warn you."

"I tried not to mention locations in my blog posts. But maybe they could track my location through my blog. Who knows?"

The bell rang. Romero walked toward the elevator before either Aria or I could move. "Will he ever leave us alone?" I asked when he was out of earshot.

"Not anytime soon," Aria said with a shrug. She rose from her chair to greet the woman in her mid-forties who entered the penthouse with two huge bags. Aria introduced me to her hairdresser and five minutes later we'd set up a chair in the bathroom and my hair was being smothered in cream that was supposed to turn my hair to its original color, not immediately but after several treatments.

Luckily I was allowed to walk around while the color reacted with my hair. Aria lent me her laptop and I settled at the dining room table. With dread, I searched the German websites for any homicide news in Munich. It didn't take me long to see the article mentioning Sid's death. The police didn't have any leads. My former roommates had to move for the time being, and I doubted they'd return to an apartment where Sid had found his end. The newspaper mentioned me, or rather my pseudonym Gwen, and that the police were looking for her because she was a witness. There wasn't a photo of me, thank God. I'd always been careful that I didn't appear in any pictures. But there was a photo of Sid with his guitar.

My stomach tightened with sadness and regret. Aria put a hand on my shoulder. "You shouldn't read that. There's nothing you can do, Gianna."

I shut the laptop slowly. There was one thing I could have done. I could have told the police who was responsible for Sid's death, so his family could find peace, but that was something I would never do. There were certain rules even I wasn't going to break. I wasn't stupid, or suicidal.

Aria's worried gaze didn't leave me as I returned to the bathroom to wash my hair. "I'm fine," I whispered, but she didn't seem to buy it, neither did I. The last twenty-four hours had been a whirlwind of emotions and change. I'd hardly had any time to reflect on everything that had happened, and I wasn't sure I wanted to. Maybe Aria was right and I should try to move on and leave the past behind. The problem was I wasn't sure I could. Didn't I owe it to my conscience and Sid that I showed some defiance, that I didn't just settle in my new life with Matteo as if nothing had happened?

chapter 15

—MATTEO—

When Luca and I returned to his penthouse that night, I felt like a fucking train had run me over. I hadn't gotten more than four hours of sleep in the last three days. The moment I spotted Gianna any thought of tiredness vanished into thin air. Her hair wasn't brown anymore. It wasn't the red she'd had before she'd run away but it was close and she looked fucking amazing even with her swollen lip.

I sensed something was off though. After dinner with Aria and Luca, we returned to our own apartment. Gianna hurried into the bedroom as if she couldn't wait to get away from me; unfortunately for her that was the room I wanted her in anyway. I followed and closed the door with a bang. Gianna sent me an annoyed look but didn't say anything. Instead she turned her back to me and rummaged in the drawers. I walked up to her, slipped my arms around her waist and pulled her against me. "You are thinking too much. Why don't you let me distract you?" I sucked the skin over her pulse point into my mouth. At first she tensed but then she relaxed against me.

"How do I know you're not going to play with me again?" Her voice had a strange quality to it but I wasn't in the mood to talk emotions.

I kissed my way down to her collarbone and slipped my hand lower, cupping her pussy through her clothes. She arched into me. I smirked against her skin. She smelled of flowers and her very own delicious scent. "Don't worry. I want to taste you all night long. I want to make you come over and over again."

She trembled against me, then her hand clamped down on mine, pressing me harder against her. She made a greedy sound in the back of her throat. I licked her shoulder as my fingers slipped under her skirt and panties, brushing her wet folds. I stifled a groan at the feel of her arousal. It took all my self-control not to dip my tongue into her pussy right away. I parted her velvety lips, brushing my fingertips over her slick skin before slipping a finger into her. She leaned her head back against my shoulder at the same time as she reached back and grasped my cock through my pants. I growled, then thrust against her palm.

I slid another finger into her. Fuck, she was so tight. Her inner walls clamped around my fingers like a vise. I couldn't wait to replace them with my cock. I was too fucking horny to take things slow or be gentle. I fucked her with my fingers, relishing in the feel of her juices on my skin, and the sounds coming from her mouth. She moved her hips in rhythm with my thrusting and her grip on my cock tightened almost painfully. It felt fucking fantastic. I rubbed my thumb over her slick nub of pleasure.

"God, yes," she gasped, her body stiffening against me. I kept thrusting as her orgasm rippled through her. When she relaxed, I lifted her into my arms and carried her over to the bed. I didn't give her time to recover. I pulled down her skirt and panties, and climbed between her legs, shoving them apart. My eyes took in her glorious pussy, glistening and perfectly pink. Unlike some girls Gianna wasn't shy about her body. She didn't try to shield her breasts or pussy from me. She let me admire her, returned my gaze without hesitation. She was fucking perfect.

Never taking my eyes off her, I lowered my head. She tensed when my lips almost touched her folds but I stopped to draw in a deep breath of her intoxicating scent. Gianna bucked her hips, a silent demand that made me grin. I didn't need convincing. I took a long lick all the way from her tight hole up to her perfect pink clit. My dick twitched in response to her heady taste. Fuck. I dove in, licking and nibbling. She rewarded me with breathless moans. Her fingers dug into the blankets when I sucked her inner lips into my mouth, gently teasing them until she squirmed on the bed. I took my time, bringing her close only to pull back over and over again. Gianna's moans turned into cries. Watching her body arch up in ecstasy was the best sight in the world. My hard-on was almost painful. When Gianna came down from her high, I released her and quickly scrambled off the bed.

I needed to fuck her now or I'd lose my mind. I got out of my pants and briefs but didn't bother with my shirt. Gianna surprised me by kneeling on the bed and wrapping her fingers around my cock. Her blue eyes were almost challenging when she brought her mouth down and closed her lips around my length. I groaned and my fingers brushed her hair from her face to have a better view of her mouth taking in my cock. I almost shot my cum right then, but a few mental tricks brought me back in line. Slowly at first, then faster, Gianna sucked me, her pink lips stretching around my width. I wanted to come in her mouth with her looking up at me like that, but even more than that I wanted to feel her tight pussy again. She circled my tip with her tongue before she took me almost all the way in until I hit the back of her throat.

Then she pulled back abruptly and wiped her mouth. She raised her eyebrows. "How do you like it when I stop like that?"

I chuckled. Was she trying to make me pay for this morning? She'd chosen a bad time. I climbed on top of her with a wicked grin and pressed my erection against her hot opening. Her eyes grew wide, but I didn't give her time for a reaction. I hooked my hand under her leg and parted her further before I started to slide into her. She was still tight and her face flashed with discomfort at my intrusion. I slowed further, easing into her and giving her time to grow accustomed to my cock. Yesterday I hadn't been careful because I hadn't known the truth but today I wanted to make her come with me in her. I watched her face closely until I'd sheathed myself completely in her tight channel. I paused for a moment. She gripped my shoulders, the challenge returning to her gaze. "Are you going to stay like that, or are you ever going to start moving?"

"Oh, I'll move." I punctuated my words with a short experimental thrust to see how she'd react. There was no sign of discomfort this time and I was fucking glad. I needed to fuck her now, and I didn't want to hold back. Keeping my eyes on her face, I established a hard fast rhythm, not as hard as I'd have liked but Gianna was probably still sore even if she wouldn't admit it. She was tight, clenching around my cock in a mind-blowing way. Every moan I drew from her lips felt like a fucking victory because it was obvious she was trying to keep them in. I changed the angle and drove even deeper into her. Another moan slipped out.

I reached between us, pressing my fingers to her clit. I needed her to come. My own orgasm was already close and there was no fucking way I'd come before her.

I thrust hard and deep, and Gianna's eyes grew wide, her face twisting with pleasure. She grasped my back, fingernails scratching my skin and I lost it. I fucked her even harder, losing every shred of control. Lust clouded my vision as I spilled into her. I growled against her slick throat, drawing in her scent as

I spent myself in her pussy. Gianna breathed heavily when my body stilled. I raised my head and smiled down at her flushed face, even when she scowled. It was almost adorable that she was still trying to keep up the show.

Slowly I pulled out of her. She winced, then quickly masked it.

"Sore?" I asked as I stretched out beside her. I touched her stomach. She didn't push me away, only shrugged in response.

I moved closer and kissed a spot right below her ear. "Has sex turned you mute?"

"You wish," she muttered, her voice slower and more relaxed than usual.

"No, that would be boring. The things coming out of your mouth are more entertaining than you think."

She gave me a look. "I'm glad I amuse you."

"Me too."

Like last night I waited for her to fall asleep before I relaxed. I wasn't sure if that would ever change.

The next few days followed the same routine until one night when Gianna's breathing didn't slow like it usually did. I was fucking tired and quickly losing my fight against sleepiness.

"You always wait for me to fall asleep first," she said into the dark, startling me awake.

Of course she'd noticed. "Sometimes I forget how observant you are."

She turned around, facing me in the dark. I could make out the white of her eyes and the contours of her head but not much more. "Why?"

"I'm a wary bastard."

"Do you think I'd kill you in your sleep?"

It was hard to gauge her emotions without seeing her expression and I fucking hated it. "Have you been thinking about it?" It was meant to sound like a joke but came out way too serious.

"No, I can't stand the sight of blood."

"That's the only reason I don't have one of my own knives stuck in my back?"

"No. Killing you wouldn't get me out of this apartment. I don't know the code for the elevator."

"That's a relief," I muttered. I wasn't sure if she was teasing or not. "You don't seem that unhappy in our marriage."

"We've been married for only a few days, and you're never around, that's a plus. And maybe I'm a good actress."

"I guess it's good that I don't trust you then."

"Yes," she said seriously.

"I suppose you want to scare me?" I asked in a low murmur, leaning so close to her that I could feel her breath on my cheek.

"I don't think there's anything or anyone that could scare you," she whispered back.

"Everyone's scared of something. Why would I be different?"

"Because you are the scariest person I know."

I paused. She didn't sound like she was kidding. "Are you scared of me?"

Silence was my answer.

I reached for her arm. "Gianna?"

"Yes," came her sleepy reply.

"Why?"

But her breathing had calmed. She had fallen asleep. What was I supposed to do with her admittance? I'd never given her reason to fear me. Okay, she'd seen me do some scary shit, but I'd never done anything to her. It took me a long time after that to fall asleep.

The next day Gianna didn't mention our conversation from the previous night. I had a feeling she hated that she'd been honest. I'd never shied back from a topic but I didn't ask her again why she was scared of me. I wasn't sure I wanted to know.

Gianna kept touching her lip during breakfast. It wasn't swollen anymore.

"Let me take a look," I said, pushing her hand away. "I think we can pull the stitches."

She grimaced. "Now?"

"Scared?" I asked because I couldn't help myself.

"No, of course not," she said. I wondered if she referred to more than the stitches. I got up and led her into the bathroom where I kept my medical kit. Gianna didn't protest when I lifted her onto the washtable and stepped between her legs this time.

I took small scissors from the kit. "Open your mouth."

She did, but gave me a warning look as if she thought I had something naughty in mind. I grinned and kissed her ear. "Do you know how kids always get a treat as reward after they see the doctor?"

She rolled her eyes but didn't push my hand away when I pressed it against her center through her jeans.

"Be a good girl and you shall be rewarded."

I drew back, enjoying the scowl on Gianna's face. She didn't get the chance for a retort because I started working on her stitches. It didn't take long and Gianna winced only twice. "Done," I said, setting down the scissors and tweezers. "Do you want your reward now?" I rubbed her pussy.

She glared.

"You just have to say the words." She pressed her lips together. "No?" I said, taking a step back, and stopped touching her.

"As if I need you for that," she said snidely, and then she opened her jeans and shoved her hand inside.

I exhaled as I watched her fingers move under the fabric. "Fuck." I stepped up to her and ripped her jeans and panties down her legs.

Gianna didn't stop caressing herself. Her slender fingers rubbed her clit nimbly while she watched me through narrowed eyes. It was the hottest thing I'd ever seen.

"Open your legs a bit wider," I ordered. To my surprise, Gianna obeyed. Her eyes were clouded with lust as she teased herself. Damn, I could see how wet she was.

I leaned back against the wall, tugged down my zipper and pulled out my cock. Gianna stroked herself even faster when I wrapped my hand around my hard-on and started jerking off.

"This is messed up," she whispered. She didn't take her eyes off my cock and I couldn't take my eyes off her fingers that worked her pink nub.

"Who cares?" I growled. "Put a finger in your pussy."

She slipped one finger into her tight opening.

"Another one," I demanded.

She barely hesitated. But I couldn't fucking take any more. I staggered forward, shoved her hand away and buried myself deep in her. She shuddered around me as her orgasm rippled through her. After a few thrusts, I came too.

"This is so messed up," she said again, her voice heavy with sex.

I didn't pull out of her yet. Instead I rested my forehead against her shoulder and caught my breath. "Messed up is good."

"I knew you'd say that."

"This thing is fucking annoying," she said after another round of sex that evening, wiggling her leg with the ankle monitor in the air. It had bothered me too the few times I'd come into contact with it during sex, but I wouldn't risk taking it off. Not only would Luca blow a gasket, I'd also have to supervise Gianna myself 24/7 without the monitor.

"You'll get used to it." I tried to pull her against me but she slipped away, moving to the edge of our bed.

"No cuddling as long as I have to wear this thing," she said.

I laughed. "As long as you don't ban sex."

"Maybe I will do that."

I moved my hand down from her stomach and ran a finger over her clit. "Why would you want to punish yourself like that?"

"You are an arrogant bastard. Maybe you think your cock is magic, but let me tell you something: it isn't." She didn't shove my hand away from where it was stroking her. Maybe she didn't notice but she'd even parted her legs a bit more to give me better access. I lightly traced her soft folds. I loved her silkiness and the way her body responded to me. I didn't increase the pressure, only lightly brushed my fingertips over her pussy. She was probably still oversensitive so I needed to be careful if I wanted to guide her toward another peak. Her lips parted and her breathing quickened ever so slightly. I leaned over her and sucked her nipple into my mouth. Pushing her over the edge this time was ever better because I wasn't busy with my own lust. I could completely focus on Gianna, her labored breathing, hooded eyes, hardening nipples as she succumbed to her orgasm.

I didn't even care when Gianna turned her back to me afterward, trying to punish me by not reciprocating. I'd gotten what I'd wanted.

"You realize that sex is all there is between us, right?" she said angrily.

"Sex is important."

"Sure, but it's not all there is."

"It's not all there is," I said, annoyed.

"Yes, it is, and there won't ever be more. Don't think I like you just because I like to fuck you."

"Thanks for the heads-up," I growled.

—GIANNA—

I was still annoyed at myself during breakfast, especially because Matteo's expression was far too smug despite my harsh words. Maybe he thought I'd been joking, or maybe he didn't care.

My body had a mind of its own, always eager for his touch. It didn't help that Matteo looked like a male model with his tight white shirt and messy black hair. He was sex on legs, and knew it.

"We are invited to dinner at one of the leading families this week, so Aria and you should probably go dress shopping."

I dropped my spoon with the yogurt. "You want me to attend a social event with you?" I couldn't believe he'd drag me into public so quickly. We'd been married for two weeks and the gossip mills were probably still going strong. "Everybody will be talking behind my back."

Matteo shrugged. "I don't give a damn what they think and they know better than to say anything in front of you or me."

"I know those women, they won't miss an opportunity to talk trash about someone, especially me."

"Ignore them. It's not like their opinion matters. They will always talk shit about you. That's all they can do."

I didn't care what they said, but I'd never enjoyed myself at social functions and I doubted that would change any time soon. "I know, but I hate these gatherings. Everything about it is false. People who wouldn't hesitate to thrust a knife into your back smile into your face if they hope to gain something from it."

For a long time I'd thought I was anti-social and just didn't like to be around larger groups of people but during my time on the run, I'd attended several parties and I'd never felt out of place. Even though I'd been pretending to be someone else then, I'd still felt truer to myself than I ever did around the people in our world.

"You'll get used to them."

"I don't want to. That's why I ran away."

Matteo searched my face with a curious expression, then his lips twitched. "So you didn't only run from me?"

"Don't get your hopes up. You were definitely one of the main reasons," I said.

"But not the only reason."

I rolled my eyes and took another sip from my coffee. "Do I really have to attend the dinner?"

Matteo rose from his chair and startled me with a quick kiss on my mouth. "Yep. I won't suffer through it alone now that I have a wife who can share my anguish. Just do what I do when I have to talk to idiots, imagine how it would feel to slice their heads off."

Despite how often I'd pushed him away, Matteo seemed intent on making it work between us. Why did he have to be so stubborn? Couldn't he finally grow tired of me and give me the chance to get away? "That's easy for you to say, but not all of us make a habit out of killing people."

Images of Sid wanted to anchor themselves in my brain again, but I couldn't bear them right now and forced them away.

"Then imagine how it would be to watch me kill the people that annoy you. As your husband it's my duty to kill your enemies after all." Matteo smiled his cocky grin, his eyes lit up with humor. My stomach fluttered in a scary way and I quickly tore my gaze away from him and emptied my cup.

"I'll go up to Aria and talk to her about going shopping. I need to be a good wife after all," I said mockingly but somehow it felt wrong. My emotions were confusing me, everything about my new situation did.

"You should probably buy some new clothes for you," Matteo said as he put his gun holster on.

"Is that an order?"

"I didn't know it was necessary to order a woman to buy clothes. Isn't that your favorite hobby?"

"Really?" I almost laughed. "Not all women are the same."

"Oh, I know." There was that smile again.

My eyes lingered on his gun, trying to remind myself that this was who he really was. The smile that made my stomach do flips was only a mask.

I stood abruptly. "You and Luca will be gone all day again?"

"Why? Do you and Aria have another escape planned?"

"Haha," I muttered, then raised the leg of my jeans, revealing the black ankle bracelet. "I can't, remember?"

"It doesn't stop you from making plans. Don't tell me you're not still thinking about escaping?"

I considered lying but instead opted for the truth. "Of course I am thinking about it. Did you think good sex and a ring around my finger would suddenly make me change my mind?"

"Only good, hm?"

I snorted and headed toward the elevator. Matteo joined me inside, his eyes resting on my hand.

"You are wearing your ring. I thought you'd throw it away the first chance you got."

I peered down at the gold band with the fine line of diamonds. "Did you carry it the entire time you were hunting me?"

Matteo smirked as if he knew I was avoiding his question, and I was. I hadn't even considered throwing the ring away. It seemed like such a waste. At least I hoped that was the only reason.

"Of course," he said. "I always knew I'd catch you eventually and I knew I would have to make you my wife before you ran off again."

His confidence was exasperating. It was also incredibly sexy. I was glad when the elevator doors slid open and I could walk away from Matteo's smile and my own unwanted thoughts. Luca passed me with barely a nod and joined his brother in the elevator.

Aria's welcome was much warmer. She was beaming all over her face as she headed my way and hugged me. "I still can't believe that you're living so close to me. I really missed having you as my confidante."

"I suppose there aren't many trustworthy women around here," I said, my blood boiling when I remembered how Luca's cousin Cosima had tricked Aria into walking in on Grace and Luca.

"Now that you are here, I don't care." Aria peered down at her elegant gold watch. "How about we head out for coffee now and then go shopping. Luca said we were all invited to the Bardonis' Christmas party."

I sighed. "Yeah. Matteo told me I had to attend."

"At least we can suffer together. Believe me, Luca isn't too excited about that invitation either. Bardoni wants his son to become Luca's Consigliere because in the past the Consigliere has always been one of the Bardonis, but

Luca wants Matteo and nobody else."

"So this party is going to be even more awkward than I thought. Everyone is going to scheme against Matteo and me. Oh, joy."

Aria smiled apologetically. "It won't be too bad. Now let's go shopping. I need some fresh air."

Of course Romero accompanied us as we headed out to buy dresses. Maybe I would have enjoyed myself more if I didn't have to be careful not to flash my stupid ankle monitor whenever I tried a dress on. From the look on the face of one of the vendors, I was fairly sure I didn't manage to cover the bracelet with the hem at all times. I realized I'd barely thought about escape in the last few weeks. Too many things had happened. And then there was Romero's constant surveillance whenever I went somewhere with Aria. Moreover, the ankle monitor was making it entirely impossible. I'd have to figure out a way to convince Matteo to take that thing off. Once that was taken care of, my desire to run away would probably return with full force.

chapter 16

—GIANNA—

I'd known all along that the Christmas party at the Bardonis' house was going to be a huge flop, but it was even worse than I'd thought. The only good thing about this ordeal was that Matteo had Sandro take off the ankle monitor so I could wear my cocktail dress without flashing that thing at everyone. That would have been the talk of the evening, no doubt.

The Bardonis lived in a townhouse, which had been decorated to an inch of its capacities. They'd even set up a massive angel, which had been carved from ice, in their front yard. The decoration was white and gold, expensive crystal baubles adorned the massive tree. It screamed money, and felt so impersonal that I was sure an interior designer had arranged it. Mrs. Bardoni didn't appear as if she'd ever moved a finger for anything. She was also at least twenty years younger than her husband.

She and her husband greeted Aria and Luca first, and while their smiles hadn't been exactly warm or honest, they turned positively fake and condescending when it was time to greet me.

I shook Mrs. Bardoni's hand with a polite smile, or at least I hoped it looked polite. Her expression was as if an untalented sculptor had tried to carve a smile into a statue. The smile of the ice angel outside had been warmer than hers. When Mr. Bardoni turned to me, I had to suppress a shudder. He reached for my hand but while he'd barely brushed Aria's skin, his lips pressed firmly to my hand and then his tongue darted out and licked my skin. The accompanying leer he sent my way almost made me punch him. I quickly retracted my hand, only barely managing not to wipe it on my dress, and only because the silk was too beautiful to come in contact with that asshole's slobber.

Matteo was in conversation with Mrs. Bardoni who was introducing him to a young woman my age. It was obvious that the old hag was trying to set Matteo up with her daughter. Anger bubbled up in me but I knew better than to show my emotions. When I finally turned my eyes away from the scene, I found Aria watching me with a worried expression. I gave a small shake of my head. Matteo tore himself away from Mrs. Bardoni and her daughter, and wrapped his arm around my waist. He scanned my face as he led me into the living room where the remaining guests had gathered. "You look pissed."

I shrugged. If I told him what Mr. Bardoni had done, things would become ugly. "Looks like you have a fan," I said instead, nodding in the direction of the Bardoni daughter whose eyes followed Matteo.

"Jealous?" he asked, smirking.

"You wish." But was I?

We didn't get the chance to talk more, because other guests approached us, and while most of them were acting polite, I could see in their eyes that they despised me. I had a feeling that they would show me what they really thought of me the moment Matteo wasn't around. They soon got their chance. While Matteo and Luca joined the other men, Aria and I strolled toward the buffet. Of course we weren't alone for long. Soon the bitch Cosima, Matteo's stepmother, Nina, as well as Mrs. Bardoni, and a few other women joined us. Aria's presence still offered me some protection from direct insults, but none of the women bothered talking to me. It was as if I wasn't even there. Even Aria's attempts to include me in the conversation failed. I didn't care. I hated these women, hated their fake smiles and nasty personalities. But the worst was watching Aria being polite to Cosima despite what that bitch had done.

Eventually I excused myself and headed toward the terrace door, which allowed a view into the small snow-covered garden. My reprieve was very short-lived however.

"Beautiful, isn't it?" a high female voice said.

Nina Vitiello stood beside me, her mouth stretched wide in the imitation of a smile. She no longer wore black. Her husband's funeral had been more than a year ago. She linked our arms to my utter disdain and led me outside despite the cold. I knew this wasn't going to be pleasant. Even though she was Luca and Matteo's stepmother, she'd never come to visit. I had a feeling she was scared of her stepsons.

The moment we were away from privy ears, she turned her back to the windows and faced me with a face devoid of any pleasantness. She reminded me of an ugly toad. "You might be parading around like you are one of us, like you belong in our circles, but if it weren't for Matteo, nobody would invite you."

I raised my eyebrows. Did she really think I gave a damn? I'd never wanted to be part of this world, that was why I had run away. It took immeasurable control on my part not to say what I wanted. Instead I tried to return to the party but Nina Vitiello held my arm, obviously not done. "A decent girl would have died from shame after being caught with another man. The only reason you're still alive is Matteo's good-heartedness. That boy is too dutiful. Although nobody would have blamed him if he'd discarded you like a dirty rag after what you did.

If my husband were still alive, he'd have fed you to our dogs."

Dutiful and good-hearted? That didn't sound like Matteo.

Deep breaths, Gianna. Don't cause a scene.

Again I tried to leave, but her fingers dug into my skin. "Aren't you ashamed of yourself? You've dishonored your family, and now you are bringing shame to the name Vitiello. Your mere presence is an insult to every honorable woman in this house. Your existence is sin."

I couldn't help but laugh. "Sin? You want to talk to me about sin?" I pointed toward the windows, behind which New York's worst criminals were gathered. "That room breathes sin."

Nina Vitiello lifted her chin. "Do us all a favor and kill yourself."

I wrenched my arm away, shocked. "I won't ever do any of you a favor." I turned and headed back inside. Matteo spotted me from across the room where he was talking with a younger version of Mr. Bardoni, Luca, and a couple of other men. I quickly looked away, hoping he wouldn't approach me. I wasn't in the mood to talk to him now. Aria was still where I'd left her, completely entrenched in conversation.

I crossed the room as quickly as possible, pretending I didn't hear the whispered "whore" a couple of people called me. Despite my best attempts not to let those insults get to me, I felt relief when I finally left the living room and found myself alone in the front hall. I needed to find the bathroom to freshen up and clear my head before I entered that room again. I was seriously worried that I'd attack someone if I didn't get a grip on myself. Taking a deep breath, I went in search for the restroom. I hoped I'd come across someone leaving the bathroom so I didn't have to open every single door. I definitely wouldn't ask Mrs. Bardoni to point it out to me. Unfortunately the only thing I found was Mr. Bardoni who must have been following me. The leer the bald idiot sent my way made me want to puke.

—MATTEO—

If Bardoni thought I hadn't noticed the way he'd eye-fucked Gianna when we'd arrived, he was even more stupid than I thought. If it weren't for Luca, I would have plunged my knife into the fucker's face right away. But Luca was a new Capo and couldn't use any more trouble, so I had promised him to stay on my best behavior. As the party progressed I slowly came to the realization that I might have to break my promise.

Gianna was trying to put on a brave face but I could see how upset she was after a talk to my bitch of a stepmother. I didn't want to know what the old goat had said to Gianna. She would never dare say something to my face. She was scared of Luca and me, had been for as long as I could remember.

Unfortunately, it took me a few more minutes before I could finally follow Gianna after she'd fled the living room. Luca's warning glance almost made me want to laugh. I had no intention of doing something stupid, except for having a quickie with my wife to lift her spirits. What was wrong with that?

When I stepped out into the lobby, I didn't see Gianna anywhere. I paused, listening closely, but the sounds of the party behind me were drowning out everything else. What if she'd run? I should have told Romero or Sandro to keep an eye on her at all times, but I hadn't wanted to embarrass her further. People had enough to gossip about as it was.

I headed in the direction of where I remembered the bathroom to be, hoping I'd find her there. A deep voice made me quicken my steps and when I came around the next corner I found Gianna alone with old Bardoni. One look at her face and I knew she was on the verge of a freak-out. She didn't see me as I approached, her narrowed eyes directed at Bardoni.

"Why don't you show me what you learned in Europe. I bet you're very talented with your lips. That's why Matteo was so eager to marry you, hm?"

Bardoni said and reached for Gianna's arm. Before she or I could react, he pulled her against him and fucking kissed her while groping her breast. My blood boiling, I stormed toward them, pulled my knife, shoved Bardoni away from Gianna and slammed my blade into the soft spot below his chin, piercing his fucking brain. Gianna gasped and stumbled back against the wall, her eyes darting from my knife to my face.

"Fuck," I muttered. I chanced a quick glance around, then dragged Bardoni's body toward his office, leaving my knife in his chin so blood didn't shoot out.

"You killed him," Gianna whispered harshly.

"He shouldn't have touched you." I nodded toward the door. "Open that for me." After a moment of hesitation, she stumbled forward and pushed the door open for me. I dragged Bardoni inside and Gianna quickly followed me inside before closing the door.

I put Bardoni down in his desk chair, then took a step back. This was bad. Luca would kick my ass when he found out.

"What are we going to do?" Gianna asked in a toneless voice from her spot near the door.

"We are going to make it look like I didn't kill him."

"Your knife is in his head."

I grinned but sobered when I saw Gianna's expression. It reminded me of the look she'd had after Sid had been shot. Sometimes I forgot that not everyone was as used to blood and death as me.

Slowly she came closer, gaze frozen on the body. "Why did you kill him?"

"Because he was an asshole."

Gianna stopped beside me and dead Bardoni. She looked like she couldn't quite believe what she saw. She raised her arm as if she was going to touch the corpse to convince herself of its existence.

"Don't touch anything," I ordered a bit too harshly, gripping her wrist to stop her.

She stared up at me with huge eyes. After another moment, she nodded almost robotically. She looked like she was going into shock. That was the last thing we needed.

Ideally I would have gone in search of Luca but I couldn't leave Gianna alone with the body. If someone came in, she'd have more trouble dealing with that person than I did.

I touched her cheek to bring her attention back to my face. "Go and get Luca," I told her.

She hesitated.

"Go."

"Okay." She whirled around, crossed the room in a rush and slipped out. She closed the door silently. I really hoped she wouldn't give everything away because she was so freaked out.

I lowered my eyes to Bardoni. I really loved the sight of my knife in his skull.

"Matteo?" I heard Luca's quiet voice a couple of minutes later. I jogged toward the door and opened it a crack. When I saw Luca standing in the corridor, I ushered him in.

"What do you want? Gianna didn't say anything," he said, but shut up when his gaze settled on Bardoni behind the desk. "Oh fuck."

"Bardoni had an accident," I said with a shrug.

Luca gave me a look. "Fuck, Matteo, what did you do?"

"If you ask me, I think good old Mr. Bardoni killed himself," I said.

Luca circled the body, then he glared at me. "It's because of Gianna, isn't it? Bardoni did or said something that annoyed you and you lost your shit. I knew the girl would bring nothing but trouble."

"The asshole has been on your death list for a while. He's been stirring up shit. You are glad he's gone, admit it. We've discussed having him killed countless times. I decided to finally act."

"Of course I wanted him dead, but not in his own fucking home at his Christmas party. Damn it, Matteo. Can't you think first and shoot second for once?"

Luca was right. I should have chosen a better time to kill Bardoni, but he shouldn't have talked shit to Gianna, and he most certainly shouldn't have touched her. He'd dug his own fucking grave.

"I'll call Romero. He's keeping an eye on Aria and Gianna but we'll need him here to deal with this fucking mess." Luca ran a hand through his hair, sent me another glower, then picked up his phone and called Romero.

A couple of minutes later, someone knocked. Luca held up his hand to stop me from opening it. Instead he went and let Romero in. Romero's eyes scanned the scene before him before focusing on me. "You killed him?"

I raised my arms. "Why did it have to be me?" It was a rhetorical question. It was almost always me doing the killing at improper times.

"Because you're the crazy one," Luca muttered, then said to Romero, "Can you make this look as if Bardoni killed himself?"

We all looked toward the dead asshole, hanging limply in his chair, lifeless eyes still expressing surprise at his early demise.

Romero grimaced. "Few people stab themselves in the brain."

"There's always a first time for everything." I chuckled but fell silent at a look from Luca. "Oh, come on," I said. "It was funny."

Luca's lips twitched but he was too stubborn to admit I was right. I knew he was more than a little glad that I'd gotten rid of Bardoni for him. "Search the room for a gun that could have blown his fucking head off. I don't need the Bandonis on my back right now. I want this matter dealt with quietly."

"No matter how we make it look, the Bardonis will suspect something. They won't believe it was suicide. Bardoni was far too narcissistic to end his own life," I said.

"Maybe I should put a fucking ankle monitor on you, too," Luca growled. "You are a ticking time bomb."

Romero stopped searching the drawers of the desk. "Even if the Bardonis suspect something, they won't say it aloud. If they don't have proof, they won't seek retribution."

"I wouldn't count on it," I said. "But we'll make sure they won't get a chance for revenge."

"Maybe you should pull your knife out of Bardoni's head. Nobody will believe it was suicide with your blade stuck in his chin," Luca said.

I walked toward the body and slowly pulled my knife out, then quickly took a step back before blood could get on my clothes. I checked my white shirt for any specks. My black trousers and jacket would hide blood better, but luckily I was clean. The same couldn't be said for Bardoni's clothes. Blood was quickly soaking his shirt and trousers.

Romero pulled a high-caliber Smith & Wesson from a drawer in the cupboard behind the desk. "This could do."

"Good," Luca said with a nod. "Matteo and I will return to the party. Wait about five minutes before you blow his head off, then get the fuck out of here. Matteo and I will hopefully be here first and in the commotion nobody will notice you are gone."

Romero was already busy figuring out the best angle to shoot Bardoni and barely reacted when Luca and I slipped out of the room quietly and closed the door. The corridor was deserted except for Gianna who was lingering at the end, looking anxious.

"Make sure she doesn't let something slip," Luca ordered. "And we'll have a talk about this fucking matter later."

"Don't worry. Gianna can lie if she has to."

"Oh, I don't doubt she can lie very well if she wants to. But she's not exactly the most trustworthy person."

"She's my wife," I reminded my brother with a bit too much force.

"That's the problem." He walked off back to the party before I could reply, and I headed toward Gianna.

—GIANNA—

I couldn't believe Matteo had rammed his knife into that man's chin. It had been a horrible sight, seeing Bardoni with dead, shock-widened eyes. He had been an asshole, and I certainly wasn't sad to see him gone, but seeing my own husband kill him without a second thought had been horrible. Matteo had acted so quickly, no hesitation, no preparation. Every move had spoken of experience. I'd known he was good with the knife of course. Even in Chicago people had talked about his skills but it hadn't prepared me for watching him actually use a knife on someone like that.

After I'd told Luca to find Matteo, I waited in the corridor. Aria had gone back into the living room; it would have looked suspicious if all of us had suddenly disappeared. And people were very eager to talk to Aria so her missing would definitely have drawn attention. Nobody would mind my absence however.

I'd barely waited for a minute, when Romero hurried past me toward the office. People always said I was unpredictable. I had nothing on Matteo.

I wrapped my arms around myself. My heart was still pounding in my chest, and I couldn't stop checking my surroundings nervously.

I was still trying to come to terms with my feelings for what happened when the door to the office opened and Luca and Matteo stepped out without

Romero. Luca passed me without a glance. He probably blamed me for the mess his brother had caused. I didn't think Matteo needed much of an incentive to kill, but naturally I realized that I had been the reason for Bardoni's death.

Matteo had acted out of jealousy and possessiveness. Seeing another man touching me had made him snap. Matteo scanned my face as he approached me. I probably looked pretty upset. The problem was I didn't feel nearly as upset as I knew I should. I couldn't bring myself to be sad about Bardoni's death, no matter how much I tried.

Matteo's movements were so lithe, so self-assured. And somehow, despite everything, I felt myself drawn to him, even to that dangerous side he'd showed me today. Matteo wrapped an arm around my waist and led me toward the front hall. Instead of returning to the living room, he steered me into a small guest bathroom near the front door.

"What the hell are you doing?" it burst out of me. "I won't make out with you after you killed someone."

Matteo gripped the back of my neck and pulled our bodies flush against each other before pressing his mouth to mine, kissing me hard. I panted for air when he drew back. His lips brushed my ear. "You look so fucking sexy. I could fuck you in a room with a dead body and wouldn't care."

"I don't doubt it," I muttered, but I didn't try to pull back. His warmth and strong body steadied my trembling limbs. Maybe the events were affecting me more than I thought.

"But that's not why we are here," he murmured.

A loud shot carried through the house. I jumped. "What—"

"That's why," Matteo said calmly. "We're going to pretend we had a quickie. We don't want people to think we had something to do with Bardoni's unfortunate end, right?"

He ruffled my hair, then his own before unbuttoning his top two buttons.

He raised his dark brows. "Ready?"

I nodded.

"Remember we don't know anything. We are shocked, and surprised."

Matteo ripped open the door, and headed out, pulling his gun. The lobby was filled with other guests, most men with their weapons drawn. Confused looks were exchanged. Luca and Bardoni's son ran toward where the gunshot had come from. Several people gave me and Matteo disgusted looks. They seemed to believe the lie Matteo wanted them to. It probably helped that they all thought I was a whore.

"Stay here," Matteo said. "I'll have to see what's going on." He looked so honestly worried and alert as if he really didn't know why a shot had sounded. Nobody would doubt him. If I didn't know better, even I would have believed in his innocence after that show.

He hurried toward the crime scene. I could only watch in stunned silence. Matteo was a master manipulator.

chapter 17

—GIANNA—

It was way past midnight when we finally got home. Most of the other guests had left long before us, but Luca and Matteo had to stay as heads of the Famiglia and pretend they were trying to figure out what had happened. Nobody had suspected them, at least not openly. To be honest, neither Bardoni Jr. nor Mrs. Bardoni had looked too distraught. Their tears had been crocodile tears if I'd ever seen any. Maybe he'd been as unpleasant to them as he'd been to me in the short time I'd spent with him.

I couldn't believe my life had changed from waitressing in Munich to covering up my husband's crimes. After a quick shower, I slipped into bed. Matteo was still arguing with Luca in our living room. This was one of the few instances where I understood Luca's anger completely.

I lay on my back, staring at the ceiling as I listened to their voices. The ankle monitor lay on my nightstand, mocking me. Maybe I should have used tonight's confusion to escape. Luca, Matteo, and Romero had been busy cleaning up their mess, and I had been without my stupid ankle bracelet. It had been the perfect opportunity. Then why hadn't I run? I doubted anyone would have stopped me.

Because of Aria? I wished that was the only reason, but as I'd stood in the lobby waiting for Matteo to return, I hadn't even considered escape. Why wasn't it at the forefront of my brain anymore? Six months ago it had been all I could think about, had been an obsession that had consumed me, and now it sometimes felt that I only thought about running because I felt that I was supposed to do it.

It was confusing. I wasn't as miserable as I'd worried I'd be living with Matteo. Of course, he was a crazy-ass killer, but it wasn't as if I wasn't used to that kind, and it actually made life exciting even if I hated admitting it. Living life as a normal person, doing normal things, earning money with normal jobs, had been an incredible experience, but for some reason it had never felt like more than a distraction.

The door opened and Matteo strode into the bedroom. He wasn't wearing his jacket anymore and half of his shirt buttons were already unbuttoned. He flashed me his usual grin before he disappeared in the bathroom.

I could have pretended to be asleep to avoid talking to him but for some inexplicable reason I wanted to talk to him. When he emerged from the bathroom in his boxer shorts, flashing his lean muscled torso, I almost cancelled my plans. But that would really have felt too wrong. A man had died, albeit a horrible man, and having sex so shortly after his death would have felt utterly wrong.

Matteo slid under the covers and reached for my waist, pulling me toward him. His eyes were hungry. There was no sign that he even still remembered what he'd done not too long ago. His lips claimed mine and I let his tongue in, let the kiss consume me until my body was humming with pleasure and I forced myself to push him away before I did something for which I'd despise myself tomorrow morning.

Matteo flung himself on his back with a groan. "This is because of Bardoni, right?"

I glared. "Maybe I'm just not in the mood. You aren't that irresistible."

"If you say so," he said in a low voice that sent a traitorous shiver down my spine. The bastard was way too manipulative.

I decided to steer this conversation toward safer grounds. "So will Luca punish you?"

Matteo chuckled. "Luca has never punished me for anything. He's used to my proactivity."

"Proactivity?"

Matteo winked and I almost reached for him again. Instead I pulled the blankets up to my chin as another barrier between us.

"Luca looked furious."

"He'll get over it. He always does. He would have had Bardoni killed anyway. It was only a matter of time."

I had a feeling this wasn't ordinary bedtime talk. "When did you kill your first man? Kindergarten?"

Matteo propped his head up on his arm, smirking. He ran a finger down my arm in a very distracting way. "No. I was a late bloomer in comparison to Luca."

"Really? That seems unlikely."

"Not really. Luca made sure I didn't get in trouble when I was younger. He was a protective big brother."

"I can't even imagine Luca being a kid, much less him making sure you stay out of trouble."

"He did. Is that really that surprising? Didn't Aria try to protect you when you were younger?"

"She still does," I said with a grimace.

"See. Luca's the same way. Of course now I'm making it harder for him to keep me in check, just like you make it hard for Aria."

"I think there's a huge difference between the kind of trouble I stir up and the trouble you cause."

"Give it some time. I have a feeling you haven't reached your full potential yet."

A laugh bubbled out of me. Damn it. Why did he have to say things that made me laugh? "You didn't answer my question. When did you kill the first time?"

"It was a few weeks after my thirteenth birthday."

"That's what you call a late bloomer? Most guys that age worry about their sprouting pubic hair and not killing someone."

"Oh, I'd come to terms with my pubic hair a long time before," he said in a teasing voice. "And most guys aren't the second son of the Capo of the New York Famiglia."

"Good point. But Luca can't really have protected you very well if you had to kill when you were still so young."

Matteo's gaze became distant. "He did what he could. Our father wanted me to kill one of the boys Luca and I had been hanging out with occasionally because he'd tried to get out of the mob."

My stomach tightened. "And?"

"Luca pulled his gun and killed the guy before I could. Father was majorly pissed. He beat Luca within an inch of his life."

The idea that Luca had done something so considerate for his brother was strange, but it wasn't all that surprising if you watched how those two interacted. It was obvious they cared for each other, cold-hearted bastards or not. "Luca is huge. How could anyone beat him?"

Matteo smiled wryly. "Luca could have wiped the floor with our father if he'd tried, but he never fought back. Father was Capo and would have put Luca down like a rabid dog if he'd raised his hand against him."

I sometimes forgot that things weren't all sunshine and rainbows for men. They had more freedom when it came to promiscuity and going out but they had their own burdens to bear. "I guess your father found someone else for you to kill pretty quickly after that." I'd barely known Salvatore Vitiello but he'd seemed like a creepy fuck.

Matteo nodded. "He found out about another traitor a couple of months after that. He made me slice his throat."

Girls weren't given many details about the induction ceremony, but Umberto had often let something slip when he'd guarded us. Usually the first kill of an initiate happened from afar with a gun. "He didn't let you shoot him?"

"No, it was probably meant as additional punishment because I'd wormed my way out of killing the first time. Shooting is easy, it's less personal. Using a knife is dirty work. You have to get close to your victim, have to get blood on your hands."

I held my breath. His voice had become very quiet. Slowly I raised myself up on my arm. I wanted to touch him but I didn't. "That sounds horrible. Could you do it?"

"What do you think?"

There was the scary shark-grin. The one that made me believe Matteo was capable of anything.

"You killed him."

"I did. It was messy. He was tied to a chair, so he couldn't fight back but it still took me three tries to cut his jugular. I was covered in blood from head to toe. I still found blood under my nails the next day."

"Then why do you prefer knives to guns? You really don't seem to mind getting your hands dirty anymore."

"In the beginning it was to prove to my father that I was tough and that he hadn't broken me like he'd probably intended. And once I got really good with the knife and everyone admired me for my skills, it seemed like a waste to give it up."

I searched his face but it was blank. I couldn't tell if it was the whole truth, or if he was keeping the worst of it to himself: that he'd come to enjoy the more personal kill. For a moment we stared at each other until it became too personal again and I lay back down and turned on my back.

"Did you ever consider killing Luca? If he were dead, you'd become Capo. You wouldn't be the first Made Man to kill a family member to climb the career ladder," I asked.

Matteo's expression hardened. "I would never kill my own brother. I don't care about becoming Capo, and even if I did, I still wouldn't get rid of Luca to improve my position. Luca's got my back and I've got his. That's the way it's always been."

"That's good. It's important to have people you can trust," I said honestly. Loneliness was a big problem in our world. You had always people around you, but you could trust no one. There was only one person I trusted absolutely and that was Aria. Lily was too fragile and young for many of my secrets, and Fabi was a boy and Father's influence on him was growing by the day. And I couldn't even talk to them anymore.

"What will it take for you to trust me?" Matteo asked curiously.

"A miracle." I turned my back to him and shut off the lamp on my nightstand. The look in his eyes had stirred something in my chest that terrified me.

Matteo shut off the other lights, then leaned over to me, kissing my ear. "Who doesn't like a good miracle?"

Matteo's arm was heavy around my waist, his breath hot against my neck, and the leg that was thrown over mine was cutting my blood flow off; then why did it feel strangely good to wake next to him?

I pushed his arm off and slipped away, and quickly got up. Matteo didn't wake. His hair was a complete mess and his face looked honest and almost gentle in sleep. I reached out but stopped myself before I could actually brush my fingers over his forehead. What was wrong with me?

I took a step back. My eyes landed on the discarded ankle monitor on the nightstand and an idea crossed my mind. I snatched up the monitor and rushed into the bathroom with it. The thing couldn't be destroyed with water. After all, you could shower with it, but maybe I could flush it down the toilet. Not that Matteo couldn't ask Sandro to bring a new monitor, but the gesture would send a nice message. I plunged the monitor into the toilet and flushed. Unfortunately it got stuck.

"Did you just flush down your ankle monitor?" Matteo asked in a voice raspy with sleep.

I whirled around. He was leaning in the doorway, arms crossed over his naked chest and an amused expression on his arrogant face. Heat rushed into my cheeks. "I tried, but it got stuck."

Chuckling, Matteo advanced on me and we both stared down into the bowl. "And who's going to get it out of there now?"

"You?"

Matteo reached down but I grabbed his arm.

"Aren't you going to put on gloves or something like that?"

"It's clean and I can wash my hands afterward," he said with barely disguised amusement. "My hands have been covered with worse, believe me."

I released him with a shrug. "Do what you want."

He retrieved the ankle monitor and put it on the washstand, then shoved down his boxer shorts and strode toward the shower, presenting his firm butt to me. He turned on the water and stepped under the stream before facing me again with a raging hard-on. "Wanna join me?"

I grabbed my toothbrush. "No, thanks."

It took a lot of restraint not to watch Matteo while he showered. I had a feeling he was taking his time on purpose. The water shut off and Matteo stepped out, drying himself with his towel. He nodded toward the ankle monitor. "You realize that it's still working, right?"

"Oh, come on. I didn't run away last night. You don't need to put that thing on me again. I'll behave."

"Really?" Matteo asked, dropping the towel and stalking toward me. "That doesn't sound like you."

I rolled my eyes. Two could play this game. I pulled my shirt over my head, then slid my panties down my legs before straightening, completely naked. Let Matteo deal with that.

As expected, Matteo's eyes traveled over my body and his cock twitched in response.

I smiled smugly. "I really hate the monitor. I don't want to wear it again."

Matteo leaned against the washbasin, so close that our bodies were almost touching and I could smell his minty shower gel.

"How about a little bet?"

I had a feeling I wouldn't like what he was going to suggest, but I motioned for him to keep talking.

"If I manage to give you an orgasm today, then we put the ankle monitor back on. If you manage to resist my skills, we throw that thing in the trash."

"Only one?"

"Greedy girl," he said teasingly, his dark eyes sparkling with excitement. "I thought you weren't attracted to me? Are you worried your body won't be able to resist me?"

I wished he was wrong, but my body really was a horrible traitor. I'd lost count of the times we'd had sex in our short marriage. "No, of course not. But one orgasm seems setting the bar very low for you, don't you think?"

"Oh, I don't know. We both know how stubborn you can be, and I promised Luca to put that ankle monitor on you. I can't make it too easy for you to get rid of it again." His eyes were drawn to my breasts, then lower. "So what do you say? Resist an orgasm until midnight and you'll be free of the monitor."

I backed away from him to be safe. "Okay."

"Of course you can't just avoid having an orgasm by not letting me touch you. You have to give me a fair fighting chance."

I huffed. "A fair chance? What is fair about this?"

Matteo shrugged. "Deal?"

"Deal," I said grudgingly before dashing into the shower and closing the door. It wouldn't stop Matteo, but he didn't try to follow.

Grinning, he walked toward the bedroom. "I'll be waiting for you."

Okay, I needed to put myself in a mindset of complete calm, needed to figure out a way to make me immune to whatever Matteo was going to do. Problem was my pulse was pounding with excitement when I thought of what he was going to do. Damn it. I closed my eyes and turned the water on cold. Gasping for breath, I started shivering and slowly my arousal abated. After a couple more minutes, I stepped out of the shower, frozen to the bone and hopefully turned off enough to resist Matteo at least for the moment. I headed into the bedroom. Matteo lay on the bed in all his naked glory with his arms crossed behind his head.

I was actually glad for his self-assured smile because it only strengthened my resolve to resist him. Straightening my shoulders, I walked past the bed, determined to head toward the dressing room. "Shouldn't we get up?"

Matteo's grin widened. "We have some time. Or are you scared of losing our bet?"

I walked toward the bed without another word. Matteo's eyes followed every move I made. I should have made a bet that he wasn't allowed to come. That bet I would have won without trouble judging from the hunger in his gaze. Matteo pulled me down on top of him and kissed me. He took his time, his hands only lightly stroking my back, and yet the pressure between my legs was already close to unbearable.

I tried to think of something else. Anything really, and somehow Matteo seemed to sense that I was drifting away. He flipped us over so he hovered over me, and then my torture began. His mouth closed around my nipple, nibbling and licking, before moving on to my other breast and lavishing that one with the same amount of attention. I lay my palms flat against the bedspread, trying to calm my breathing and racing pulse.

Matteo cupped my other breast, and squeezed harder than expected. I arched up at the intense sensation, then quickly relaxed again. I couldn't make it too easy for him. He'd be even more smug if he got me aroused so fast. Peering up at the ceiling, I focused all my attention away from Matteo's teasing lips. He chuckled against my sternum, then licked a trail down to my navel. "So stubborn."

I knew the moment Matteo parted my legs, he'd see how much my body craved his touch. There was nothing I could do about it. Maybe there was a way I could have an orgasm without Matteo actually noticing? By now that was almost my only hope because I was fairly sure my body was going to betray me.

With a wicked grin, Matteo moved between my legs and pushed his palms below my butt and then he pressed his mouth to my heated flesh. I bit back a moan at the feel of his tongue. His eyes were on me, so possessive and hungry that it turned me on even more.

I closed my own eyes tightly, trying to block out what Matteo was doing, but he was making it difficult.

"Delicious," he murmured, then took another lick. "You taste so good, Gianna. I want to eat you out every day." He dipped his tongue into my opening before drawing the softest circles with the tip of his tongue, only to enter me again. I pressed my lips together to hold back a moan. His hands pushed my legs even further apart and then his fingers gently opened my lips to give him even better access. His tongue barely brushed me, so soft my toes curled from the intense sensations. "You can pretend this isn't doing anything to you, Gianna, but your body betrays you."

Damn it, as if I didn't know it.

"Are you going to keep your eyes closed the entire time?" he asked in a mocking tone.

My eyes shot open and I glared at him.

He lifted his head with his damn shark-grin, his chin glistening with my juices. "That's better," he murmured before he lowered his gaze back down to my center and rubbed his thumb lightly over my clit. His tongue slid over my inner thigh before lightly biting down. More wetness pooled between my legs and Matteo's smile widened even more. "See, you like this." He slid his thumb between my folds, then lifted it to his lips and licked off my juices. "Hmm." I knew I should close my eyes again but it was impossible. Instead I braced myself on my elbows to get a better view. This was a losing battle anyway, I might as well enjoy it fully.

Matteo raised his eyebrows. "Upping the ante?" He dove back down and I threw my head back, not even bothering to keep the moan in. Fuck the stupid bet and the stupid ankle monitor. My calves started spasming and the tremor spread through my entire body as pleasure coursed through me. There was no thinking of hiding my orgasm. No chance in hell.

I arched off the bed, letting pleasure consume me. Loud cries fell from my lips and I let them out without restraint.

Eventually, I caught my breath. Matteo pushed himself up on his elbows. The look on his face made me regret my weakness. "Maybe one orgasm was really unfair," he said in a raspy voice.

"You think?" I whispered breathlessly. "How about an additional bet? All or nothing?"

"I'm listening."

"If I manage to make you come, you lose and I won't have to wear the ankle monitor again. If you resist, I'll put that thing back on without protest."

Matteo sat back on his haunches, presenting his rock-hard cock. I leaned forward and curled my fingers around his length with a challenging look. "So what do you say?"

"Why should I risk losing if I can only win the same thing again."

I licked my lips and squeezed his cock once. "Are you scared of losing?" I repeated his earlier words.

He chuckled. "Of course not. The bet's on. I'm in your hands."

"Lie down," I ordered, not wasting any time. I'd win this bet no matter what.

—MATTEO—

I flopped down on my back beside Gianna and crossed my arms behind my head. Gianna looked pretty confident. My cock was already hard from licking her, and she probably thought I wouldn't last very long. She didn't know me very well.

She knelt beside me, then lowered her head very slowly, her eyes glued to me, challenging and sexy as fuck. Did she know how much her gaze turned me on? That look alone made my cock twitch. Gianna curled her fingers around my base and swirled her tongue around my tip before she took all of me into her fucking hot mouth. I loved seeing my cock disappear between her pink lips. When I hit the back of her throat, I almost groaned.

Gianna smiled around my width as if she knew exactly what she was doing to me. And then she started to hum, and the vibrations went straight to my balls.

"Fuck," I growled, which only seemed to spur her on more. She bobbed her head up and down, eyes on me, and massaged my balls in the best possible way.

"You're so good at this," I said.

She rolled her eyes at me, and damn, if that didn't make her even sexier. Her red hair stuck to her forehead and cheeks as she took me deep into her mouth.

I wasn't going to last forever. I'd never really thought I could win this bet, never actually wanted to win. All I wanted in this moment was to come in Gianna's hot mouth. I raked my hands through her gorgeous locks. The muscles in my thighs tightened but I fought the sensation off. It was too fucking amazing to be over so soon, and knowing Gianna I might have to wait a while before she gave me another blowjob. She looked like a sex goddess. Fuck. I'd wanted to see her like that for a long time, had fucking daydreamed about it. I jerked my hips, and felt my balls tightening. Gianna sucked even harder. Not that I needed any more convincing. All I wanted was to spill into her. And then I fucking exploded. Gianna didn't pull back. Fuck, she kept sucking even as I shot my cum down her throat. With a long moan, I let my head fall back and my body became slack. Gianna lifted her head and wiped her mouth with a wide smile. "I win."

I laughed quietly. "You did. Congratulations."

"So I won't have to wear the ankle monitor ever again?" she asked with a hint of suspicion.

"That's the bet." I didn't tell her that I felt like the real winner. I'd never liked seeing her with the ankle monitor; it had always felt like a sacrilege to cage her in like that. I was glad that she wouldn't wear it anymore, even if that meant I had to keep a close eye on her, and that Luca would probably punch me.

chapter 18

—GIANNA—

The next morning after I'd showered and dressed, I enjoyed my newfound freedom, even if it was small. Matteo had kept his promise and stashed the ankle monitor in a drawer. I didn't have to wear that stupid thing, at least for now. I doubted Matteo would still keep his promise if I tried to run again.

We'd both lost our bets and yet we both felt like winners. Life with Matteo was an enigma. He was already leaning against the kitchen counter, drinking coffee when I came out of the bedroom. His smile was so smug I had trouble stopping myself from wringing his neck. I grabbed a cup for myself, then leaned across from him. "Do you ever feel regret or guilt?"

Matteo's eyebrows climbed his forehead. "Regret?"

"Yes, you know that feeling normal people have when they've done something wrong?" I took a sip. I wasn't even sure why I was asking, except to wipe that annoying smugness off Matteo's face.

For a long time Matteo only looked at me until I couldn't stand it anymore and pretended my coffee was really interesting. Why did I suddenly feel guilty for asking that question?

"There's little time for guilt and regret in my life," Matteo said. His voice was quiet and devoid of humor; I couldn't help but look up, trying to gauge his mood, but as usual he was making it difficult.

"So you *do* feel it sometimes?"

"Occasionally. But I've learned a long time ago that it's not clever to dwell on the past. I prefer to focus on the future." With that, his usual charm was switched back on. He strode toward me, set his cup down on the counter, and braced his arms beside me. "Do you ever regret running?"

I opened my mouth to say "no" but for some reason I hesitated. That moment of hesitation was all the answer Matteo needed.

"Why?"

"Because it got someone killed," I said quietly. I'd managed to forget Sid and his horrible end, but now it all came back. I could have kicked Matteo for bringing the memory back. Especially because I'd come to realize that the life I'd run from wasn't as horrible as I'd wanted it to be.

Matteo's expression said he didn't give a fuck about that, and it was pretty much what I'd expected. "I can tell you without a doubt that I don't feel guilt over that guy's death," he murmured. He ran a hand down my side. "I would have killed every guy that touched you. But we both know I don't have to because despite plenty of opportunity you were a good girl."

The way he said "good girl" made my blood boil. I was still trying to come up with a clever comeback when the elevator rang, announcing a visitor. Matteo pecked the tip of my nose with a superior expression before staggering off toward the elevator. I couldn't believe him.

I was still glaring at his back when the elevator doors slid open and Aria walked into the apartment. She was talking on the phone. To my surprise Matteo moved into the elevator, leaving us alone. I suspected he could lock the elevator from the outside, so I couldn't leave unless I took a dive out of the window and ended up as a blood splatter on the sidewalk down below.

"Who are you talking to?" I asked as Aria headed toward me.

She gave me a bright smile and held the phone out to me. "Lily and Fabi want to talk to you but Father forbid them from calling you, so..." She trailed off. Of course, I'd suspected something like that. Father had made it pretty clear that he didn't want me around them anymore.

"Thanks," I mouthed to Aria before taking the phone from her and pressing it against my ear. "Lily?" My voice was shaky and I had to clear my throat.

"Oh, Gianna! I was so sad when Father didn't let me say goodbye to you. I've been begging him to let me talk to you but he got really mad and now I'm grounded."

Grounded had always felt like a strange term for our punishment. We had never been allowed to go anywhere alone anyway, so being grounded only meant that we had to stay in the house even more.

"I'm sorry," I said, trying to keep my anger for our father back. Lily still had to live under his rule. She didn't need to get in trouble because of me. I walked over to the living area and sank down on the sofa. Aria perched on the edge beside me. "How's school?" I asked.

"Boring. But at home is even worse. Since you and Aria moved out, nothing fun ever happens anymore," Lily murmured. My heart ached for her. I'd always had Lily, and for a long time Aria, but Lily would have to survive for years without that kind of support. Of course she still had Fabi but he was a boy and would soon face very different challenges. "What about Fabi?"

"He's being a pain in the ass," Lily said. In the background I could hear my brother say something. "You are!" Lily retorted. "Oh shut up. It's my turn now. You can talk to her later." There was the sound of grappling and then there was Fabi's voice in my ear. "Gianna!"

"Shhh, you fathead," Lily hissed, obviously taking the phone back. "Nobody can know that we're talking to her." For a moment there was silence as if they were both listening for sounds, then Lily spoke again. "Is Romero there with you?"

I laughed. "That's why you're calling? I thought you wanted to see how I was doing," I said in a mock hurt voice.

"Of course I want to know how you're doing."

"I'm fine." There was a pause. Deciding to stop torturing her, I added, "And Romero isn't here." I glanced at Aria and she whispered "upstairs." "He's at Aria's place, discussing important mob business with our husbands." Sarcasm dripped from the words. "Do you want me to go upstairs and ask him to talk to you?"

"No!" Lily blurted. "He'll think I'm in love with him."

"Aren't you?"

Silence. Poor Lily, I didn't have the heart to tell her that there was no chance in hell that Father would ever allow an alliance between my sister and a mere soldier, especially one from New York. Love just wasn't something that mattered.

"How do I know if I'm in love?" Lily whispered after a while.

Yes, how? I hadn't been in love with Sid or anyone else. I wasn't in love with Matteo.

Right?

"I don't know," I admitted.

"Aren't you in love with Matteo?"

"Why would you think I was? I ran away, remember?"

"But you're married now."

"Marriage doesn't equal love."

"It did for Aria," Lily said. My eyes darted to Aria who was frowning at me.

"You're right. Maybe you should ask her then." Before Lily could say another word, I handed the phone to Aria. "Lily wants to know how it feels to be in love."

Aria took the phone from me, her blue eyes full of concern. She listened to Lily for a moment before she said, "That's hard to put into words. Love is when you feel safe in someone's arms, when he's the first thing you want to see in the morning, love is surrendering. You risk getting hurt but you don't care. You are willing to give someone the power to break your heart. Love means seeing someone at their worst and still seeing the good in them, love means someone is perfect for you despite their imperfections." She grew quiet, eyes distant.

I didn't have to ask; I knew about whom she was thinking. I swallowed hard. I could have never said what Aria had just said. Unwantedly an image of Matteo's cocky grin flashed in my mind. I'd definitely seen him at his worst that day he'd tortured the Russians.

"But how do I know when I'm in love?" I heard Lily's whine through the phone.

Yes, how?

"It's a gradual process. I don't really know when exactly I started loving Luca. For a long time I thought I hated him."

I pushed to my feet, suddenly restless. This wasn't a topic I felt comfortable with. It made my chest feel tight, made me start to panic in an odd way. I hurried into the kitchen and made myself another cup of coffee. After a couple of sips, I returned to Aria who gave me a questioning look. I raised my cup as a way of explanation. "Here," she said, handing the phone back to me.

"So what else is new?" I asked lightly.

I could practically hear Lily roll her eyes. "Are you going to come to our Christmas party?"

I opened my mouth to say yes, because I'd always been there, then I realized I probably wasn't wanted anymore. "I don't know. Things are difficult at the moment."

"You mean Father doesn't want you to come."

"The only reason I would want to come is you and Fabi. I don't care about anyone else. And maybe you and Fabi can come visit New York in the New Year."

Lily was silent. "Father said he won't ever allow us to go to New York again after what you did."

That shouldn't have shocked me as much as it did, I suppose. Of course he wouldn't let Lily out of his sight. He couldn't risk another one of his daughters turning into a slut. "We'll figure something out. I'll ask Matteo if we're going to Chicago."

Facing Father again was the last thing I wanted to do. For all I cared I would never set foot on Chicago ground again, but the idea of never seeing Fabi and Lily again was even worse.

"Promise?"

"I promise," I said. "Now give me Fabi before Father realizes you're talking to me and not Aria."

"Hi," came Fabi's voice.

"I bet you've grown another two inches since I last saw you."

"When I grow up I'll be at least six feet tall," he said proudly.

"Six feet four at least. You'll probably be taller than Luca."

"That would be so cool. I could kick everyone's ass. Everybody would have to be nice to me and respect me."

I smiled wistfully. Soon enough people would do that anyway. The cute boy would be replaced by a ruthless killer. "That would be cool," I agreed. "So do you have any new knives?"

Fabi had a huge collection of knives. A bigger collection of knives than a ten-year-old should have. Of course Father supported my brother's fascination with weapons.

"No," Fabi said, sulking. "Father is angry at me."

"Because of me?"

Fabi didn't say anything at first but I knew he was shrugging in that cute way he had. "I don't like how he screamed at you."

"I don't like it either, but you have to try not to make Father angry too often, Fabi. I don't want you to get punished." Now that I wasn't available as Father's favorite punching bag, I worried Fabi might have to bear the brunt of his anger.

"Okay," he said. "I miss you."

"I miss you too."

We hung up and I handed the phone back to Aria.

"Are you okay?" she asked.

I nodded half-heartedly. "The party is next weekend, right?"

"Yeah."

"I guess I'm not invited?"

Aria grimaced. "Even Luca and I aren't sure if we should be going."

"Why?"

"Things are really bad right now. Luca has enough trouble in New York. And he doesn't want to deal with Dante Cavallaro or Father in addition to that."

"Fabi and Lily will be really sad if you don't come to visit."

"I know," Aria said with a sigh, leaning against the backrest. "That's what I've been telling Luca. I even suggested I could fly over alone with Romero, so Luca could take care of business here."

"Let me guess. He hated that idea."

Aria laughed. "Yeah. He doesn't trust the Outfit and won't let me go there without him."

"I kind of have to agree with him. I wish we could go together though."

"Maybe next year. Father can hardly stay mad at you forever."

"Father will still be mad at me when he's roasting in hell."

As expected, I wasn't invited to my family's Christmas party. Officially, Father couldn't have denied me entrance as Matteo's wife, but not only would that have been very awkward but Matteo also didn't want to risk taking me back to Chicago so soon. That night after my body had won over my brain once again and succumbed to Matteo's charm, I lay naked in his arms, his chest pressed up against my back. I wasn't sure why I always fell asleep with his arms around me, and worse why I was sometimes longing for his closeness during the day too. So far I'd managed to resist that second notion at least.

"Will I ever see Fabi and Lily again?" I whispered into the silence.

Matteo's arms around my waist tightened. "If they were part of the Cosa Nostra, Luca could do something, but your father only has to listen to Cavallaro."

"I know," I said almost angrily. I knew how things worked in our world. "But can't we invite my family over for some kind of gathering? Father wouldn't reject a direct invitation, right?"

Matteo propped himself up and stared down at my face. "Your father would definitely follow the invitation, but he wouldn't have to take your sister and brother with him. Many men keep their families out of it for security reasons."

I nodded.

Matteo watched me for a long time and it was starting to make me feel naked in a very different way. I shot him a glare. "What?"

"Luca is very convincing. Maybe he can ask your father to allow Liliana and Fabiano to come for a visit after Christmas. Your father could send his own guards with them if he doesn't trust us."

"Why would Luca do that? He and Aria are still welcome in Chicago."

"If I ask Luca, he'll do it."

"And why should you ask him? Aren't you in enough trouble already because of Bardoni and getting rid of my ankle monitor?"

Matteo twirled a strand of my hair around his finger. "I'd do it for you. You are my wife and I want to make you happy." His smile was teasing and yet what he'd said had sounded sincere.

My heart thudded dangerously, and new panic rose up. What was happening? Fear of my own emotions got the better of me. "If you really care about me and want to see me happy, let me go. All I've ever wanted was freedom and a normal life."

The moment the words left my mouth, I realized I wasn't sure if they were still the truth.

Matteo's expression shut off, something hard and cold settling in his eyes. He lay back down and extinguished the lights. I almost apologized and reached out for him.

His lips brushed my ear. "I guess then that means I don't care enough. Because letting you go? That's the one thing I'll never do."

After that conversation, our interactions in the next few days were reduced to sex once again.

To my surprise, I missed our banter. I even missed Matteo's stupid cockiness and that annoying shark-grin, but most of all I missed falling asleep with his fingers tracing the soft skin of my inner forearm.

Christmastime was definitely turning into my own personal nightmare. Matteo and I were invited to three more parties, all of them either hosted by high-ranking mobsters, or business men with close connections to the mob. All of them too important to offend by not attending. I really hoped Matteo wouldn't kill any more hosts though. The Bardoni debacle so far had been without consequences but I still wasn't entirely sure it would stay that way. At some point people would undoubtedly get suspicious.

Now that I wasn't wearing an ankle monitor anymore, Sandro was my shadow, and when Aria and I went anywhere together, Romero was always there as well. It was ridiculous. Even without a technical device every aspect of my life was out of my control. Married bliss, my ass.

I fixed a wayward strand, which had fallen out of my updo, and brushed my hands over my new dress. With all the social events looming in my future, Aria and I had done another big shopping trip. I was starting to feel like one of those trophy mob wives I'd despised all my life. Shopping, social events, and warming their husband's bed was their whole world, and also mine. I glared at my reflection. I even looked all the way like a trophy wife with my hair in that elegant updo and the gorgeous dark green cocktail dress that hugged my curves. Even my huge wedding ring and the diamond necklace screamed trophy wife. It took all my self-control not to rip the dress off my body and cut my hair off. How could I have become what I'd hated for so long? And how could I be okay with it?

"Aria and Luca are here," Matteo shouted. "We need to get going." This was more than he'd said to me outside of the bedroom since that night. With a sigh, I turned away from the mirror and headed toward the living room where Aria, Luca, and Matteo were waiting. Matteo looked marvelous in a slim-fit black suit, white shirt, and black tie. It was so cliché mobster, but he pulled it off with ease. That man always looked good. His eyes did a quick scan of my outfit and my body responded with a familiar shiver. I'd read about looks that were like sex, but I'd always considered them urban legend. But Matteo had that look down to a T.

I kept my face unaffected as I walked toward them. Aria was an apparition in her dark red dress and with her golden curls. In the past I'd often felt like I could never compete with her but I'd come to realize that I didn't have to. Luca towered over my sister in a similar suit like Matteo, but it did nothing for me. I stopped beside Matteo and his hand immediately went to my hip. Did he even notice how possessive those small gestures were? In the past, my first reaction to them would have been annoyance followed by a rebuff, but now it seemed almost natural. I wasn't sure why this was the case, why I molded so easily into the life that had been cut out for me even before my birth. Some people would probably seek an explanation in fate or faith. I'd never considered either option to be valid. I didn't like the idea that some bigger outer thing controlled who I was and how my life would develop.

"Hey, where are you?" Matteo asked, squeezing my hip lightly. I blinked, focusing on him. I hadn't even realized we'd stepped into the elevator.

I shook my head. "Thinking of all the ways this evening could end badly," I lied.

"As long as Matteo keeps his knife in his holster and you keep your mouth in check, things should go smoothly," Luca muttered, sending both Matteo and me a glare. "Tonight is important. Several of the attending businessmen are under pressure from the Russians. I want to show strength and make a good impression. It would be even better if you could manage not to offend the wives."

"Why me? What about Aria?"

"Aria knows how to behave herself. She's the perfect lady whereas you are anything but."

Aria touched Luca's chest. "Be nice to my sister."

"I'm not rude to everyone. Only people I don't like," I said pointedly.

"Which will be everyone at the party," Matteo interjected. "They are insufferable, believe me." We exchanged a grin, then as if remembering our "kind of" fight from a few nights ago, looked away from each other. I could see Luca give Aria one of those secret looks they always shared.

"Just behave yourself," Luca said. "Both of you. It's like God's sent you two to me to test my patience."

Aria giggled and hit Luca's shoulder lightly, but her eyes were sparkling with adoration. Would I ever look at someone like that? I wasn't sure if I wanted to. It seemed like she was baring her soul for everyone to see and she didn't even mind.

Together we stepped out of the elevator and into the freezing cold parking garage. I shivered. I hadn't taken a coat with me because I only had to walk from the elevator to the car and then from the car to wherever the party was taking place, but now I regretted it. It was mid-December after all. One month since Matteo had caught me. Sometimes it was hard to believe so much time had passed already.

Matteo let go of me, removed his jacket and put it over my shoulders. His warmth and scent enveloped me, and I caught myself drawing in a deep breath.

"Thanks," I said half-embarrassed.

Luca had done the same for Aria despite the short way to the car. Aria and I settled in the back of Matteo's Porsche Cayenne while Luca and Matteo sat in the front. It seemed the men weren't worried anymore that I'd try to jump out of the driving car to escape. Maybe they, too, had noticed how easily I'd settled in.

Aria leaned over to whisper in my ear. "I know you don't want to see it but you and Matteo are like you were made for each other."

I shot her a look, ignoring the way my pulse sped up with an emotion I didn't even want to think about. "Don't even start."

Aria shrugged. "It's the truth. And he's really trying. They aren't perfect but they are trying to be good to us. You don't look unhappy."

I wasn't exactly unhappy, but I tried to attribute it to Aria's constant presence in my new life. It was the convenient explanation. I didn't say anything, couldn't come up with a witty reply that wouldn't sound utterly fake.

We sat in silence after that and yet I felt like my silence was more of an answer than I liked. I was actually relieved when we finally pulled up in front of a luxury apartment building not unlike the one Matteo and I lived in. A doorman rushed toward our car and opened my door. Good thing he didn't see both Luca and Matteo reach for their weapons, always ready for an attack.

I thanked the guy who looked like he was barely my age, and got out. Aria followed quickly. We handed the jackets back to our husbands before walking into the brightly lit lobby. Another doorman waited next to the elevator and clicked the correct button for us.

As we rode up toward the top floor, Matteo leaned close and murmured, "Don't forget to behave yourself." He winked at me when he pulled back and I knew we'd be in trouble. Matteo's expression promised that he had absolutely no intention to be good tonight.

The party took place in a huge penthouse overlooking the city. It was not quite as big as Luca's but definitely showy. The walls were covered with drawings by Picasso, Warhol, and Miró, all of them originals, and I had a feeling the furniture was as pretentious, but everything had been removed to fit two long tables for eighty guests into the room as well as a dozen bar tables where guests could mingle before dinner.

The noise level was overwhelming despite the size of the penthouse and there wasn't anything Christmas-y about the decoration except for an abstract glass Nativity scene on the mantle and an even more abstract glass Christmas tree in one corner. Aria and I looked at each other and almost burst into laughter.

My mood dropped the moment the host and hostess, a middle-aged couple that looked even more fake than their tree, approached us. I braced myself for the disgusted once-over, but the woman smiled at Aria and me the same way.

The hostess who introduced herself as Miriam practically *beamed* at me, though it looked almost scary because her face was frozen from too many Botox treatments. "You must be the beautiful new bride," she said, and kissed me on both cheeks.

"Yes, thank you," I said, startled.

I darted a confused look at Matteo. He must have read it right because he leaned toward me while the host and hostess spoke to Luca and Aria. "They aren't part of our culture. They don't give a crap about our rules and morals," Matteo whispered.

The hostess turned back to us. "Dinner starts in thirty minutes. But please help yourself to our delicious hors d'oeuvres and champagne." She pronounced champagne in an odd French accent, which almost made me laugh again, but I pulled myself together and smiled politely instead. The woman had been kind to me, so I had to act accordingly, even if Luca thought I was incapable of pleasantness.

I glanced around, only spotting one familiar couple, that I assumed must be part of the mob or I wouldn't have recognized them. Apart from that, we were blissfully surrounded by strangers, who didn't call me slut under their breaths, or look down their noses at me. This was a straight-up social event that normal people, *well* normal *rich* people attended. I relaxed. Maybe this wouldn't be too bad.

"Come on. Let's fill up on some champagne. We'll need the buzz to carry us through the boredom," Matteo said. Luca shot him a scowl, but Matteo merely grinned and led me toward an unoccupied bar table. I grabbed a glass and took a deep gulp. That was the one good thing about living in our world; nobody gave a damn if I was of legal age to drink. The bubbles prickled delightfully on my tongue. It had been a long time since I'd had good champagne. The last time was at Aria's wedding.

Matteo smirked.

"What?" I asked, checking my dress for any stains.

"You look like a sophisticated lady."

"I'm not a sophisticated lady," I said quickly and was about to take another gulp of champagne but stopped with the rim against my lips. With a glare, I set it down. "I'm not."

"I didn't say you were. I only pointed out that you look it."

He was right. I fit in, which brought me back to my earlier problem. Why was I becoming more like a trophy wife every day? I downed the rest of my champagne in one large gulp, not at all ladylike, making Matteo laugh, and I couldn't help but do too. It felt good to laugh with him, and even better to see mirth banish some of the darkness in his eyes.

Miriam called for everyone to settle around the tables, and asked us to sit next to her with other important guests. Unfortunately Aria had to sit across from me, so I couldn't even talk to her in case I got bored. I was wedged between Matteo and a woman I didn't know. Luckily the first course was served almost immediately, so I had something to do. Miriam as well as the other women around us were more interested in Aria anyway, probably because she was Luca's wife and knew how to do proper small talk.

Suddenly I felt Matteo's hand on my knee. I shot him a look but he was immersed in a conversation with Luca and the host. I took another bite of my carpaccio but stopped mid-chew when his hand began its ascent higher, toward the lacy edge of my hold-ups. I had to suppress a small shiver at the sensations his light touch sent straight to my center. I clenched my legs together and tried to focus on the conversation Aria was having with the other women. The corners of Matteo's lips twitched in reaction. Of course that wasn't the end of it. When was it ever?

Matteo's fingers slipped between my legs despite my attempts to lock him out, and then his fingertips slipped under the edge of my panties and lightly stroked the crevice between my leg and vulva. I reached for the glass and took a deep gulp of the wine.

"What do you think, Gianna? Would you be interested?" asked the hostess Miriam. Her eyebrows were raised but due to all the Botox, the rest of her face was static, and her expression resembled one of mild boredom.

My eyes darted to Aria, hoping she'd help me out. I had no clue what Miriam was talking about. Matteo's fingers had distracted me completely.

"I know you love modern art, and it's not easy to come by a private tour through the Guggenheim. I'm sure Matteo can spare you for a few hours," Aria said with a meaningful look.

I could have kissed her. She always saved the day. "Yes, I'd love to—" Matteo's fingers slipped between my lower lips, gently nudging them apart, finding me wet and aching, the stupid bastard. He was still talking to Luca and the other men as if nothing of interest was going on under the table.

Aria and the other women were watching me expectantly. I cleared my throat and kicked Matteo's leg hard, before I said, "I'd love to take you up on that offer." Could I sound any more sophisticated? Trophy wife all the way.

Matteo's finger traveled up my slit until it reached my clit where he started to draw small circles. I pressed my lips together to stop a moan from slipping out. Thankfully, Miriam went on another monologue about a trip to the Caribbean and I was back to pretending to listen. Only Aria gave me the occasional odd glance, as if she thought I might not be feeling well.

If only she knew. The waiters entered the room with our main course, but I hardly cared.

Without even intending to, I parted my legs a bit more, giving Matteo more room to explore my wet folds. His fingers slipped up and down, teasing my opening, before they returned to my throbbing clit. I clutched my wine glass. It wouldn't have surprised me if I'd broken it in two from my tight grip. My breathing was shallow. Matteo kept up the slow rhythm, driving me closer and closer toward release. I should have pushed his hand away, should have stopped this madness before this turned into the most embarrassing night of my life, but need had taken over and banished any hint of reason. After a few bites of veal, I put my fork down. I was hungry for only one thing.

Matteo slipped a finger into me and I barely managed to keep in my whimper. I was getting so close. Could I even be silent?

But I was too far gone to care. Matteo still wasn't looking at me. Instead he was completely focused on the conversation, or at least he pretended to be. I hated him for his acting talent. He brought me closer and closer, taking his time. God, this was the most delicious torture.

His skilled fingers became the whole center of my being until suddenly, without a warning he pulled them away. Shocked, I stared at him, only to realize that the waiters had returned with our dessert, chocolate mousse. Matteo gave me a grin.

I wanted to rip his clothes off and have my way with him, bring him to the brink, only to deny him release. Matteo dipped a finger into the mousse, the finger he'd used to finger me, and slid it into his mouth, licking it clean. "Hm. Delicious."

My body was humming with desire, but in that moment I wanted to push Matteo's face down into the stupid mousse. He picked up his spoon and calmly started eating. Aria gave me a questioning look when I didn't move.

I grabbed my own spoon a bit too tightly and tasted the mousse. It was delicious, creamy and very chocolaty, but now all it did was remind me of Matteo's fingers and what they had done mere moments before. Two could play this game. Once I was done with my dessert, I slipped my hand under the table and reached between Matteo's legs. I found him already hard and that knowledge made me ache even more. I considered stroking myself instead of teasing Matteo, but banished the idea. If I wanted to win this game, I needed to play. My fingers closed around Matteo's erection. He sucked in a quiet breath before his eyes met mine, one corner of his mouth lifting. I massaged him through the fabric of his pants, feeling him grow even harder and bigger. Unfortunately my own body responded too.

Matteo turned his head to an older guy across from him who'd asked him a question and I used the moment to find his tip and start rubbing that. Matteo had had it easier. He didn't have as many barriers between his fingers and their goal, but as I worked the head of his cock, I could see from the flexing of his jaw that Matteo wasn't completely unaffected. And unlike me, he would have a hard time hiding his arousal if he got up, and an even harder time if he came in his pants. The thought made me smile.

Aria leaned across the table toward me. I really hoped she wouldn't notice anything. "What's the matter with you? You're acting strange," she whispered.

I shook my head and mouthed "later," but my hand never stopped its work under the table. I hoped Matteo was getting close. It was hard to tell. He'd angled his face away from me and was actually conducting a coherent conversation with the old man. I squeezed a bit tighter, getting annoyed, and finally got another, albeit small reaction. Matteo tensed briefly but then visibly forced himself to relax. I could have screamed in frustration.

I was about to squeeze again, even harder when his hand found mine under the table and pulled it away. I would have clung to his erection if I hadn't been worried about injuring him. Even if I'd never admit it to anyone, I loved Matteo's cock, and particularly the things he could do with it. I chanced a look at Matteo and met his gaze. There was hunger in there, but also something else, something that made me want to go running for the hills, because I had a feeling I knew what it was and I was pretty sure I was starting to feel the same. I wrenched my hand away from his hold, pushed my chair back and straightened.

With a small smile at the other guests, I said, "Excuse me." Without another look at Matteo, I headed straight toward where I hoped to find the restrooms.

It took all my self-control not to run down the long corridor branching off from the main area of the apartment. When I entered the restroom, I released a harsh breath. My cheeks were flushed, but not so much that anyone would suspect anything. That was what I hoped at least. I gripped the edge of the washbasin and squeezed my eyes shut. My heart was slamming against my rib cage. Suddenly someone gripped my hips. My eyes shot open and I stared into the mirror. Matteo towered over me, his gaze practically burning with want. He pressed his hips against my butt. "You left too soon." His hand slipped under my dress while his other hand pulled down his zipper.

"What are you doing?" I hissed with a glance toward the door. "What if someone comes in?"

"Who gives a fuck? Let them get the show of their lives. It's probably been years since those bitches got to see a cock." He pushed my panties aside and thrust two fingers into me. I jutted my butt out, giving him better access. My body seemed to be acting on its own accord even when my brain was screaming at me to push Matteo away.

"Matteo," I gasped. "Lock the stupid door."

He moved his fingers in and out in a deliciously slow rhythm. My hips moved against him, forcing his fingers deeper into me.

"Do you really want me to stop so I can lock the fucking door?" He licked my spine from the edge of my dress up to my hairline, then met my gaze in the mirror. I shivered. He slammed his fingers into me again, hitting a sweet spot deep inside of me. His eyes seemed to bore into me, trying to reveal my darkest deepest secrets. My heart lurched, and I knew I'd be doomed if I didn't stop this madness soon. Sex, that I could deal with, but these moments of silent understanding, these long looks full of too much meaning, they were starting to chip away at the walls I'd taken years to build.

Matteo cupped my breast through my dress, kneading and pinching my nipple in an almost painful way that made me grow even wetter. I closed my eyes to avoid his eyes and soaked in the sensations. Matteo thrust his fingers into me over and over again. I bit down on my lip to keep the sounds in. Matteo's lips clamped down on my pulse point, sucking the skin into his mouth. I arched, pushing my butt against his hand with all my might as my orgasm jolted through me.

"Look at me," Matteo ordered, and my eyes flew open, meeting his. "Yes, like that. Fuck, you are so fucking wet and hot."

I dropped down to my forearms with a shuddering breath, enjoying the last waves of pleasure while Matteo slowed his fingers. He lifted my skirt even higher. I heard him unbuckle his pants and then he wrapped his arms tightly around my chest, pulled me against him and rubbed his tip over my opening. Then he slipped in inch by inch. I tried to jut my butt out, needing to feel him all the way in me, but he didn't let me. If possible, he slowed even more, edging into me.

"Fuck me," I whispered harshly.

He reached up and tilted my head to the side before claiming it with his mouth, his tongue taking possession of me. He had finally sheathed himself completely in me and then after a moment of stillness, he started slamming into me. My hands shot out to grip the edge of the washstand. Matteo drove my body against the cold stone as his cock thrust into me, deep and hard.

"Fuck, you feel so good," Matteo rasped. I moaned in response. It did feel better than anything ever had. Everything about this did. God, what was happening?

I tried to shut my brain off and only focus on the way Matteo's cock filled me up, how he removed himself almost completely to drive me insane only to slam back into me. The edge of the washbasin dug into my palms as I clung to it. Matteo's hands moved down, clasping my hips. I threw my head back, gasping and whimpering as I tumbled over the edge again with Matteo close behind. The sound of his moans spurred me on even more. A moment before we both slumped forward, our gazes met in the mirror again. And then I knew why I'd hardly considered running in the last couple of weeks, and it terrified me like nothing ever had.

I quickly looked down, trying to catch my breath, and calm my pounding heart and pulse.

Matteo kissed my shoulder blade. "I'm fucking glad that you are mine."

I stiffened and would have pulled away if I wasn't trapped between the washstand and Matteo's body.

When Matteo eventually pulled out of me and we straightened our clothes and cleaned up, I couldn't meet his gaze. I wasn't embarrassed by what we'd done. That ship had sailed. I was confused and terrified by what I'd seen in my own eyes.

—MATTEO—

During sex there were moments when I was certain Gianna was falling for me, but then always came the time afterward and I wasn't sure if I'd imagined it. In the past I'd always had girls crushing on me even when I never gave them reason to, but Gianna was a difficult nut to crack, and sometimes I caught myself wondering if maybe she'd never fall for me and was only fucking me to get on my good side. Gianna was clever, maybe she was trying to wrap me around her finger with sex so I'd grant her more freedom and she could run away again.

Gianna put a few strands that had fallen out during our quickie back into her updo. She was frowning at her own reflection and pretending I wasn't there.

When we left the bathroom, she still ignored me. Then she stopped suddenly. "We can't enter together. Everyone will know what we did."

I shrugged. I didn't give a fuck. Gianna was my wife and I'd fuck her whenever I felt like it. "We've been gone for a while. They're probably suspecting already."

"Great," Gianna muttered but then she squared her shoulders and headed back to the tables with the other guests without another glance in my direction. So we were back to playing games?

That night I woke to an empty bed. I jumped to my feet, and searched the room for a sign of Gianna, but she wasn't there. How could she have run? I didn't bother putting on pants. Grabbing my gun holster on the way I stormed out of the room and into the living room.

I had to call Luca and tell him. He'd be furious. He hadn't been happy when I'd removed Gianna's ankle monitor. My eyes made out a slender figure in an armchair close to the window. Gianna.

I relaxed and discarded my gun holster on a sideboard before I crossed the room toward her. She must have pushed the armchair closer to the window so she could look out. Her legs were pressed up against her chest and her face rested on her knees. She was fast asleep. But even in sleep her brows were drawn together. I wasn't sure but she looked as if she'd cried. I stopped beside her, staring down at her sleeping form. She must have moved very quietly for me not to hear her. I was a light sleeper. She'd even managed to put on pajamas. My gaze darted to the elevator console. Had she tried to crack the code and escape? The alarm would have alerted me to any attempts, and yet the suspicion remained. I hated that I didn't trust her. It wasn't as if I was used to trusting people, except for Luca, but I wanted to trust my wife. Of course it was difficult to develop trust when Gianna didn't even have the chance to prove herself.

If I gave her more freedom, and she didn't try to run, then I could start trusting her, but I had a feeling I'd never see her again if I did. I was too selfish and possessive. I didn't want to lose her, even if that was what was best for her. My eyes returned to her face and the sadness that seemed to be edged into it.

I slipped my hands under her body and lifted her into my arms. She didn't wake as I carried her back into our bedroom, back where I wanted her and where she belonged, but where she didn't want to be.

I put her down on the bed, but I didn't lie down next to her. I was too angry at myself for my wimpy thoughts. What did it matter if Gianna wanted to be my wife? What did it matter if she'd rather return to Munich and find some other idiot like Sid? She was mine and I wasn't a good guy. I didn't give a damn about other people's feelings. I felt on the edge, like I needed to hit something to get a grip. With a growl, I grabbed my gym clothes, put them on, grabbed my car keys and left the apartment.

I punched the code into the elevator panel and rode it down into the parking garage. I mounted my motorcycle, shot out of the garage and raced through the city toward our gym. Apart from a guard, it was deserted, which was a pity because I would have loved to actually spar with someone, instead of a fucking dummy.

I didn't bother with boxing gloves. I wanted to feel every hit. Facing the dummy, I started pummeling it, alternating between kicks and punches.

I was still at it when the gym started filling up with familiar faces. Nobody disturbed me. Apart from a short nod, they stayed the fuck away from me. They all knew what was good for them.

"Trying to kill a poor dummy?" came Luca's drawl.

I landed another hard kick against the head before I turned around to my brother. He wasn't wearing gym clothes. "What are you doing here?"

"Looking for you."

"Why?"

"Because you weren't there when I came to pick you up in your apartment this morning."

"You went into my apartment while I wasn't there?"

Luca rolled his eyes. "I didn't touch your wife, but I left Aria and Romero with her."

I nodded, trying to calm the fuck down. I was still on edge. I wasn't even sure why.

"Take a shower and get dressed. You look like you need a drink," Luca said in his Capo voice.

I didn't protest. I felt like a truck had run me over. I must have been in the gym for hours. It was already light outside. Luca and I went to one of our dance clubs. Except for the cleaning ladies, it was still deserted. I grabbed a whiskey bottle from the shelf, and Luca and I settled at the bar. In most social circles it was probably considered too early for alcohol. Luckily we didn't have to obey those stupid rules.

Luca and I emptied our glasses, then he fixed me with his big-brother stare. "So what's going on? Are you already growing tired of your obnoxious wife?"

I downed another glass of whiskey, waiting for the familiar burning to turn into warmth that spread in my chest. "Why do you ask?"

Luca cocked one eyebrow. "Maybe because you prefer spending the night in a sweaty gym than in bed with your young wife."

"I couldn't sleep."

"And you couldn't come up with something more entertaining to do than kickboxing a dummy?"

"You're starting to grate on my nerves," I said.

Luca ignored my warning tone. "To be honest I'm surprised you lasted this long with her. If I spend more than ten minutes in a room with Gianna, I want to seal my ears with hot wax."

"I'm not tired of her. I actually like Gianna's *obnoxious* personality. She spices things up. Life would be boring if she were like the other trophy wives."

Luca narrowed his eyes. "Aria isn't just a trophy wife."

Of course he was allowed to get angry when I even remotely insulted Aria but he could talk shit about Gianna all the time. "I didn't say anything about Aria. But I prefer my women…"

"Annoying and foulmouthed," Luca finished for me, before he took the whiskey bottle out of my hand. "Then what's the problem? Why are you sulking like a whiny bitch?"

I was waiting for one of my usual clever comebacks to pop into my mind, but I drew a fucking blank. That was serious bullshit. "I'm starting to think that Gianna might always hate me. I thought it was her way to be interesting and a challenge, a sort of game at the end of which she'd come to her fucking senses and fall for me like all the girls I've pursued before her, but I'm pretty sure Gianna is a challenge I'm losing. She won't come around. I think she hates this life a bit more every fucking day."

Luca scanned my face. "This is really bothering you."

He said it as if that was the biggest fucking surprise of his life, as if I was a fucking robot that wasn't capable of emotions. "That, coming from you," I said with a smirk. "Before Aria I wasn't even sure you were capable of liking anyone, least of all a woman."

"You make it sound like I'm a fag. It's not that I didn't like women. They were just not something I considered useful outside of the bedroom."

I shook my head. "How the hell did you get Aria to love you? It's like the fucking eighth Wonder of the World. Are there any new drugs you're not telling me about?"

"You're wasted, Matteo."

"I'm not. If you'd stop hogging the fucking whiskey, I might get the chance to be in a couple of hours." I ripped the bottle from his hand and took a swig. "Gianna is like a tiger in the fucking zoo, caged in. It's fucking depressing to watch her look for a way to escape captivity."

"Did she try to run again?"

"How could she? I'm keeping her on a tight leash."

"You're not thinking about letting her go, are you?"

I didn't think I could, and I didn't want to. I was selfish and that wouldn't change any time soon. I still wanted Gianna. I wanted her gorgeous body in my bed every night, and my cock in her tight pussy. I wanted everything from her, most of all the things she was refusing to give me. "Would you let me?"

"No. The Famiglia is already displeased as it is. You'd look even weaker if you'd let her run away again. I really don't need the additional trouble. Not to mention the fucking Outfit would probably declare fucking war on us if we managed to lose Gianna again. Her father is being a real pain in the ass." He gave me his Capo look, which was meant to intimidate the rest of the world, but was useless on me as he fucking well knew. "You won't let her get away. You're stuck with her until the bitter end, and she with you. I don't care if she's fucking unhappy and if she hates you, she'll just have to deal."

"Wow, you're full of sunshine and rainbows today, aren't you?" I knew he was right, and really it wasn't like I'd tell Gianna she could go but somehow his words managed to piss me off anyway. "You realize the only thing stopping Gianna from slicing my throat at night is that she can't see blood. Do you know how reassuring it is to fall asleep beside someone who's probably fantasizing to see you dead so she can be free." She'd never said it in so many words but sometimes I thought I saw it in her eyes. Or maybe I was so fucking messed up that I was always thinking the worst of others.

"I hope you're joking," Luca said dryly.

"Who knows?" I emptied the whiskey bottle. I could feel the first treacherous signs of a nice buzz. I grinned. "Sometimes she's definitely trying to kill me with her eyes."

"Maybe then you shouldn't sleep in a room with her. She might get over her fear of blood at some point."

"Nah. Not anytime soon. And she isn't the violent type, not really."

"I wouldn't count on that. She can be really unhinged."

"You weren't worried about sleeping beside Aria when she still despised you so why should I?"

"You can't compare Aria to Gianna. They are like two different species. And I trust Aria absolutely. She caught a fucking bullet for me."

"Must be nice," I muttered. "Gianna would probably applaud my shooter."

chapter 19

—GIANNA—

Matteo was in a strange mood, had been ever since he'd found me in the living room two nights ago. He hadn't said much, which was unusual for him. I wasn't sure if he was angry at something I'd done, and I didn't really care. That night I'd promised myself that I'd have to stop whatever was going on between him and me. I'd sworn to myself that I'd never become one of those women, that I'd never marry a Made Man, and much less develop feelings for him.

Christmas was only five days away but we both definitely hadn't caught the holiday spirit yet. There wasn't a single piece of Christmas decoration in our apartment. I'd considered asking Matteo to buy a tree and decorate it together, but then the panic had set in again and I hadn't said anything. Instead I'd accepted the strange mood between us almost with relief.

Matteo was gripping the steering wheel in a steel grip as we drove away from the last Christmas party of the season. The hosts had rented a deserted warehouse and turned into a winter wonderland with fake snow and a real ice bar. Aria and Luca were still there but Matteo's bad temper had caused Luca to send us away early. He'd probably worried that Matteo would end up killing someone again. I couldn't blame him.

The road was covered with a fine sheen of frost which glittered in the glare of our spotlights.

"You know what's funny?" Matteo asked in a tight voice.

I glanced toward him, his tense body and dark expression.

"Whenever you think I'm not watching, you look like you might be happy and then the moment our eyes meet, it's like 'poof' and the happiness is gone."

I wasn't sure what to tell him.

"Why do you insist on being miserable?"

Before I could formulate an answer, Matteo suddenly floored the gas. I was pressed into the seat. "What are you doing? You don't have to kill us because you're pissed."

Matteo peered into the side mirror. "I'm not trying to kill us. I'm trying to save our lives."

Something collided with our trunk. I glanced over my shoulder. Headlights of another SUV filled the rear window.

"Who are they?" I asked.

"Russians would be my guess. I noticed them too late. Fuck. This happens when I get distracted by other shit."

We were the only cars in this part of the industrial area. Matteo twisted the steering wheel and we shot around a corner into a narrow street between two high storehouses.

"Head down," Matteo barked.

I obeyed at once. Struggling against my seat belt, I leaned forward. A second later, our pursuers shot at us. The rear window exploded and shards rained down on us. Matteo didn't react, he kept driving like a madman. He'd somehow even managed to pull his own gun.

I clutched the seat, my head pressed against my legs as I jerked back and forth with every twist and turn of the car. The tires were screeching, gunshots whistling through the air, glass bursting. A new shower of shards rained down on me as the side window in the back exploded as well.

"Fuck," Matteo snarled while he tried to get a connection with his phone, probably to call Luca. Fear was clogging my throat tightly. Fear for my own life was only a small part of it. Seeing Matteo in clear line of fire terrified me even more. He couldn't duck his head. One bullet and everything could be over.

We turned another corner and I slammed against the door. I squeezed my eyes shut, fighting my rising sickness.

More shots rang out and Matteo let out a hiss. I peered to the side. Matteo was still driving and shooting at our pursuers, but he was bleeding from wounds in his arm and shoulder. That moment another bullet grazed his head, blood spurting everywhere, even on my face. Matteo didn't even seem to care; he fired another round of shots. Suddenly we were spinning, the car out of control. I wrapped my arms around my chest as I was thrown around in my seat. Through half-closed eyes I saw our car shooting toward a massive wall and then there was an earsplitting crash as we smashed into it. My body jerked forward, the air rushing out of me as I was flung against the safety belt. It cut into my collarbone, and my vision turned black. Then something soft exploded in my face, stopping my impact.

I didn't know how long I hung limply in my seat belt, my face buried in the deflating airbag as I tried to catch my breath. My ears were ringing but eventually that faded and silence greeted me. With a groan I sat up, ignoring my throbbing headache. Smoke was rising from our crushed hood, slowly filling the car through the broken windows. I blinked to get rid of the dots dancing in and out of my vision. My entire body was sore but nothing seemed to be broken. At least I could move.

I turned to the driver's side and stilled. It was dark in the car. Our lights were smashed but from somewhere a distant glow illuminated what was around me. Matteo was slumped over the steering wheel. Like many mafia cars, the driver didn't have an airbag because it was a bother during car chases. Blood plastered his dark hair to his forehead, soaked his shirt and dripped down on his pants. So much blood. He must have hit his head against the steering wheel or maybe the dashboard when we'd collided with the wall.

Was he dead?

He wasn't moving, and I couldn't see if he was breathing. I held my breath, listening for a sound. There was nothing. I blinked, then peered over my shoulder to see where our pursuers were. Their car had smashed into another building and had already caught fire. They were definitely dead. Was our car going to start burning too? I needed to get out.

Wasn't this the chance I'd been waiting for? Matteo and I were alone. Nobody was here to stop me from running. I could leave and be free. I unbuckled myself, then glanced at Matteo again. I needed to check if he was dead, but somehow I couldn't. What if he was really gone? What if he was dead? My throat felt tight and raw. My lungs refused to work as panic settled in my body. God, what if he was dead? What was wrong with me? Hadn't I wanted him out of my life six months ago? This was my chance, probably the only chance I'd ever get. The smell of gas drifted into my nose, and the smoke inside the car was starting to burn in my eyes. Matteo was a killer. He wasn't a good man. If you asked most people, they'd say he deserved death.

With shaky fingers I reached out and touched Matteo's shoulder. He still felt warm but that didn't mean he was alive. Slowly I inched my hand up until I brushed his blood-slick throat. My fingers ghosted over his skin, finding nothing, pressing and searching, until finally a soft pulse beat against my fingertips.

I exhaled, relief slamming into me like a hammer. Still alive. He was still alive. Thank God. With a sizzle and a pop fire shot out under the hood of the car. I gripped the door handle and pushed but it didn't budge, distorted from the crash. Panic spread in my chest as smoke and heat filled up the car, and I started clawing at the door. I shifted, tugged my sleeve down my hand and roughly cleaned the window frame from broken remains before I climbed out of the car headfirst. When I finally felt solid ground under my feet, I almost dropped to my knees because my legs were shaking like crazy. The entire hood was burning now and Matteo was still in the driver's seat. I rushed around the car, toward his door, praying that it wasn't stuck like mine. I didn't think I could drag Matteo through a narrow window without his help. I gripped the car door and tugged as hard as I could. With a screech it flew open and I landed on my butt. I caught my breath, then stumbled to my feet and grabbed Matteo's arm. He hadn't been wearing a seat belt so I could pull him out of the car without trouble. He plopped down on the asphalt a bit too hard and I winced, then quickly hooked my hand under his armpits and pulled him away from the car that was catching fire way too quickly.

Matteo was heavy and dragging him away from the car with my aching body hurt like hell, but I didn't stop until I was sure he was a safe distance away in case of an explosion. I let go of him before I straightened and wiped the blood from my palms on my pants. Matteo's eyes were closed, his face turned to the side, showing his striking profile. Strands of hair stuck to his bloody forehead and a puddle of red was quickly spreading around his head, trickling from his head wound. I could see his chest rising and falling. My eyes searched our surroundings. The car of the Russians was already a flaming mess, dark plummets of smoke rising into the sky. We were in the middle of nowhere, an abandoned industrial area nobody set foot in without reason. But the smoke would certainly attract attention. Somebody would find Matteo before it was too late.

Right?

I should run. I should *want* to run. I started backing away from Matteo's unmoving form on the ground, ignoring the way guilt corded up my throat. He'd forced me into a marriage I'd never wanted. He knew I would use the first chance I got to escape. I took another step back. Matteo had chosen a path of danger and death. Even if he died today, it was what he'd chosen for himself.

This wasn't the life I wanted.

I turned around, then paused. I closed my eyes. Distantly flames crackled. Someone would find Matteo in time. And even if they didn't, I shouldn't care.

I didn't care about him. I *didn't.* And I definitely *shouldn't.*

I should hate him. I should hate what he was and what it meant for me. I should that he couldn't give me up no matter how often I pushed him away. Why couldn't he give up?

I started walking away, one small step after the other. Once I was out of town, I would call Aria and ask her about Matteo.

It will be too late for him then.

Maybe.

Or maybe not.

Matteo was tough. A head wound wouldn't kill him.

I chanced a look over my shoulder, my eyes finding Matteo's unmoving body, sprawled out on the concrete. Behind him the cars were burning, tingeing the illuminated city sky black with their smoke.

Funeral black.

The pool of blood around Matteo's head looked black from my vantage point, and it had grown even more. "I don't want to love you," I whispered as I jerked to a halt, clenching my eyes shut. But I did. I did love Matteo.

My eyes flew open, I whirled around and began walking back, then started running, getting faster and faster, until I was racing. I dropped to my knees beside Matteo, fumbling in my pockets for my phone but coming up empty. It was in my bag. My gaze went to the burning car where I'd left my stuff. Stupid Gianna.

I reached into Matteo's pocket and exhaled a shuddering breath when I grabbed his phone. Not wasting time scrolling through his contact I hit speed dial.

"I'm not in the mood to talk to you, Matteo. You acted like a major asshole tonight," Luca's sharp voice rang in my ear.

I let out a sob.

"Gianna?" I could hear Aria in the background but couldn't hear what she was saying.

"He's dying," I said after a moment, sounding flat and voiceless.

"What are you talking about? Give me Matteo."

"I can't. Russians attacked us. There's so much blood, Luca, so much blood."

"Is Matteo alive?" For the first time since Aria almost died, Luca sounded worried.

My eyes darted to the body beside me. To my husband.

Was it my imagination or had Matteo's chest stopped moving? I pressed my palm against his blood-soaked shirt. There was nothing. "He's not breathing. He was a moment ago, but he's not anymore." Hysteria found its way into my voice.

"Gianna, you have to do CPR. I'll be there soon. I have your GPS coordinates. But you'll have to get him breathing or it'll be too late."

I didn't say anything, only stared at the man I loved. I'd wanted to hate him, had given it my all, and in the beginning there had been hate, so much of it, but not all of it had been directed at Matteo, and now hardly any seemed left, and it felt ridiculous to hold onto what little I still harbored.

"Gianna?" Luca's voice sliced right through me. I could hear commotion in the background, the sound of a car springing to life. I put Luca on loudspeaker and cupped Matteo's face, then pressed my lips against his and blew air into his lungs. I tried to remember how often to press as I rested my hands against his rib cage. I didn't know the first thing about CPR except for what I'd seen on TV. Why had I never paid better attention? What if Matteo died because I was doing something wrong?

Luca's next words tore through my thoughts. I'd forgotten he was on the phone. "I know you feel like Matteo trapped you, that he ruined your life, but no matter what you think, he didn't do it to make you miserable. For some unexplainable reason Matteo loves you. You don't have to believe me. You can keep hating him but don't leave him alone, not now. If you help me save his life, I'll grant you freedom. I swear it on my honor and my life. Aria is here. She's witness. You will get money, a new identity and even protection from the Outfit if you want. It's all yours if you save his life."

"Okay," I said as I pressed down on Matteo's chest again. I wasn't even sure why I said it.

"You have to do chest compressions. Hard and fast. Don't worry about breaking his ribs. Thirty pushes, two breathes. *Fast.*"

I sped up my compressions, then bent over Matteo to breathe into his mouth twice. "He's not reacting!" I gasped as I started everything from the beginning.

"Keep doing it."

And I did, even as my fingers cramped. They were red and sticky with blood. I couldn't even see through my eyes anymore. They were blurry with tears. Why couldn't I stop crying? I cried over a man like Matteo but had hardly shed a tear over Sid.

"We'll be there in ten minutes," Luca said. "How's Matteo?"

I didn't reply. I pushed harder against Matteo's chest and then he drew in a shallow breath. I froze, almost scared I'd imagined it. I quickly leaned over his face and felt the gentle breeze of his breath against my cheek. I brushed shaky fingers over his throat, finding his pulse. It wasn't as fast and strong as usual, but it was there. I closed my eyes for a moment, squeezed a few annoying tears away and then I opened them. I sank down on my butt and stretched out my legs. I wanted to cradle Matteo's head in my lap but worried about hurting his neck, so I merely rested my palm against his chest to reassure myself of his steady heartbeat. His blood was starting to soak my pants but I was beyond caring.

"Gianna? Are you still there?"

"Yes. Matteo is breathing again."

There was a pause. "Good," Luca said quietly. "Stay where you are."

"Don't worry." I tilted my head back and stared up at the sky littered with stars and hazy with smoke. The gentle rise and fall of Matteo's chest was almost like a lullaby and my eyes started to droop. My headache had gotten even worse. I probably had a concussion.

The roar of an engine made me turn my head. Two cars were racing in our direction. The one in the front was Luca's Aston Martin and the one in the back belonged to his crony Romero. I quickly pulled my hand away from Matteo's chest and rose to my feet, even as my vision swam.

The Aston stopped with fuming tires and Luca jumped out. He stormed toward Matteo, barely sparing me a glance as he knelt beside his brother and felt his throat. He did a quick scan of Matteo's injuries and then Romero and Sandro were already beside him.

Someone touched my shoulder and then Aria appeared in my field of vision. She wrapped her arms around me and I sagged against her, feeling drained. "Are you hurt?"

"Maybe. Probably. I don't know."

"Get her away," Luca said. "Take my car and drive her to our apartment."

I pulled back to look down at him. "Where are you taking Matteo?"

"To the hospital. This is too serious for our doc," he said, then smiled coldly. "Don't worry. I'll honor my promise. When I return to the apartment, we'll make the necessary arrangements to ensure your freedom." His eyes were hard. I had a feeling he wouldn't have minded much if I'd died in the crash.

"Maybe Gianna wants to go to the hospital with Matteo," Aria suggested softly as Luca and Sandro lifted Matteo carefully and carried him over to the jeep. Romero was talking to soldiers on the phone, making arrangements to keep the police out of this.

"She doesn't," Luca said firmly. "Help her gather her things from Matteo's apartment, so we can get her settled in her new life before my brother returns home."

Why didn't I protest? Why couldn't I admit my feelings even now?

Aria gave me a searching look but I shrugged, ignoring the heat behind my eyeballs and the tight feeling in my chest as I watched them take Matteo away. "We can follow them in our car," she whispered.

I swallowed, then shook my head. "No. Luca's right. I need to pack up my things."

Frowning, but without protest, Aria led me toward the Aston Martin.

—MATTEO—

Every inch of my body hurt and my head felt like it was filled with cotton. Groaning, I tried to open my fucking eyes, which seemed to be glued shut. Resisting the urge to peel them open with my fingernails, I slowly opened them a tiny bit, then finally fully. Luca was sitting in a chair next to my bed.

A fucking hospital bed. "Don't tell me you took me to a fucking hospital?" I rasped, then coughed. Fuck. I felt like death warmed over.

Luca leaned forward, a wry smile on his face. Did he have to look so damn worried? I wasn't a kid who needed his protection anymore. "Now that you're swearing again, I'll consider moving you to my penthouse. Romero is already looking forward to playing nurse."

I was reaching for the needle in the back of my hand to pull it out but paused when his words sunk in. "Your penthouse?"

"You'll need to rest a few days. And I know you, so there needs to be someone to keep an eye on you."

He was watching me carefully. As if he was trying to gauge if I could take the bad news. "Did something happen to Gianna?"

"No. She's fine." He paused.

"Spit it out. Damn it!"

"I made a deal with her."

"Stop fucking around. Tell me the fucking truth. I can take it."

"When she called me, you weren't breathing. I was worried she'd use her chance to run."

"My life against her freedom," I said with a dark laugh.

"She agreed. Now she's home with Aria, packing her bags."

"We need to protect her from the Outfit. Her father won't accept it."

"You want to protect her?" Luca asked incredulously.

"She's still my wife. And I'll protect her as long as she'll let me."

"She'll leave as soon as I've set everything up. You better forget about her sooner than later."

I glared. "Would you just forget Aria because someone told you to?"

"Aria wouldn't need bribing to save my fucking life."

I jerked the needle out of my hand and sucked the blood away that welled up before I swung my legs out of the bed, despite my splitting headache. My eyes scanned the table beside my bed for my knives and my gun holster. They weren't there. Damn it. I felt fucking naked without them.

"Fuck," Luca muttered. The bastard grabbed my shoulders to stop me from standing. "I didn't mean to get you all riled up. You're supposed to stay in bed."

"I don't give a damn. I'm not a fucking toddler. Stop patronizing me. I've dealt with worse shit than a headache." I shrugged his hands off and slid off the edge of the bed. Big mistake. The moment my bare feet hit the floor, I swayed. Luca steadied me. With a groan, I sank back down on the bed. "What did they give me? I feel as if someone put roofies in my drink."

Luca gave me his most patronizing expression. "I told you to stay in bed."

"Shut up." I blinked a few times. It did nothing to banish the dots from my vision. "I want to get the hell out of here. I'm fine."

"You're fine when I tell you. I'm your Capo."

I opened the drawer in the bedside table, but my weapons weren't in there either. "Where are my knives?"

"In the car. I could hardly roll you into the hospital armed to the teeth."

I clenched my jaw, then pushed myself to my feet again. This time I hardly swayed at all.

Luca glowered at me. "Goddammit, Matteo. Why can't you listen for once?"

"Don't give me that bullshit. If our situations were switched, you'd be out of the fucking hospital already." He didn't bother denying it. I knew him. "Let's go."

Luca thrust a bag at me. "Sandro picked up a few clothes for you. The ones you were wearing during the crash have to be burnt."

I got out of the embarrassing hospital gown and slipped into clean jeans. "What about underwear? Maybe Sandro likes it if his junk jiggles around in his pants, but I prefer another barrier between my balls and the zipper."

Luca snorted. "I wonder what it will take to shut your big mouth. Almost getting killed and having your wife leave your sorry ass obviously isn't enough."

I stopped buttoning my shirt. I knew he was joking. And he was right. Nothing ever got me down. Not when our mother died, not when Father beat the crap out of me, not when I was bleeding like a pig. Then why the fuck did mentioning Gianna feel like a fucking punch to the gut? Damn it. I was turning into a pussy. I sent Luca a forced grin, but he was already scrutinizing me with a frown.

"Don't tell me you're so eager to get out of the hospital because you hope to walk across Gianna and talk her into staying with you. She won't. The selfish bitch wants freedom."

I stalked toward him, getting right in his face. "Don't call her a bitch." Then I fucking swayed and had to grab Luca's shoulder to stop myself from making a faceplant. So much for being threatening. Damn it.

Luca only stared.

"I swear if you don't stop giving me that fucking pitying look I'm going to beat you to a bloody pulp," I muttered.

"I don't pity you. Pity is for people who got into a bad situation with no fault of their own, but you chose Gianna. You saw how volatile and fucking annoying she was and you still wanted her. You were turned on by her bitchiness. You got yourself into this mess. Now you have to deal."

"Cold-hearted bastard," I said, glad he didn't try to console me.

Luca smirked. "Always."

I shoved my shirt into my jeans and slipped into my shoes. "Sandro is a fucking asshole. No socks either? Is he a nudist or what?"

"He probably thinks you are."

I headed for the door, trying to walk as tall as possible despite my wobbly legs. Luca walked too close. He probably thought he might need to catch me if I fainted. "Stop hovering. People will think you're my sugar daddy."

Luca ignored my comment. "What do you remember before you woke up?"

Back to business, thank God. "A bunch of cock-sucking Russians chased Gianna and me. I got rid of the first car pretty quick. A bullet between the brows got rid of the driver and the resulting crash of the other fuckers. The second car was more trouble. I don't remember what happened to them."

"They burnt in their car. Charcoal all of them."

"What about my car?"

"Charcoal."

"Great."

"Could have been worse. You didn't look good when I first saw you."

I reached for the tender spot on top of my head. A few nurses watched us as we passed them, but they didn't stop us. Luca had probably already settled everything in advance.

"You're lucky they didn't shave your entire head. Knowing how vain you are, you wouldn't have stopped bitching about it."

"You know how to cheer me up," I said.

Luca was busy texting someone. He barely glanced up.

"You're warning Aria that we're coming, aren't you?" I couldn't help but wonder if Gianna was still with Aria, if they were making plans for Gianna's future without me. Luca had offered Gianna freedom on a golden platter. She'd be stupid not to go through with it. A life away from the mafia was something she'd always wanted. Away from me. She'd finally get her wish.

Luca spared me the barest glance. "It's for the best, believe me."

Annoyance zipped through me. Luca had always tried to dictate my life—look out for me as he called it—and it had only gotten worse since he was also my Capo. "I can handle Gianna. I'm not a pussy, Luca. I won't break down and cry because my wife wants to run as far away from me as possible."

"I know." He stuffed his phone back into his jacket. Of course I knew he'd already told Aria everything she needed to know.

We arrived at Luca's car. He opened the door for me. "Don't think I'll put out just because you're being a gentleman," I told him as I half fell into the seat. I hoped Luca thought I had done it on purpose and not because my legs had gone on strike.

"Don't worry. Your back door is safe." Luca shut the door in my face before he rounded the car and slipped behind the steering wheel. He started the car and slid out of the parking lot. "Do you want me to organize someone who can distract you? Maybe not today because of your head. But in the next couple of days."

I snorted out a laugh. "You mean a hooker?"

Luca gave a one-shoulder shrug, not taking his eyes off the street. He had his poker face on and it annoyed the crap out of me, because I wasn't sure if this was a test or if he was being serious. A few years ago, I'd have said he was dead serious. Luca had never had trouble moving from one woman to the next, but that had been before Aria.

"First of all, I might have a concussion but I'm not dead, and that means I don't need a pity fuck. If I want a woman, I can find one myself and don't need to pay someone."

"You haven't seen yourself in the mirror yet."

I checked my reflection in the rearview mirror. "Okay. Maybe I'd have more trouble than usual." I had two black eyes, both of them swollen and bloodshot, and there was a bluish lump below my hairline. Not to mention that my hair was a matted mess.

"You'll scare the shit out of every woman you approach."

"So what? It always worked for you."

Luca chuckled. "So is that a no?"

"A big fat one. I don't want to fuck anyone but…" Realizing the fucking trap I'd just walked in I snapped my mouth shut. Damn it.

"You're not going to give her up, are you?" Luca said in a resigned tone.

"No."

"I swore on my honor to grant her freedom but I can break my promise if that's what you want. It's not like I haven't done worse before."

"No. I don't want you to break your oath. And it would only make her hate me more. You can't force Gianna to do anything. She needs to come back to me freely. That's the only way."

Luca shook his head. "Matteo, even you must realize how futile it is to hope for that. She'll run and never come back. Are you willing to risk that?"

"Yes."

"Then you're a better man than I am. I would never let Aria go."

I glared out of the window. It sounded easy: letting her go, giving her the chance to find her way back to me, but I wasn't sure I could go through with it. I wasn't better than Luca. But I was a hunter and sometimes a chase was useless, sometimes you had to wait for the prey to come to you. I wasn't a patient hunter, but this time I would try.

chapter 20

—GIANNA—

Aria kept throwing glances my way, her pale brows drawn together in concern. "Are you sure you don't need to see the doc?"

"I'm fine, really," I snapped, then felt bad for it. Aria was always on my side. She'd done so much for me in the last year, even gone against Luca. "Sorry. I'm exhausted." The smell of smoke and blood lingered in my nose, a vivid echo of the earlier events.

"It's okay. You've gone through a lot," Aria said gently.

My thoughts drifted back to Matteo. I hoped he'd be fine. He was tough, but he'd lost a lot of blood. Maybe I should have let Aria drive me to the hospital to make sure he was alright. I wanted to be with him, wanted to be there when he woke and hold his hand while he was unconscious. I wanted to tell him that I was tired of the games, tired of pretending that I didn't care for him, when I'd already lost my heart to him. It was futile trying to lie to myself. I knew I'd come to love Matteo, even his arrogance and shark-smile. He was still a bad man, a murderer and criminal, but I knew now that I wasn't much better. I had no doubt that I would have been like Matteo if I'd been raised like him and not sheltered from life like all the women in our world. It was an ugly truth, one I'd prefer to deny, but it was the truth, and it was time to admit it and own up to the life I was obviously meant to live. The words lay on the tip of my tongue.

"You can take a quick shower, and then I'll help you pack everything."

"Oh, sure," I said distractedly. Pride had always been my problem, even now when I knew it was only hurting me, and Matteo.

Aria glanced my way. "Luca will keep his word. You don't have to worry. He's never broken his promise. And he knows I'd never forgive him if he'd lied. You'll be free."

Free? What was freedom worth if it meant ignoring what my heart wanted? "I know."

"You don't look happy."

I wasn't happy. But why? For months I'd wished for nothing more than to figure out a way out of this marriage, out of this life, out of this world, and now that I finally got my wish, I didn't feel anything. How could I have been lying to myself for so long? And why couldn't I admit it, especially not to the outside world? Why did it feel as if admitting I loved Matteo was the ultimate defeat? "I'm still recovering from the crash. That's all," I said on autopilot. I wondered how long that lie would work.

Aria didn't look convinced but she didn't push the matter. I leaned my head against the window and closed my eyes, not in the mood for conversation. I needed to sort through my emotions as soon as possible, but the splitting headache definitely wasn't making it an easy feat.

I must have dozed off because suddenly Aria was nudging me awake and we were parked in the underground garage. She gave me an encouraging smile, and for some reason it made me feel horrible. I quickly scrambled out of the car, unable to meet Aria's compassionate gaze. I rushed toward the elevator, a few times almost tripping over my feet. Aria caught up with me and called the elevator down with a press of the button. "What's the rush? You don't have to worry that Matteo will come home while we're still packing. They'll probably keep him in the hospital overnight. He looked really bad."

I leaned against the cool wall of the elevator. Did Aria really think that would cheer me up? Was I such a horrible bitch that people thought I'd be happy that someone was seriously injured?

Of course they did. Luca had thought he had to offer me a ticket to freedom so I didn't let his brother die. I was nothing but a heartless, selfish bitch in his mind. And judging from Aria's words, she agreed with him.

My throat corded up. Maybe they were right. "I'm not worried," I said calmly. It was easier to play the part they all expected me to play.

Aria nodded, but she didn't stop watching me. We were leaning across from each other and I could see my reflection behind her in the mirror. We couldn't have been more different. Aria with her kind expression, angel-like hair, porcelain skin. and baby-blue eyes; the epitome of pureness. And I looked like I'd risen from hell with my messy red hair, blood-covered clothes and skin, and dark shadows under my eyes. When we stepped into the apartment that I'd shared with Matteo since our wedding, I quickly rushed into the master bedroom, and from there into the adjoining bathroom. Maybe a quick shower would help me get a grip on my heart. Luca's offer was my last chance, I knew that. If I followed my heart instead and stayed with Matteo, then that would be it. I had to let my brain make this decision.

After my shower, I still didn't feel better but at least I'd made up my mind. Aria was sitting on the bed, typing on her phone, when I entered the bedroom.

"Did Luca tell you about Matteo?" I asked immediately, my throat already tightening and panic flooding me. I should have gone with Matteo. Suddenly I couldn't breathe.

"He's doing fine. Apparently it's only a concussion and a few cracked ribs." She finally looked up and quickly walked over to me. "You look pale."

I swallowed. Matteo would be fine. Slowly my panic settled down.

"You are really worried about him, aren't you? Why don't you admit it? You can trust me, Gianna, you know that."

"Of course I worry. I'm not made from stone. I don't want anything to happen to him. I care about him, believe it or not."

"But not enough to stay?" Aria asked.

I wasn't sure what to say. All my well-laid plans in the shower seemed to crumble before me again. "I need to lie down for a while, I think. Or do we have to leave soon?"

Aria shook her head. "No, Luca will take Matteo to our penthouse when he wakes, so you won't cross his path if you stay here. And it's late anyway. Catch some sleep."

I grabbed clean clothes and put them on before I lay down on top of the covers. I could hear Aria closing the door and then silence reigned around me.

It was already light out when I woke. I was alone in the bedroom. I quickly scrambled off the bed and left the room, half expecting to find Matteo in the kitchen. He wasn't.

Aria was there. She typed something into her phone before handing me a cup of coffee. "How do you feel?"

"Where's Matteo? Is he okay? Is he still in the hospital?"

"He's fine. He's in the penthouse, sleeping off his concussion."

"Oh, right. He's at your place. That makes sense."

"Gianna, you don't have to leave, you realize that, right? It's okay to stay with Matteo."

I stared at her. It was okay, wasn't it? Okay to love a man like him, okay to accept life in the mob.

The elevator stopped with a bling and Luca walked out, his cold gaze settling on me. I had to suppress a shiver. That was what hatred looked like, and I supposed he had every reason to hate me. Sandro was a couple of steps behind him like a good lapdog.

"I hope your bags are packed. I want you out of this apartment as soon as possible."

"Luca," Aria hissed. "That's not fair."

For once she couldn't warm his cold heart. "No. That bitch needs to get as far away from my brother as possible. I want her gone. She's been ruining his life for long enough."

I glared, but deep down I wondered if he was right. Of course, I'd never admit it. "I know you think Matteo deserves better than me. But let me tell you one thing. Aria deserves better too. She's too good and pure and kind for you. You aren't even worth the dirt under her shoes. She's too loving and nice to see it, but I do. You think I destroyed Matteo's life, but I never got a choice in the matter. I didn't want to marry him. You on the other hand chose to marry Aria. You chose to destroy her life with your darkness. So get down from your high horse, you bastard. You don't deserve her and never will."

Aria's knuckles turned white from her grip on Luca's wrist. He could have shaken her off with ease but he didn't move. "I know," he said in a steely voice. "But the difference between you and me is that I'm trying to be a better man for her. But you never tried. You were always content with being a bitch."

Aria gasped. "Luca, please."

"No. He's right. I'm a bitch, and I'm leaving now. Tell Matteo goodbye from me." Wow, spoken like a true bitch. It was too late to take the words back, and I knew I would be too prideful to do it anyway. I took two of my bags that

Aria must have carried down before I'd woken, and headed for Sandro who picked up my other bags and followed me toward the elevator. I stepped inside and faced Aria and Luca, my head held high. Luca's gaze was unrestrained hate, but Aria was crying. She was pleading me with her eyes and eventually I couldn't take it anymore and lowered my gaze to the floor. The doors slid shut and the elevator started moving. Sandro didn't try to make conversation. Every look he gave me spoke of disapproval. I wondered if Luca would have had me killed if it weren't for Aria.

Sandro drove me to a hotel where I would stay until I'd found an apartment. I wasn't even sure if I would stay in New York. Returning to Chicago was definitely out of the question. I'd be dead within a week.

"Here. That's five thousand dollars. Luca will contact you with more details soon," Sandro said as he parked in front of the hotel. A doorman opened my door. Sandro didn't follow me as I got out of the car, only gave the doorman information about the reservation. The moment the doorman had lifted my luggage out of the trunk, Sandro drove off, leaving me alone. I stared after the car. Nobody was watching me. I was free.

Then why did freedom feel like my new prison?

—MATTEO—

"I don't think this is a good idea," Luca muttered as he followed me into my apartment.

"This is my home. I'm not an invalid. I won't have another sleepover at your place," I said. I was still feeling fucking dizzy but I wasn't going to admit it to Luca. I walked into my bedroom, Luca close behind me. If he didn't stop it soon, I'd kick his ass.

I stopped in the middle of the room. The drawers were ajar. I didn't have to look into them to know they were empty.

"She moved out this morning," Luca said.

"I know."

I could feel Luca's eyes on me. "You should stay with Aria and me. It's almost Christmas. Do you want to spend the holidays sulking?"

"I don't care about Christmas. And I'm not sulking. I'm supposed to rest, remember?" I pointed at my head, then walked over to the bed and lay down. "And I don't want you to watch me while I sleep."

"You will have dinner with Aria and me tonight. I don't care if I have to drag you into my penthouse, but you will be there."

I nodded. "Let me sleep."

He finally left. Of course there was no way I could sleep. My eyes darted toward the dressing room with its empty shelves. Gianna was really gone, and this time I wasn't going to hunt her.

chapter 21

—GIANNA—

I stared out of the window of my hotel room. It was dinnertime but I wasn't hungry. I hadn't left the room since I'd checked in this morning. Did freedom always feel this lonely?

My phone beeped with a message. It was from Aria.

Matteo broke down again. He's unconscious.

I called her immediately, my heart hammering in my chest. She picked up after the first ring. "Where is he?" I asked.

"At our place. He's in the guest bedroom. The doc says he needs to stay in bed. He overexerted himself too soon after the crash."

"I'm coming over."

"You are?" Aria asked in a hopeful voice.

"Yes. Tell Luca he should get used to my presence again."

I could practically hear Aria smiling. "I knew it." She paused. "I'll send Sandro over."

"No, I'm taking a cab. I'll be there soon."

When I arrived in the apartment, Luca barred my way. "What is she doing here?"

"I want to see Matteo," I said. And I didn't care if I had to knock out Luca to do it.

Luca glared. "Get the fuck away."

"Luca, please," Aria whispered.

I tried to walk past Luca but he didn't let me. "Let me see my husband."

"Matteo can't use the emotional stress right now. You leaving and then returning won't help with his recovery," Luca growled. I had a feeling his words would have been much worse if Aria weren't standing beside him. "If you stay now, you'll stay for good. I'm done with your games."

"I'm not leaving again."

Luca sent me a doubtful look but he stepped back. I didn't hesitate. I rushed toward the guest bedroom and stormed inside. Matteo was asleep. I lay down beside him, determined to keep watch over him until he opened his eyes.

—MATTEO—

A soft hand held onto mine. I opened my eyes, blinking a few times to clear my vision. I felt like a total wimp for having passed out. Fuck. I'd been shot and stabbed and even burnt before, and a stupid hit to the head brought me down to my knees. It was a disgrace. I turned my head. Gianna was curled up beside me, her hand clutching mine. Her clothes were wrinkly and her hair a complete mess as if she'd been at my side for a while.

Her face was mostly covered by her unruly hair. I felt the irresistible urge to see her expression. Slowly, carefully I sat up and brushed a few strands away with my free hand. Gianna looked like a fucking angel in sleep. Too beautiful to be real. Her thick lashes rested on her pale skin. I trailed a fingertip over her high cheekbone, enjoying the softness of her skin. Her eyes fluttered beneath her lids and then they peeled open. She blinked sleepily until her gaze finally focused on me.

I waited for her to let go of my hand and jump off the bed like it had caught fire. At the very least I expected some ridiculous excuse for why she was here, holding my hand. I doubted Luca had dragged her back. He knew I didn't want him to.

She didn't do any of those things however. Instead she sat up slowly, blinking away sleep and rubbing her eyes with the hand that wasn't holding mine. She searched the room for something. "What time is it?"

I had no fucking clue. I wasn't even sure what day it was. "You are asking me?"

She laughed once, then her expression tightened. "You scared me."

"I did? I suppose I'm a scary guy."

Gianna didn't smile. She was looking at me with an expression I'd never seen on her face, vulnerable and open. "I should have never agreed to Luca's offer. I was being stubborn. I didn't want to admit my feelings to myself. But when Aria called to tell me you'd broken down again, I was terrified that I'd lose you." She paused, her fingers on my hand tightening. I didn't say anything, wasn't sure what to say. My general solution in emotional situations was humor but it felt wrong to make a joke and I didn't want to stop Gianna from saying whatever else she had to say.

She stared off toward the window, guilt marring her beautiful face. "All I could think about when I wasn't at your side after you'd broken down was 'what if you die and all I've ever done was treat you badly and push you away.' I've been acting like a major bitch. I'm sorry."

I touched her cheek and moved closer. "You don't need to apologize for anything, Gianna. I actually enjoyed most of our arguments. They added entertainment to my days." I grinned and this time I got a smile in return.

"You should be pissed, Matteo. You know what Luca offered me in exchange for saving your life and that I agreed. Why aren't you sending me away? I would deserve it."

I shrugged. I didn't like the idea that Gianna had eagerly accepted Luca's offer, but she was here now. It had taken a while but eventually I'd realized that Gianna had to come to me on her own. Gianna would never let anyone force her to admit her feelings. I touched the back of her head and pulled her toward me. She didn't resist and when her mouth touched mine, she wrapped her arms around my neck and deepened our kiss. My hand found its way under her shirt, feeling the soft skin of her stomach and moving higher.

Gianna stopped my hand's exploration. "You need to rest. You passed out yesterday. I won't let you overexert yourself again."

I chuckled. "Come on. If you ride me, I won't have to exert myself at all. You'll do all the work."

"Yeah, right," she said. "No way am I going to risk your recovery. Luca would be so pissed if I did something stupid. He hates me anyway. I don't want to give him another reason to keep me away from you."

"Luca wouldn't stop you from seeing me."

She raised her eyebrows. "He tried to stop me from coming here yesterday."

"Why the fuck did he do that?" Annoyance shot through me. Luca always had to play the Capo and order people around.

"I suppose he was worried about you," Gianna admitted grudgingly. There was no love lost between my brother and her, so I was surprised by her admittance. "He didn't want me to play with you. He thought it was better if there was a clean cut between us and I left your life for good."

"So what made him change his mind?" I asked.

"Aria, I suppose."

"Of course," I said, though I'd hoped for another reason. I leaned back against the headboard, ignoring the slight twinge in my head at the movement. I crossed my arms over my chest, trying to look fucking relaxed when I was anything but. "I'm fine now. I won't die. You could leave now without feeling guilty."

Gianna looked at me for a long time without saying anything. "I don't want to leave."

"You agreed to Luca's offer, you said it yourself."

"I did, because Luca took me by surprise with it. You were dying right in front of me. We'd barely survived a crash and the crazy Russians, and suddenly I was offered something I'd thought I wanted. I didn't even really think before I said yes."

I nodded, but didn't say anything. I was tired of making the first move, of always pursuing Gianna. This time I wanted to hear something from her.

She sighed, her blue eyes tired. "You think I would have let you die if Luca hadn't offered me a ticket to freedom, don't you? That's what everyone thinks, probably even Aria."

I kept my expression neutral. "Isn't it the truth?"

She glared. "No, it's not the truth. When Luca mentioned his stupid offer, I had already started chest compressions. I didn't know what I was doing and probably made every mistake possible, but I wasn't just letting you die. I was doing everything I could even before Luca offered me freedom for your life. I would have never let you die, never. I know you don't have to believe me. There's no reason why you should. I could be lying for all you know."

But I did believe her. I knew how to read people and Gianna wasn't lying. I could tell how upset she was, more upset than I'd seen her in a long time. "I don't think you are."

Gianna didn't even seem to hear me. She was scowling in the direction of the window, her cheeks flushed with emotions. "I knew the moment I saw you lying in your own blood that I didn't want to lose you. I knew it, but I still didn't want to admit it to anyone. I was so stupid and stubborn. I was being bitchy Gianna like usual. And once I'd agreed to Luca's offer, I was too proud to tell him that I didn't even want his stupid freedom. I didn't want to leave you, didn't want another life. I probably would have been miserable alone but too proud to admit it if you hadn't broken down. It felt like I was giving up, like I was admitting defeat, which is so idiotic. How can love ever be a defeat?" She fell silent, eyes widening.

I had become very still, like a hunter who didn't want to startle its prey.

She licked her lips nervously. I wished I knew what she was thinking, but I had a feeling I knew. She was probably regretting ever bringing up the "L-word" and everything else that had bubbled out of her. That was who she was. Maybe she was waiting for me to say something first, to tell her I loved her, but I wasn't going to open my fucking heart to her and risk her stomping on it. I knew what I was feeling, had known it for a long time but I'd never said it to her. I'd never said it to anyone. Admitting something like that made you vulnerable and so far Gianna had given me little reason to risk that. I'd hunted her long enough. Now was her turn. I wouldn't push her in either direction. Everything from this point on would have to come from her.

"Luca's offer still stands. You are a free woman. You can walk out of this building and nobody will stop you."

"No," she said firmly. "I've run from my emotions for too long." She braced herself on her palms and leaned forward. "I want to be with you, Matteo. By God, I know I shouldn't want it, but it doesn't matter anymore. I'm sick of ignoring my heart. I love you."

She kissed me almost desperately, her hands finding their way into my hair. My head was still tender but I'd have rather cut my own throat than told Gianna to be careful. I wanted to feel her lips, her fingers, her body. I wanted all of her. "You sure you mean it?" I asked in a teasing voice when she pulled back.

She nodded. "Yes. There's no fucking doubt in my mind. I love you, Matteo. I don't care what that makes me. I don't care what other people think about me, about us. I don't even care what Aria and Luca think. All I care about is us."

I kissed her again. I'd never get enough of tasting her. "I love you, Gianna. I've fucking loved you for a long time."

—GIANNA—

Hearing Matteo say that he loved me set my heart aflame. I couldn't remember the last time I'd felt so happy. I'd thought admitting my feelings to anyone would give that person more power over me, but instead I felt freer than I had in a long time. I'd fought my emotions for so long, had held myself back for no good reason. Now that I'd said everything that needed to be said I felt relieved. Maybe all this had started as something that had been forced upon me, but today, this life, Matteo, my marriage, were my choices, and I said yes to all of them.

Matteo's kiss was demanding. There was no restraint, no sign that not too long ago he'd been unconscious. I knew it was stupid, but I wanted to feel him, wanted to show him with more than just words that I loved him. I pulled back and let my eyes wander down Matteo's body. He was dressed in only a tight white shirt and boxer shorts that did little to hide his erection. When I looked back up into his face, his gaze was transparent with lust. I'd never listened to other people's advice, so why should I start now?

Matteo wouldn't overexert himself. I would take care of him. I knelt on the bed, and gripped his waistband. Matteo smiled his shark-smile. "I thought you didn't want to risk my health."

"Oh shut up," I said quietly. "Or do you want me to stop?"

"No. Don't stop." He made himself comfortable against the array of pillows.

I smiled as I pulled down his boxer shorts, revealing his hard length. I moved between his legs so I could watch him while I sucked his cock. I cupped his balls, gently massaging them, but I didn't touch his shaft yet. Instead I watched it twitch and grow even harder under my ministrations.

"You tease," Matteo growled. "I thought you wouldn't torture me today."

He was right. This wasn't about me. I leaned forward and ran my tongue all the way from his balls up to the top, then swirled it around his tip before sucking him into my mouth. I took inch after inch of him in until he hit the back of my throat before I let him slide out again. Matteo watched me through half-lidded eyes. He gently pulled my hair back, which always got in the way, and stroked my cheeks as I licked and sucked his tip, knowing that it was where he was most sensitive. I traced the tip of my tongue along the ridge of his tip slowly. Matteo's breathing quickened, his abs tightened but he didn't take his eyes off me or stop touching my face. It felt like he was revering me while I was revering him.

I sucked a bit harder, feeling him getting closer. His fingers against my scalp tightened occasionally and he released a harsh breath every time my teeth scraped him lightly. He started pumping his hips, pushing his length deeper into my mouth and I let him. I was growing wet and the pressure between my legs had mounted to almost unbearable proportions but I was determined to ignore my own needs for today.

Matteo's motions grew frantic. I clamped my lips tightly around his cock as he thrust into me over and over again. "I'm coming," he rasped. I didn't pull back. Instead I cupped his balls tightly and met his gaze. The muscles in his shoulders flexed and his body seized up with his orgasm. Eventually he stilled. I pulled back and wiped my mouth with a self-satisfied grin.

Matteo chuckled, a low sound from deep in his chest. He reached for my shoulders and pulled me on top of him, claiming my mouth in a firm kiss. His hands glided down my back to cup my butt and squeezed. My core tightened with arousal. Before I could make up my mind, if I should allow Matteo to exert himself even more, a knock sounded. I tensed, my eyes darting toward the door, which was already opening.

Luca stood in the doorway, his gaze taking everything in without an expression. It wasn't hard to guess what we'd done. After all, I was lying on top of a bottomless Matteo who was groping my butt.

My face flamed with embarrassment.

"You really shouldn't barge into someone's bedroom like that," Matteo said in amusement. He didn't look embarrassed at all, but after everything I knew about him that didn't surprise me anymore.

I stayed exactly the way I was, even though Matteo wouldn't have cared if I'd moved away and bared his cock to his brother.

"You should be resting," Luca said dryly, gray eyes piercing me with an unreadable look. Was he angry? It was hard to tell. Recently he'd always been pissed around me. Not that his presence made me much happier.

Matteo gave my butt a firm pat, his grin turning annoyingly smug. "I feel very well rested."

Luca shook his head. "I give up," he said. "You two do whatever you want. I don't even want to know what's going on or not going on." He turned around and closed the door behind him.

I pushed away from Matteo and slid off the bed, trying my best to straighten my wrinkled clothes, but now there were also stains on them. They were an absolute mess.

"Hey, I thought we weren't done yet. I didn't even get to touch your pussy."

"And you won't. Luca was right. You should rest. You've had enough excitement for the day," I said sternly. Matteo was already growing hard again and he didn't bother to hide it.

I huffed. "I'm going to change and clean up, and then return with something to eat for you. In the meantime, please pull your mind out of the gutter."

Matteo winked. I stifled a smile and slipped out of the room. Aria and Luca were in the dining area, talking in hushed voices. Of course, I knew exactly what they were discussing.

Aria noticed me first and fell silent. After a couple of seconds of silent scrutiny, she smiled brightly at me. Luca didn't share her enthusiasm though. I ignored him. "Could you give me some of your clothes? I really need to change and shower."

Luca raised his eyebrows. "Do you need to make yourself presentable so you can leave?"

I met his gaze. "I'm not leaving. Not ever again."

Aria was practically bouncing when she stepped up to me and linked our arms.

"We'll see," Luca said simply. Aria shot him a glare before she led me upstairs toward their dressing room.

"Don't listen to him. He's protective of Matteo," Aria murmured. She pulled jeans and a long-sleeved shirt from her drawers and handed them to me.

Luca's protectiveness of Aria and Matteo was one of the few things I liked about him. "I know. I haven't given him any reason to trust me with his brother."

Aria watched me curiously as I undressed. "So will you move back into Matteo's apartment?"

I paused on my way to the bathroom. It wasn't as if I had already settled somewhere else. I hadn't even started considering where to live after I'd moved out. "Yes. I will move back in and be his wife. Probably not a good wife, but it's not like Matteo didn't know that when he married me."

"Matteo doesn't expect you to be a perfect wife. He likes you for who you are, flaws and all."

It was the truth, even if I'd been blind to it for so long. I stepped into the shower but didn't immediately turn the water on.

Aria sank down on the edge of the bathtub. "Are you sure you can do the same? Accept all of him, even the bad?"

There was plenty of bad in Matteo, in every Made Man really, but I'd come to realize that there was in me as well. Maybe not as much, but it was there. It was in all of us. I'd tried to become someone else, some kind of ideal I'd thought I needed to be, but that had never been me and never would. Matteo had held up a mirror to my face and showed me who I really was and where I belonged. I'd hated it, had fought it tooth and nail, but it was time to be brave.

"Yes. I love him, the bad and the good," I said firmly. Aria smiled as if I'd given her some huge present. Smiling back, I turned the water on, and really let the words sink in, their truthfulness.

I'd never be okay with everything Matteo did, would never do even half of the things he had done and was going to do in the future. But I'd realized I didn't have to be happy about every aspect of his life. As long as Matteo treated me with care and respect, as long as he loved me, and I loved him, things would work out.

I'd stand by him and support him as best as I could, because he was mine and I was his.

epilogue

—GIANNA—

It was late April and today was the first warm day of the year. The temperature had finally climbed over 70°F. The ocean was still too cold to swim in it, but I didn't care.

I wasn't sure what it was about the beach and the ocean breeze that made me feel free. I stormed down the vast lawn of the Vitiello mansion toward the bay. Matteo was close behind me, and catching up judging from his steps. I sped up even more, not daring to throw a glance over my shoulder to check.

My feet hit the sand. It wasn't exactly warm; the water would be worse, but I didn't slow. I stormed right toward the soft waves. The moment my calves hit the water my breath caught in my throat and I stumbled to a stop. This was definitely still too cold to swim. I almost fell forward because of my momentum. Teeth chattering, I was about to back out again when warm hands gripped my waist and lifted me up.

"No! Don't you dare!" I screamed.

Matteo chuckled and then I was thrown through the air and landed with a splash in the freezing water. My muscles seized for a moment, then I burst through the surface and panted for breath. I scowled at Matteo who was grinning at me. He was up to his stomach in the water and didn't seem to mind the cold. "You bastard," I brought out through my chattering teeth.

My entire body started shaking. I wrapped my arms around my chest to make a show out of my freezing. Matteo's brows drew together and he came toward me, actually looking worried. The moment he was in arm's reach, I attacked. I lunged at him, grasping his shoulders and trying to dunk him under the water.

I should have considered how used Matteo was to physical fights. He used my momentum to catapult me up and swing me over his shoulder. "Hey!" I shouted in protest but he only clapped my butt and started carrying me out of the ocean. "Where are you taking me?"

"We need to warm you up," he said wickedly.

Excitement jolted through me but I made a show out of kicking my legs and hammering my fists against his back. He carried me to the right toward a corner of the lawn that was shielded from the mansion by bushes. A blanket had been set up. He had planned this!

He laid me down on the blanket and hovered over me. My body was covered in goose bumps, and not just from the cold.

"How about I lick every drop of water off your skin?" Matteo murmured as he leaned down and licked a hot trail up from my belly button to my collarbone.

"What if Aria or Luca come down here?" I whispered as he pushed my bikini top down, baring my breasts to the cold. My nipples hardened even more, and then Matteo's hot mouth closed around one. I cared less and less if someone caught us.

"They won't," he whispered against my skin. And that was the last time we spoke in a long time. His lips and hands found every place on my body, banishing the cold and leaving only heat and want. When he finally entered me, our bodies pressed together, it felt like everything was falling into place.

Even without the breeze and the blue sky, I would have felt free. It had taken a long time but I realized I could feel free, be free, even when I was bound to Matteo.

In the evening, Matteo and Luca set up a barbecue on the patio. The weather was holding up and we could eat outside. Aria went inside to grab the salad she'd prepared while Matteo headed toward the wine cellar for something to drink. That left me alone with Luca who was manning the barbecue grill. I set the table, pretending he wasn't there. Things between Luca and me were tense; they'd never been not tense, but they'd gotten worse since I'd accepted his offer months ago.

I took a deep breath. This had to stop. Luca was not only Matteo's brother, he was also Aria's husband. We had to make a truce at some point. I put down the last plate, wiped my hands and then strode over to Luca who was turning the marinated lamb chops around on the grate. As if he could sense my attention, he glanced up. It was futile trying to read his expression. I bridged the remaining distance between us. Most of our interactions hadn't exactly been civil. My go-to response to him was usually snarkiness, but I was doing my best to keep my expression open and as friendly as possible.

Luca raised one dark eyebrow when I stopped beside him.

Suddenly I felt ridiculously nervous. "I know you don't like me," I began. "But I think we should try to get along better for Aria and Matteo."

I managed not to squirm when he scrutinized me. What was he thinking?

"I didn't like you because I hated how you treated Matteo."

"Okay," I said slowly, not sure where to go from there.

"But I'm starting to change my mind."

"You are?"

He turned another lamb chop. "I'm starting to think that maybe Matteo was right and you two aren't the worst match."

"Thanks?" I said, unsure if it was meant in a positive way. "You are really bad with compliments."

"I'm not in the habit of handing them out. And don't tell my brother I said he was right. He's cocky enough." His eyes went to something behind me and I turned and spotted Matteo heading in our direction, his arms loaded with several bottles of wine.

"He is," I agreed with a smile. Luca gave me what could be considered his version of a smile, and some kind of silent understanding passed between us.

Matteo set the wine bottles down on the table before joining us and wrapping his arm around my waist. "What are you two gossiping about?"

"You," Luca and I said at the same time.

"Is that so?" Matteo lifted one eyebrow.

Aria came back from the kitchen, eyes darting between us. She pressed up against Luca with a confused look. "What's going on?"

"Your husband and my wife are discussing my many wonderful traits," Matteo said.

I nudged his side. "You are way too cocky."

Matteo kissed my ear. "Admit it, you love my cockiness."

"Done."

"Your declarations of love still make my knees go weak," he joked.

I stood on my tiptoes. "Your cockiness isn't the only thing I love about you." I let my eyes wander the length of him.

"I need some bloody lamb to cancel out this disgusting display of sweetness," Luca muttered, but I didn't miss the tender look he'd given Aria when he thought no one was paying attention.

Matteo swept me into his arms and kissed me. Luca grumbled something else but I didn't listen. All that mattered was Matteo.

THE END

BORN IN BLOOD MAFIA CHRONICLES

Bound By Honor
Aria & Luca

Bound By Duty
Dante & Valentina

Bound By Hatred
Gianna & Matteo

Bound By Temptation
Liliana & Romero

Bound By Vengeance
Cara & Growl

Bound By Love
Aria & Luca

Read Fabiano's story in the first book of the Camorra Chronicles, a new spin-off series to the Born in Blood Mafia Chronicles:

Twisted Loyalties
Twisted Emotions
Twisted Pride
Twisted Bonds

about the author

Cora Reilly is the author of the Born in Blood Mafia Series, the Camorra Chronicles and many other books, most of them featuring dangerously sexy bad boys. Before she found her passion in romance books, she was a traditionally published author of young adult literature.

Cora lives in Germany with a cute but crazy Bearded Collie, as well as the cute but crazy man at her side. When she doesn‘t spend her days dreaming up sexy books, she plans her next travel adventure or cooks too spicy dishes from all over the world.

Despite her law degree, Cora prefers to talk books to laws any day.

Printed in Great Britain
by Amazon

61420169R00160